SUCCUBUS HUNTED

THE (UN)LUCKY SUCCUBUS

L.L. FROST

SUCCUBUS HUNTED

THE (UN)LUCKY SUCCUBUS BOOK 4

Copyright © 2019 by L.L. Frost

All rights reserved. No part of this publication may be reproduced, distributed, or transmitted in any form or by any means, including photocopying, recording, or other electronic or mechanical methods, without the prior written permission of the writer, except in the case of brief quotations embodied in critical reviews and certain other noncommercial uses permitted by copyright law.

This is a work of fiction. Names, characters, businesses, places, events and incidents are either the products of the author's imagination or used in a fictitious manner. Any resemblance to actual persons, living or dead, or actual events is purely coincidental.

Cover design by L.L. Frost

Book design by L.L. Frost

Printed in the United States of America.

First Printing, 2019

ALSO BY L. L. FROST

THE VEILS UNIVERSE

The (un)Lucky Succubus

First Serialized in Succubus Harem

Succubus Bargain

Succubus Studies

Succubus Mission

Succubus Hunted

Succubus Dreams

Succubus Trials

Succubus Undone

Succubus Reborn

Succubus Ascended

Demonic Messes (And Other Annoyances)

Drunk Girl *(novella)*

Doom Dog *(novella)*

The Cleaners

The Witchblood

The Fox God

Tally & Her Witches

MONSTERS AMONG US

Monsters Among Us: Hartford Cove

First Serialized in Hartford Cove

A Curse of Blood

Bathe Me In Red

A Feud to Bury

FIRE AND ICE

"Call Tobias and Kellen. We need to talk."

My words hang in the air for a moment as Emil processes my sudden appearance in his office.

His morning coffee steams on the corner of his desk, his laptop not even open yet for business. He must have just arrived in the office.

My eyes move to the hidden door on the right that leads to Tobias's office.

"Emil, I need you to call Tobias and Kellen," I repeat. My bones hum with urgency, the hag's voice continues in a loop, filling my ears until I hear nothing else. *The Hunters are back. The Hunters are back. The Hunters are back.*

Frosty white brows furrowed, his hand moves toward the phone on his desk. "What's going on?"

Before I can answer, Emil's office door crashes open.

Faster than I can blink, four black-clothed men swarm inside with guns raised. The smell of ozone comes with them, along with a heady mix of bedroom sheets and passion.

Incubi.

"Put your hands where we can see them and keep your wings sheathed!" the leader yells as he levels his weapon on me. Sharp purple eyes watch my every move. "One hint of feather and your corporal form *will* be destroyed."

My tongue flicks out, tasting the power in the air.

These are old incubi, but not so old they can mask their power level like my mentor, Landon, can. Even so, they're far stronger than I am, with bright balls of energy in their cores to pull from. With all four working together, they can unmake me before Emil can tell them I'm safe.

My bones shake to flee their threat, but I lock my knees. Hyper-speed does me no good against my own kind. Eyes wide, I lift my hands, the book I hold knocking me in the temple.

"Drop your weapon!" the leader commands.

Confused, my gaze flicks to the dirt encrusted book before I let it drop. The precious contents survived years of being used as a leg support for Landon's butterfly garden, it can survive a tumble to the nicely carpeted floor of K&B Financial's president's office.

With me secure, they drop out of hyper-speed, and another of the men turns to Emil, revealing two distinctive slits in the back of his armored shirt for his wings to slip free if needed. "Sir, we sensed a high-level energy fluctuation in your office! Have you been injured?"

Emil spreads his fingers on his dark desktop, frost creeping across its pristine surface. "I hardly think I'm in danger from one small succubus, Leonard."

He snaps to attention. "The power level we sensed was off the charts, sir! Destruction level." Then his neon-green gaze shifts to me, and his tongue flicks out to taste the air. As uncertainty clouds his face, his voice turns accusatory. "You're just a baby."

Rising onto my toes, my chest puffs out. "I am *not* a baby!"

His feathery white brows lift, as if I just proved his point. Which maybe I did.

Deflating, I drop back to my heels. "I arrived by way of the Librarian."

"Yes." Frost coats Emil's voice as the temperature in the room plummets. "Something that should not have been possible. I was assured the wards around the doors prevented any portals from activating."

"Well, I didn't exactly come through a doorway," I point out, then lift my hands higher when the lead security guy's eyes narrow. "Come on, I'm obviously not a threat. Tell them, Emil."

"*If* you're really Adie," Emil concedes.

I twist to face him. "Excuse me?"

"Your arrival in my office is somewhat suspicious." The glacial blue fades from his eyes to leave only white. "You could be a shapeshifter, designed to look like my succubus in order to put me at ease."

"Okay, first of all"—I hold up a finger—"I do *not* accept that claim. We are still in the dating phase. And two"—up comes another finger—"If you don't pull that popsicle out of your ass, I'm throwing away every single straw in the house, and you can just lick chocolate-flavored ice cubes from now on."

"How dare you speak to Mr. König with such familiar—"

"It's fine, Leonard," Emil interrupts, the white fading from his eyes to reveal blue pools of amusement. "That's Adeline Boo Pond. You'll find her name on the safe list."

"But to show such disrespect," he sputters. "She should be removed. We can find you another succubus, one with more—"

"Um, excuse me." I snap my fingers to bring his neon focus back to me. "I currently have that delicious, vanilla ice cream cone of a Destruction Demon under contract, so you can take your offer and—"

Emil's cool power prickles over my skin. "Ms. Pond."

"Don't you 'Ms. Pond' me." Disregarding the weapons still unholstered in the room, I point to the four incubi. "Those prickles you're feeling right now? Those are *mine*. If you let even one snowflake under your skin, I will file an energy theft grievance against you."

"Adie," Emil purrs, turning my name into a caress.

"Don't you use that sexy tone on me." I shake my fingers at him, realize that looks weird, and drop my hands to my hips instead. "If you think we're not having a talk about all these sex demons you and Tobias apparently have squirreled away right next to your office, you are in for a big surprise."

"Oh?" Coolly, he circles the desk, motioning to the security team. "You may leave for now. We will revisit this portal issue at our next meeting."

"Yes, sir." Saluting, the guns finally go back in their holsters, and the men, the *incubi*, file out.

Through narrowed eyes, I watch them leave and shut the door once more.

If Tobias and Emil had such ready access to so many sex demons, why'd they chase me down? I seem a little unnecessary at the moment, compared to what they already had on hand. The thought sends my wings razoring against my spine with dissatisfaction.

I don't like to be unnecessary.

Icy fingers brush my arm, and I shift my glare to my ice demon.

Emil caresses my tense jaw. "You're unhappy."

"Damn straight I'm unhappy."

"That pleases me." His touch moves up to my lips. "Your jealousy is welcome."

"I'm not jealous," I growl against his fingers. "I'm mad."

"That also pleases me." He leans down to blow

frosty air across my face that nips and stings before it sinks beneath my skin in a tingly rush of pleasure.

My lips part on a hungry gasp, catching his next breath in my mouth. It skates across my tongue to slide down my throat and chill my lungs, turning my nipples to hard, needy peaks. I catch his wrist, my lips closing around his fingers to lick the ice from his nails. Energy melts into my core, suffusing my limbs with the power of snowstorms.

Yes, all of this is *mine*. If any of those incubi touch Emil, I'll rend them limb from limb with my bare hands. My hand clenches around Emil's wrist, his bones creaking. *Mine*.

Cold lips brush my ear. "I can't fire them, no matter how displeased you are."

Possessiveness shivers along my bones, and I push his hand away to fist the collar of his pristine dress shirt. "Then, I'll just make sure there's nothing of you for them to take."

Ice creeps down my arms and fills the small space between us with snow. "I look forward to the challenge."

Gaze fixed on the ice crystals on his mouth, I spring forward.

A file folder snaps between us, the manila dry and unsatisfying against my lips, followed by the mudslide of Tobias's irritation. "Need I remind you both this is a place of business?"

I barely register his sudden appearance beyond the interference it poses to my claim on Emil.

"You're not usually so fastidious, Tobias," Emil growls as he steps away from me. My hands tighten on his shirt to prevent him from going far as I turn my glower on the catalyst demon at our side.

His black eyes fix on me as he responds to his business partner, "And you're not usually so lax."

"I was challenged." Frozen fingers wrap around my wrist, squeezing to force my fingers to release.

I growl, teeth bared and willing to risk broken bones.

The folder in Tobias's hand begins to smoke, filling the office with the scent of scorched paper as he lowers it to his side. "What has you in such a jealous rage?"

I bare my teeth at him. "Emil is *mine*."

"She had the misfortune of meeting our security team," Emil informs him.

Tobias's thick brows arch. "What about them?"

"She apparently objects to them being incubi."

"Few demons are as fast or can universally drain power from other demons. They're perfect for first defense security," he points out, his tone making it clear this should be obvious.

Emil finally forces my fingers to unclench from his collar and steps out of range. "Which is why I refused to fire them."

My focus snaps back to Emil. Frost casts rainbows across his cheekbones, and the blue tinge to his lips begs to be licked away. Far too much power to tempt a hungry demon. I should have sucked him dry the other day when we lay in bed together, not let him distract me with silly things like pleasure and foreplay.

I move to close the distance between us, ready to rectify that mistake now.

Tobias steps into my path, his scent changing to burning forests as his irritation shifts to anger. Instinctively, I skitter back as the memory of ash and fire clogs my throat. I hate myself for the reaction, for my body's unwillingness to separate Tobias's scent from the demon who attacked me. His interference does the job of knocking me back to my senses.

Hurt flashes across his face before he masks it with impassivity. "Did you have a purpose for being here beyond this jealous tantrum, Adie?"

Against my spine, my wings rustle with

unhappiness at my inability to control my instincts. Both in my need to possess Emil and in my unwarranted rejection of Tobias.

"Yes." I cast him an apologetic glance as I circle wide around him to reclaim my abandoned book, brushing more of the potting soil from the cover.

Emil twitches, his fingers fluttering toward a trashcan next to his desk as the dirt circles toward the freshly vacuumed carpet.

Before he gets distracted and brings out the dustbuster, I hold the book up for them to see. "This."

Tobias and Emil still, the temperature in the room both dropping and rising at once to create a mini cyclone in the space between them.

"Why do you have that book?" Tobias bites out, anger adding the weight of landslides to the room.

"The Librarian gave it to me." I point to the symbol on the front, fear rolling in my gut. "Someone's been painting this on the back door of the bakery. She says it's the Hunters. That they've marked me."

In contrast, Emil's voice softens, the first flake of snow that heralds a new ice age. "When did this begin?"

"A few days ago." I hug the book to my chest. "The same time I encountered Domnall."

His name leaves a bitter taste of sludge, ash, and bile in my mouth. My bones ache with the memory of his attack, of being burned from the inside out, forced to choke down his horrible power then vomit it up once more.

Cool hands touch my arms, snapping me back to myself, and I meet Emil's understanding gaze. A part of me wants to reject him, to scoff at his concern, to not be weak before him. But the soft part of me, the same part that refuses to hurt humans, whispers of the comfort to be found in his embrace. The two sides war within me in a standoff that leaves me rigid beneath his grasp.

With a quiet curse, he takes the choice from me with a sharp tug that crashes me against his solid chest. Unable to stop myself, I shove my face into the crook of his neck, drawing his winter chill into my lungs to wash out the memory of fire.

Shivering, I whisper, "This does not make me weak."

"Hush." He strokes my long, white hair, pulling the blue tips through his fingers.

The gesture settles my nerves, and my eyes open to meet Tobias's. Blatant yearning fills his gaze, shocking me to my core. Without thought, my arms reach past Emil, fingers open and grasping for the demon who stands out of my reach.

Surprised, he steps forward and tentatively slides his hands into mine. His heat pushes back the chill of Emil's arms, a warm fire on a cold night. I pull him closer, shifting my grip to his forearms, then his elbows, trying to touch more of him.

His chest hits Emil's back, and the ice demon's head turns with a low rumble of warning. My teeth sink into the side of his throat, right above his jugular, in a warning of my own.

Emil's pulse leaps beneath my lips. "You demand much, Ms. Pond."

Breathing in his frosty scent, I roll my eyes up to stare at Tobias. "Yes."

Tobias's pupils expand, blotting out the whites until only black voids stare back. "What do you need?"

So many responses for that question, too many to put to words, but one is certain. "Bring Kellen here."

STEAMROLLED

"I worried this might happen." Kellen lounges back on the center of the office couch. Electricity crackles in the air to join the mini cyclone generated by Emil and Tobias.

"What do you mean?" I shiver and huddle in one of the chairs dragged over from its place in front of the desk.

When his gaze shifts to me, lightning skitters across his pupils. "A Hunter was spotted in town. He was taken care of, but when there's one…"

"He was a scout." A low-level earthquake accompanies Tobias's words.

Emil leans forward from his place on the far end of the couch. "Tell us everything the Librarian said."

My gaze skips over them, the three demons of destruction cuddled together on the couch while I sit opposite them, like someone on interview. Not that I want to be closer to them right now. My skin aches from the level of energy they throw off. It's a struggle to absorb it as fast as they generate it. I couldn't handle being in direct contact with them right now.

I thought I was keeping up on their energy draws better, but right now, they reveal untapped depths. How much do they hold back when I'm with them? My bones rattle with the warning of their danger, even as my core hungers to consume them.

Clutching the arms of the chair, I force myself to stay in place. "She said I was marked. Someone's been spray painting my door with that symbol." I nod to the book that rests on the coffee table between us. "I thought it was some neighborhood punks."

Tobias's mouth opens, and Emil shushes him quietly.

I cast my ice demon an appreciative glance and make a mental note to bake something special for him. Yes, I know a fully trained demon probably would have recognized the symbol right away. No, I don't need Tobias to point out my stupidity right now.

Kellen makes a rolling wrist motion with his hand for me to continue.

My fingers dig into the armrests as I force myself to admit the next part. "She said I was targeted because they know I'm weak. How do they know I'm weak?"

"They have tools, spells they've crafted from pieces of other demons." Disgust fills Kellen's voice. "Divination and the blood of our kind."

"The more powerful you are, the better you can mask your energy to pass as human." Tobias leans back, his arms spread over the back of the couch. "Even if you returned to Dreamland and fed properly, you wouldn't be able learn the skill for another fifty years. Maybe a hundred at how slowly you feed and the rate you burn through your reserves."

Angry at the dig, I lean forward, my nails digging furrows into the armrests. "Well, maybe if someone didn't interrupt my feeding—"

"That was *not* going to end in your favor," he interrupts. "You're thousands of years too young to take on any of us."

"Sounds like I missed some fun this morning." Kellen covers a yawn, his jaw creaking with the effort.

We woke him with our call, and it reminds me I haven't slept since yesterday. Between cleaning Landon's house and my trip to the Library, the entire morning had passed. Emil must have just arrived at work when the Librarian plopped me down in the middle of his office.

I won't have much time to rest before I need to go in for my shift at the bakery. I should probably hire another supervisor.

Tally can't cover for me every time something pops up, but the idea of bringing on another person right now scares me. How can I knowingly put a new person at risk? Maybe I should shut down the bakery, at least until this matter with the Hunters is resolved.

The idea brings with it a rush of anxiety. I only just got it up and running, with steady customers and a good income. If I close now, I'll have to restart from scratch. And how will I support my newly acquired imps? The first rent payment on their new house is due to Kellen at the first of the month.

"Back to the topic at hand," Emil's low voice pulls me out of my spiral of despair. "What else did the Librarian say?"

"That I needed to power up—"

Kellen settles back on the couch, eyes closed,

and pats his thighs. "Well, come over and sit on my lap, then."

I ignore the invitation. "And that I needed to speak to you guys. And seek out…" My brow furrows as I struggle to remember the name. I was panicking at the time, so… "He Who Consumes?"

Kellen stiffens, his eyes slitting back open to cast sparks across his cheekbones. "No."

"Excuse me?" I straighten in my seat. "The Librarian was really firm on all of this. I think we should listen to her."

"Trust me when I say you want to stay far away from *He Who Consumes*." His lip curls around, and derision fills his voice. "He's bad news where you're concerned."

I look from Kellen to Emil and Tobias, but the stony expression on their faces declares there will be no help from their quarter.

Kellen thrusts to his feet. "If that's everything, I'm going back to bed. Adie, you're welcome to join me to start on that power increase if you like."

I spring to my feet. "But we need to be planning!"

He waves a hand in dismissal. "Yeah, I'll take care of it."

My mouth drops open in shock, but Emil and Tobias simply nod.

"See that it's more discreet, this time," Tobias warns, the burn of lava backing up his words.

"I *know*," Kellen snaps and, somehow, I get the impression this isn't the first time Tobias has berated him for whatever they're covertly discussing.

Kellen's focus shifts to me, his fiery eyebrow arching. "Will you be joining me?"

The Librarian said to stick close to the guys for protection, and while Kellen's highhandedness irritates me, I can't exactly hang out in Emil's office until I go into work today. And my car is still parked in Landon's driveway.

How the hell am I going to get it back? Take a bus? Do buses even go out to his house? What's the possibility of tearing my mentor away from his video games long enough to bring me my car?

Slim. Very, very slim.

I stare at Emil and Tobias. "So that's it? Planning session over?"

"The Hunters won't get near you." Tobias stands and picks up the book from the table, extending it to me. "But read this so you know what to look out for."

Angry, I snatch it from him and flip open the

book. Demonic writing squiggles and crawls across the pages, refusing to form legible words. Frustration spikes through me and I want to scream.

Snapping it closed once more, I grab my abandoned dress shoes from where Emil tidily stowed them next to the sofa and tuck them under my arm.

"Fine." I join Kellen at the office door. "But we're only snuggling."

He yawns again, unconcerned. "Good, because unlike you, I can't fuck in my sleep."

Kellen's heavy arm flops across my face, waking me for the third time since we climbed into his bed and the storm demon passed out.

We started out in a nice, energy-drawing spoon position, which Kellen quickly rolled out of as soon as he fell asleep, starfishing in the middle of the bed. When I tried to cuddle back up to his side, he shoved away.

Resigned, I had moved to the edge of the bed and fallen asleep, with only my feet on his leg for contact. That's when I learned Kellen was a restless sleeper and not someone to share a bed with. Abusive to the extreme in his sleep.

He moves around like he dreams of being a steamroller, and I'm the uneven bump he needs to flatten out. The arm in the face is the last straw.

I crawl out of the bed and grab my clothes from the floor before I march downstairs. Circling the fireplace, I climb up the opposite set of stairs to my room on the third floor. There, I find Tac sprawled on top of my pillows, smashing my carefully constructed nest. My favorite purple, sequined pillow winks a greeting from beneath his large, wedge-shaped head.

"Tac, bad!" I yell and run over. Tossing my cell phone onto my nightstand, I drop my clothes to bop him on his giant kitty nose. "Bad, kitty!"

Saucer-sized, green eyes slit open, and his lip curls back in a growl to reveal teeth the size of daggers.

My hands move to my bare hips. "Don't you take that tone with me! That's *my* nest! How am I supposed to get any sleep now?"

He snorts a hot breath across my face that blows my hair back and closes his eyes, ignoring me.

Annoyed, I climb up onto the bed and shove against his furry shoulder to no avail. The enormous cat monster weighs a ton and can turn into an immovable mass at a moment's notice. He barely shifts, even when I brace my feet against the headboard and shove.

Exhausted, I sag against his side. I could probably move him if I used some of the energy in my core, but I'm supposed to be conserving it right now. For a fight I've apparently been sidelined on.

Frustrated tears prickle at my eyes. It's not like I *want* to go to war with the Hunters. I'd like for them to all just vanish without our paths ever crossing. But being dismissed, after the hag specifically told me there would be a fight, just leaves me to feel *helpless*.

Sniffling, I scrub my hands over my face. Crying is not going to help and only makes me feel weaker. I need to demand to be included, to be a valid part of what's happening to me. But how do I prove myself when I *am* so much weaker on the power spectrum than they are?

Tac shifts against my back, his wings rustling, and the one closest to me lifts in invitation.

My head rolls, and I stare at the dark, furry cave created by the curve of his wing, before I slowly crawl in against his side. "This doesn't make the destruction of my nest okay."

As I snuggle in against his furry side, he begins to purr, the loud, chainsaw noise rattling through my bones and shaking out every other thought in my head. Grateful, I bury my face against his softness and fall asleep once more.

"I never, in a thousand years, would have thought I'd lose a bed partner to a demon cat," Kellen calls, disrupting my sleep once more.

Groggy, I fling a hand out until my fingers knock against the nightstand. I find my cell phone and drag it into my kitty cave. The light on the screen flares to life, illuminating soft black fur and blinding me for a moment. Squinting, I make out the time and bolt upright, only to slam my head on one of the hard support bones of Tac's wing.

With an offended grunt, the beast stands and tromps down to the bottom of my bed, leaving me cold, naked, and exposed to the bright sunlight that streams in through my open shutters.

"Well, well, well," Kellen purrs. "If that's not an invitation, I don't know what is."

I fling out an arm toward the window. "You are not welcome in my room."

"Spoilsport."

I roll onto my stomach, then up onto my knees, shaking the hair from my eyes. Kellen crouches on the ledge to my window, one leg dangling dangerously close to the floor while not technically stepping inside. Behind him, the late morning sun casts a halo of gold around his head, turning him almost angelic.

"Why'd you run away?" He flexes his fingers, and static dances between them. "You can't have been full."

"You're the worst bed partner I've ever had."

His eyes narrow. "Bite your tongue. I'm exceptional."

"Exceptionally rude," I snort.

"Psh," he scoffs. "You're exaggerating. Admit it, you left because I was too tempting, even in my sleep."

"I left before you seriously injured me with all your flailing." Rolling my eyes, I scoot off the bed and search around for my bathrobe.

"Adie, you luscious little succubus, come over her so I can—"

"Nope! I'm late for work." Giving up on the bathrobe, I head for the door. "And get out of my window! Use doorways like a normal person!"

"What's the point of being able to fly if I don't use the wings?" He calls after me.

"You're going to scare the neighbors!"

Grinning, I jog down to the bathroom and find my robe on the hook on the back of the door when I lock myself inside. I don't remember leaving it there last time, but so much has happened since yesterday, when I woke up deliciously languid in Emil's bed. Going out to Landon's, the Library, then K&B Financial seriously threw off my sense of time. It feels like days have passed instead of hours.

Once I dress and make it down to the kitchen, I find the house empty. Kellen must have gone into Fulcrum already, but he left a pink sprinkle doughnut on a napkin for me, with a little flag stabbed through it that reads: *Eat Me*. Is he trying to feed me into growing stronger?

With a grin, I scoop it up and head for the door, only to come to a stop at the sight of the empty driveway where my car usually waits.

Oh, yes. My missing car.

Sighing, I pull my phone from my back pocket and dial the number for my cousin, Julian.

It rings once before a voice drawls, "HelloHell Delivery, where we serve *all* your needs."

"Hey, Philip, it's Adie. Put me through to Julian."

"Oh, hey, Adie." The sex-kitten purr vanishes to be replaced by his normal, chipper voice. "Boss is out."

"Is he out? Or is he *Out*?" I demand. "I'm a little short on time and can't play games right now."

"No, he's really out." His voice lowers. "Has been since yesterday afternoon."

Concern ripples through me. The last time Julian disappeared, it was because our evil Cousin Cassandra kidnapped him and was using him as a snack. "Is everything okay?"

"Yeah, he was really excited when he ran out yesterday. Said something about getting his gear out of storage." Curiosity comes down the line. "Any idea what that might mean?"

"No clue." I nibble my lip for a moment. "Any chance you can come pick me up and take me to work?"

"No can do. We have a catering gig we're about to head out for." The line muffles, his voice becoming distant. "The green booty shorts, not the pink ones!" His voice comes back. "Do you want to leave a message?"

"No, I'll try his cell."

"Good luck with that. He's dodging my calls."

My shoulders sag. "Yeah, thanks."

"Have a good day!" As he goes to hang up, I hear him yell, "No, the *edible* body paint! What kind of business do you th—"

I dial Julian's personal line next, unsurprised when it rings five times before shooting me to voicemail. When my cousin wants to go off the grid, he'll stay gone until he's good and ready to be found again.

Next, I try the landline at my old apartment in the hope one of them will be able to give me a ride, but I don't even get a message service there, the line just keeps ringing until I eventually give up.

I could call Tally, and she could probably send one of her house mates over to pick me up, but they have their own jobs. I don't want to pull away whoever is at the bakery with her today. It would kill me if something happened there while she was unprotected.

Reluctant, I look up the number for the taxi company. I hate spending the money, especially if I need to shut the bakery down for a few days, or longer, but I don't see any other options at the moment.

Thumbing through the options, a car alarm from

down the street draws my gaze to the right, where the separate garage on the side of the house catches my attention. Slowly, I shut my phone off and jog down the stairs.

The guys have a couple cars in there that they don't use, and they left them unattended, which is practically an open invitation for me to borrow one. Kellen stole all of my clothes the first time I did laundry at the house and replaced them with pink yoga pants and t-shirts with the word *Yes* written on the chest and ass.

Taking one of the cars now is *practically* the same thing, right?

Reaching the garage, I open the side door and flip on the overhead light. Tobias's sports car sits directly under one of the lights, glossy black, with sleek lines that beg to be driven at top speed. Emil's more sedate gray four-door is missing, so they must have carpooled to work today. The spot for Kellen's car is also empty. At the back, a motorcycle waits, but I reject that option right away.

I'd more than likely tip it over and skin myself alive.

My focus shifts to the large, boxy shape shoved off to one side and covered in a beige dust cover. So far, I haven't given into temptation to peek under and see what it's hiding. I stride over to it and grasp one edge, whisking the cover away.

"No. Freaking. Way."

I stare, open mouthed, at the teal and lime green van, complete with happy orange flowers on the nose and sides.

My fingers clench with excitement. "Please say Mystery Machine. Please say Mystery Machine."

Heart pounding, I walk around to the side and release a loud squeal of excitement at the bubbly letters stenciled over the rear window.

Arms shooting into the air, I yell, "Yibbity-Yabbity-Doo!"

(UN)CONCERNED

"Jesse, did you already give Torch the Pink Ivory?" I special ordered the expensive Bocote wood shavings, and when I arrived to work today, the box was already open. "You know he's on a strict thorn wood diet while we're baking."

Liquid eyes wide, the little gray imp ducks out of sight behind the kitchen island. Not a hard thing to do when it stands little over four feet tall. I really wish it would choose a form already, but none of the magazines I brought in piqued its interest.

My other imps have all settled into their chosen human guises and can now move about freely without raising suspicion, but Jesse has to stay hidden. No one would look at its gray skin, large brown eyes, and androgynous body and mistake it for human.

Sighing, I crouch next to the oven and open the little hatch on the side to check Torch's food supply. Wood pellets form a dome in its metal bowl, with little curls of pink wood mixed in with the pale gold rounds. I'm seriously going to have to lock up Torch's food.

The little ignis demon comes running from the opposite side of the bank of ovens. He glows a nice, steady red that flares to a happy blue for a second as he spots me.

I smile and wiggle my fingers at him. "Hey, buddy, you doing good today?"

He flickers and pats his round belly.

Does he look bigger than yesterday? I eye his overfilled dish. Maybe I need to put him on a diet. We can't risk him growing too big and escaping his oven again.

"Okay, let's both work hard, little guy."

He flickers again and runs to his food dish, pellets spilling over the side as he digs out a pink curl and shoves it into his stomach. He flares blue again and reaches for another of the expensive shavings.

Closing the hatch, I stand to check the temperature on the oven and adjust a couple dials.

Definitely need to lock up his food supply. We can't have him burning the cupcakes.

"Master, we are low on bumble bees," Iris calls as she pulls small cakes off the cooling rack and moves them to the decorating counter.

I try not to flinch at the honorific. Since I took over their contract, I can't get them to stop with the whole *Master* business. At least, they're not calling me *The Protector of Imps*. I cringe with the knowledge that, somewhere in my history book in the Library, that title has been permanently stamped on record. Offer a little freewill to the imps, and suddenly, I'm titled.

"Okay, I'll be right there." I reach into my chef coat pocket and pull out a hairnet, fitting it over the bun I put my hair up into.

Nothing says sexy succubus like a hairnet, right?

With a deep breath of sugary, buttery air, contentment temporarily washes away the troubles of the last twenty-four hours. The bakery is my dream, and somehow, surrounded by all the happy energies brought on by humans indulging in sweets, it's hard to believe there are Hunters out there who want to harm me.

Thin arms wrap around my waist, followed by an apologetic coo.

"Yes, yes, I'm not mad." I glance down at the top of Jesse's head and pat the mesh hat that covers its limp, brown hair. "Just be careful, okay? If Torch gets big and runs out again, someone might destroy his corporeal form."

Jesse bleats in alarm and shakes its head.

"Did you see the new magazine I brought in for you?"

Its focus shifts to the side, where I left the magazine before I went to check on Torch. Reproachful, liquid eyes rise to meet mine.

"I'm not saying you *have* to choose. But you might find something in there that catches your attention." I stroke its shoulder, the form soft and malleable beneath my palms without a hint of bone. "If you stay like this, it makes it harder for you to go outside, but if that's what you want, we'll work around it."

Reluctant, Jesse releases me to go to the magazine. Long fingers roll it into a tube, and it vanishes into the pocket of Jesse's too large chef coat.

Guilt fills me for pushing the whole body issue,

and I force a smile. "Do you want to try frosting the cakes again?"

Brightening, Jesse nods and runs to fetch its step stool as I walk to the decorating counter and pull out the icing bags we'll need.

The two-way door flies open, and Perry runs inside, his beach-boy, blond hair in messy waves around his surfer boy face. "We need more espresso beans." Then, his blue eyes land on me, and he veers off course to press against my side. "Master, welcome."

"Morning, Perry," I say as I struggle to work with him so close. The imps like to brush up against me like cats whenever possible, leaving their baby powder scent behind. "How are things looking up front?"

"Ms. Tally is covering the cash register while Kelly takes a break," he informs as he rubs his cheek against the top of my head.

"That's good. Have you had your break yet?"

Before he can respond, Jesse arrives and thrusts its stool against Perry's leg, large eyes narrowed. Perry returns the glare, mashing his body closer to my side, and releases an angry chitter.

Jesse chitters back, prodding him with the stool once more to try and dislodge him from my side.

"Stop it, you two." I peek out the pass-through to see Martha peering toward the kitchen. The hopper on top of the bean grinder sits empty. "Perry, go get the beans Martha needs. Jesse, stop hitting Perry."

"Yes, Master." With one more cheek rub, Perry hurries to the hall that leads to the storeroom.

Jesse sets its stool down with more force than necessary and climbs up to stand just out of view from the customers up front. Its shoulder rubs against mine, trying to layer its scent over Perry's. I don't see the point. All mischief imps smell the same to me, but I let it go as I set one of the mini cakes in front of Jesse.

We spend the next thirty minutes frosting green grass and little bumble bees onto the tray of cakes. Jesse does most of the grass, not skilled enough yet to pipe on the bees. When we finish, I set them onto the waiting plate that Iris provides and give Jesse the extra frosting and a sheet of wax paper to practice on.

Kelly returns from his break and picks me up in a bear hug, his scruffy beard tickling the side of my face. "Welcome, Master."

"Morning, Kelly," I wheeze through the embrace. "Did you have a good break?"

"Yes," he rumbles as he sets me back on my feet. He dances in place with excitement. "Jax invited me to a hardware store."

I grin at his enthusiasm. "Exciting!"

"They have entire aisles dedicated to wood." He turns and points to the hall, where a four-by-four leans. "I bought one for Torch."

My voice goes faint. "Oh. That was… considerate of you…"

Kelly rubs the back of his tattooed neck, looking uncertain. "Jax invited me to go on a job with him to lay floors, but…"

My heart squeezes. I knew this would come eventually; I just didn't expect it so soon. I reach out to squeeze Kelly's big biker arms. "Then, you should go."

"But there's work here, Master." Pain fills his eyes, the need to please me warring with his personal desires.

"We'll arrange the schedule so you're not missed," I reassure him. "But, if one of the others wants to do something similar, you'll be expected to cover for them, too. This is a give and take type thing."

His lips thin. "But not with Jax."

My hands move to my hips. "Yes, if Jax makes them the same offer and they're interested."

Mutiny flares to life. "But Jax is mi—"

"*Mine*," Tally interrupts, her usually chipper voice tight with possessiveness. "First, Jax is Slater's, then he is mine."

I glance in surprise at the usually friendly baku demon. Today, she wears her pink hair up in two buns that somehow manage to look like cupcakes, complete with little plastic cherries on top. Now, tiny fangs pimple her bow shaped lips, and the gossamer wing tattoos on her bare shoulders shift beneath her skin. I've only seen them separate from her once, when we first met.

Kelly, for all his bad boy biker looks, cowers before the small baku demon. "Yes, ma'am. Your claim comes first."

"Go cover the cash registers." She commands.

Kelly glances to me, and I nod permission.

We wait as he scurries away before Tally turns to me, her fangs vanishing. "Adie, good morning."

"More like afternoon, now." I check the clock. "Do you need a break?"

She waves a hand in dismissal. "I am—*I'm* fine."

I suppress the grin that wants to escape at her struggle to learn contractions in an effort to fit in better with humans. With her pink hair and mahogany eyes, I think it's a lost cause, but she's trying for her roommates: Jax, Slater, Reese, and Xander.

At the thought of the half-trained witches, my mood plummets once more, and I tip my chin toward the hall. "Do you have a moment? There's something I want to discuss."

"Of course." Her pink brows furrow in concern, but she stays silent as we walk to the pantry and part-time office. As I shut the door behind us, she glances around at the packed shelves. "I spoke to Jax about your idea to convert the attic. He is most amiable."

"We might want to hold off on that plan." I walk over to lean against the desk, my arms folded over my stomach. "I had a bit of a…revelation earlier today that might affect the bakery."

"Oh?" Now, true worry fills her voice. "If it is something I can improve on, I will eat whichever dreams I need to—"

"It's not you," I rush to reassure her. "Though it may affect you and the imps." With a deep breath, I blurt, "There are Hunters in town, and they've apparently marked me and the bakery. I think we should shut down."

"Ah." Her expression clears. "And what of your men? What do they say?"

I scowl. "They're going to *take care of it* for me."

"And you doubt their prowess?"

"They seem a little cavalier about the whole thing." The anger from earlier returns. "I don't like them dismissing the danger to my people."

"Perhaps they are not thinking of your people, but only of you," she points out gently. "One of you is not that difficult to defend against the Hunters, especially for demons of their caliber. Though if that is the case, they should not have left you here alone. You should be behind wards until this matter is resolved."

"Well, *I'm* concerned for more than myself. Though I'm not sure the Hunters can hurt you." By all rights, the baku demon shouldn't even be out of Dreamland. She doesn't even register as a demon to my senses, so she probably won't show up on the Hunter's map, or whatever they use to find us. "But my imps will be easy pickings."

She shrugs. "Imps are of little use to Hunters, beyond the sport of killing. Their bodies have little substance to use in rituals."

"I would still rather they not be *murdered*."

"They can reform. They would just need to go

back through the proper channels to gain access to the human plane once more." Her gaze shifts to me. "And you would, of course, have to agree to sponsor them again. It is not without financial cost."

"I would still rather avoid the murdering thing," I grit out through clenched teeth.

"You are kind." She lifts a hand to touch one of the plastic cherries on her cupcake bun, her eyes going distant. The little fangs make a reappearance as she whispers, "Your dreams must be *delicious*."

I snap my fingers in front of her face. "Hey, just because I'm not currently in Dreamland doesn't mean you can snack on me while I sleep."

Her shoulders pull back. "I would never!"

My eyebrow arches.

"Well, I'm not saying I've never *thought* about it." She licks her lips. "Few of my kind have ever tasted a succubus' dreams."

That's because most of my kind are on the hunt when we sleep. I bare my teeth at her. "That's because we eat your kind."

The air crackles between us. Baku and succubi have an uneasy relationship in Dreamland, both hunters of the sleeping humans. But of the two, baku are usually weaker and stuffed full of human emotion. A hungry succubi or incubi will eat them whole for a fast energy boost.

Tally smiles, breaking the tension. "But *you* do not do that. It is why we are friends."

Even though she speaks the truth, she can't know it for sure, and it makes me worry about the trust she so easily hands out. Someday, someone will break that trust, and the shine that surrounds her will dim a little.

"So the Hunters are after you, and your men have told you not to worry about it. They have discounted your concerns." She tilts her head. "Why are you concerned?"

"The Librarian made this sound like a pretty big deal."

Her eyes widen. "Then, it is a big deal indeed."

"That's what I'm saying!" I throw my hands up. "But they've completely sidelined me because I'm weak!"

Out come the fangs again. "We must make it so you are not weak."

Wary, I study her gleeful expression. "I'm not going on a sexathon."

"It would do you good." She shakes her head before I can protest. "But I have something else in mind."

"What's that?"

"You are most concerned about the bakery at the moment, yes?"

I nod slowly. The wards on my bakery are basic at best. They have two basic purposes. One, keep out demons who pose a threat. Two, draw in humans to feed on their happiness.

That should have been a great plan as a way for me to *not* harm humans. But now it lets the very humans who want to harm *me* just waltz right in, because no matter what messed up jewelry or tools Hunters might carry of demonic origin, they're still human.

Tally rubs her hands together. "This is where *my* men are most helpful! We will prepare you for battle, with or without your demons of destruction."

CAGED

At five fifteen on the dot, the cellphone in my pocket vibrates. Smiling at the customer across the counter, I ignore it as I hand her a blue-rose cupcake. "Your espresso will be ready in just a minute at the coffee bar."

"Thank you." Secretive indulgence wafts from the middle-aged woman as she walks away with her prize.

A wife sneaking dessert before she heads home for the night? Mouthwatering, I breathe it in. *This*. This is what I opened the bakery for. To make humans happy, and in return, skim off all the delicious energy they exude at the height of emotion. Not as fulfilling as sex, but far less dangerous for them.

Tally left at three with Jax, promising to return later with the rest of her guys and whatever solution they concoct to help me power up and defend myself against any Hunters. I hope she's not doing something weird in Dreamland and putting herself at risk. Though it would be hilarious if my tiny manager returned sporting a *Buffy the Vampire Slayer* vibe.

My cell phone vibrates in my pocket once more, and I ignore it as I help another customer, then quickly peek at the caller ID while the next customer takes a look at the pastry display shelf. Maybe it's one of my cousins returning my call from earlier, and I can get my car back tonight after work.

The house number flashes across the screen, and I scowl before shoving the phone back into my pocket.

There's no reason for the big, bad demons to be bothering weak, little me while I'm at work.

As if to disagree, my phone vibrates once more, and I pull it out to stash in the drawer where it won't bother me. The only person I care to speak to right now is Tally, and she'll call the bakery line if it's important.

At seven, a demon walks into my bakery. A very, very angry demon.

Unlike other times he's visited, I notice Tobias

right away by the black cloud that flows ahead of him through the door. The sigil on the display case, a stylized swirl that resembles a frosted cupcake, flickers, uncertain if he's a threat. I expect him to storm straight to the counter, but he surprises me and takes his place at the end of the line.

I help the five people in front of him, my distracted gaze straying to his dark expression again and again. What could I have possibly done to piss him off this time? Is it about the chair I haven't replaced yet? I haven't exactly had time to go shopping with Kellen, what with everything going on.

My cheeks ache with the forced smile as I hand my current customer a box of four cupcakes. I can't even take pleasure in the pretty, frosting bouquet she chose as Tobias looms behind her. "Have a wonderful evening. I hope you enjoy your treats."

Not sensing the menace at her back, she lingers. "Do you plan to add more to the menu besides cupcakes? Like cookies or scones?"

I blink at her, the question throwing me. "I hadn't given it much thought, but it's an interesting idea. Why do you ask?"

"Well, it's just…" She glances at the sign

overhead. "You're a bakery, but all you have are cakes. Why not be a cupcake shop?"

Because Boo's Boutique Cupcakes lacked the delightful alliteration that Boo's Boutique Bakery has, but I keep that thought to myself. "I see your point. Thank you for the suggestion."

"Also, do you have a newsletter? And a website? I'd love to be able to place orders online." She slips a hand into her purse and withdraws a glossy business card. "I'm always on the lookout for catering ideas, and my team loves sweets."

"We're working on adding that feature," I lie while internally scrambling to figure out how to add something like that to my basic website as soon as possible. I take the card and read the name of some intel company. "I'll let you know when the feature is available."

"Thank you." She turns to leave, then spins back. "Do you deliver?"

My smile becomes strained. "Not at this time."

"You should consider it. There are a lot of small businesses around here who would utilize the service."

I nod, eager to see her leave. "Thank you for the suggestions. Have a good evening."

Tobias steps up to the counter, and I experience

instant regret. I'd rather talk more with the Intel lady than be the brunt of his cloud of anger. My bones shiver with warning.

Here be predator.

Martha hurries over, a to-go cup of tea in her hand, and silently sets it on the counter before she scurries away.

I nudge it closer to him. "Would you like a cake to go with this? I have unfrosted ones in the back."

Tobias doesn't like desserts the way Emil does, but he could use some sweetness right now to tame the acrid bite of his anger.

"Call one of your helpers to the front," he instructs, voice deceptively calm.

"They're all on break right no—"

"I can see them in the pass-through."

I twist in time to catch Iris's rainbow head ducking out of sight. "They take breaks in the kitchen. I can't disrupt their legal break time."

He leans across the counter, tone a low rumble that shivers the air between us. "Either be professional and call someone to cover the register, or let your customers see me forcibly take you."

I wait a heartbeat for him to finish that sentence. Take me…where? When he stays silent, my gaze darts around the full shop. So far, no one's paying any attention to us, but… "Tobias, what—"

"Now, Adie."

My wings rustle against my spine, urging me to run, but the humans cage me in. It's a startling flip to my first encounter with Tobias, where I used the human presence at the coffee shop to escape. Now, they become my jailer, their presence limiting what I can do without giving away I'm *not* human.

I lick my lips, taste the burn of ozone, and a quiet whimper escapes.

A warm, pillowy body presses to my side. "Master?"

I rip my gaze from Tobias to look at Martha. The motherly imp quivers with fear, and my spine stiffens. I'm The Protector of Imps, dammit, so I have to be strong. "It's okay, Martha. Can you please call Kelly out to cover the register?"

With a quick glance at Tobias, she walks to the pass-through and chitters quietly. After a moment, Kelly steps through the two-way door. For all his tough, biker exterior, he scurries to the counter, his head down so as not to draw Tobias's attention.

Anger pushes back my fear. How dare Tobias come into *my* sanctuary and scare *my* people. Reaching into my pocket, I take out two sparkle balls and set them on the counter, within sight for the two imps to discover. I can't hand them to the mischief imps directly; it doesn't satisfy their need to steal things if I do. But I can make it easy for them to find, and the prizes will help to calm them.

I make sure to rub my arm against Kelly's for good measure before I nod for Tobias to follow me into the kitchen. "Come to my office."

When we enter, we find the other imps huddled at the kitchen island, and Jesse clutches Torch's heat-proof box. They're prepared to hide, like they did when Domnall attacked.

Angry that they have reason to fear, I give them a reassuring smile. "Jesse, please put Torch back in the oven. Perry, there are tables that need to be bussed up front. Iris, please start a fresh batch of sunshine cakes. I'll be in the office, but if you need anything, just knock."

Eyes wide, they slowly disperse to their tasks, and I lead Tobias down the hall to the small pantry.

As soon as I enter, I spin to face him, rising onto my toes to be bigger. "What do you think you're doing, coming in here and terrorizing my staff?"

"You *are* aware there are Hunters in town, yes?" He shuts the door and locks it with a quiet click before he turns to me. "You didn't already forget?"

I eye the door uneasily, not enjoying being trapped. "Yes, I remember. I also remember you all sidelining me and telling me you'd *take care of it*."

"When you're in *danger*..."—he stalks closer, biting the words off. Anger rolls before him, a cloud that stings against my skin. I drop to my heels and skitter back until I slam up against a shelf—"you do *not* ignore your phone."

My mouth drops open in surprise. Is this concern? Did he think something happened to me? I draw in a relieved breath and choke on burning forests and ash.

The air sticks in my lungs, and I wheeze, "Tobias, I need you to take a step back."

Instead, he reaches past me to grip the shelf on either side of my head. "No, we are going to discuss this *now*."

I press hard against the shelf, struggling not to take another breath of burning air.

His scent grows strong. "I thought something had happened to you. That the Hunters managed to lure you out of the bakery."

I turn my head away, gasping in a ragged breath of forest fire, and my vision hazes red. The storeroom vanishes, replaced by a dark alley. Sweat breaks out down my spine, and instinct takes hold.

Desperate, I try to dart around him, panic demanding I escape, but in such a small room, with him so close, not even hyper-speed can save me.

He catches me easily, slamming me back against the baker's rack. Frantic, I scramble at his arms, claws digging bloody furrows into his forearms, and his grip tightens, his palms fiery hot where he touches. "I'm not Domnall. I'm not going to hurt you."

But he smells like Domnall. He burns like Domnall. I can't go through this again.

Lunging forward, my teeth sink into his shoulder, and I bite hard enough to taste the copper of blood even through his shirt.

He shoves me back and grips my chin to force me to look at him. Black bleeds out to fill his eyes. "Adie, I'm not Domnall."

I know that, I really do, but all I smell is ash. All I feel is fire.

Strength floods my limbs, and I break his hold, shoving him away. As he crashes against the door, his body blocks my only escape. My wings burst from my back, and I launch myself toward the ceiling, toward the too small vent.

Hard fingers curl around my ankle and yank me back to the ground. "Adie, stop!"

Coiling, I spring at him. If I can't escape, it leaves me only one recourse. Talons digging into his shoulders, I pin him against the door, my mouth latching onto his.

If I can't flee, I will destroy.

(UN)GENTLE

The demon's flesh gives beneath my claws, and I catch his pain on my lips, drinking it down before I delve deeper to latch onto his energy. I yank it from him in chunks that taste like copper and sear like coals as it rolls down my throat to burn in my belly.

Desperate to destroy what I fear, my nails burrow deeper until I find bone. Blood and meat, slick and hot, scorch my fingers with the power contained within his flesh. The daily restraint I practice not to harm those around me slides off, self-imposed chains falling away. The absence leaves me lighter, and my bones sing with the need to consume.

I tear into the demon beneath me, ripping his power out and swallowing it down in convulsive pulls that taste of lava and earthquakes, of forests set ablaze by lightning storms. The power rolls in my core, a molten mass that turns my bones to liquid, that threatens to melt my body and leave me pliant, ready to be forged anew. My bones crackle and give beneath the onslaught of power, my skin tight and fragile as it struggles to hold my shape.

Ozone and copper perfume the air.

The body beneath me groans, and large hands cup my waist, cold against my burning flesh. I growl a warning, nails digging deeper, but instead of fighting, they pull me closer, molding my body. The mouth against mine moves, lips and tongue a caress where I expect a fight.

An abyss of power waits inside him, enough energy to glut myself on and sleep for ages. And when I wake, I'll be reformed, recreated into a new succubus, one who never has to fear again, one who can stand equal to Landregath the Great Devourer, who could bat Cousin Cassandra aside without concern, who could hold the human masses in sway and feast on their desires.

And the demon within my clutches offers that power without struggle, body pliant beneath me, hands offering support.

I blink the red haze from my eyes, and Tobias's black gaze meets mine.

Flinching, I rear back, yanking my talons from his flesh. My hands lift to my mouth in horror. Long tears rip apart the front of his blood-covered dress shirt, buttons missing and collar agape to expose the torn flesh beneath. Fresh blood pumps from his shoulders and fans downward in a gory ombré.

Copper fills my nose, and I pull my hands away to stare at the blood that coats my fingers and palms, the flesh stuck under my nails.

Oh, god, what did I do? How could I do that to him? His stolen power roils inside me, more than I've ever taken from him before, and the urge to vomit clenches my stomach. This was not freely given. It was taken, ripped from him. I used Tobias the same way Domnall used me.

Whimpering, I scramble off of him, sticky, red handprints dotting the floor as I crawl away.

Strong hands catch me, and my wings bap against his hard body. I strain against his hold, a pathetic mewl escaping. "No. I'm sorry. I'm so sorry."

"Hush. It's okay." With implacable force, he pulls me back into his lap. Dry lips dance across my cheek. "Take more. Take as much as you need."

"No, I can't." I turn my head away, my belly full

and tight from all the energy already stolen. "I'm so sorry, Tobias. I never meant—"

None too gently, he clasps my jaw and brings my head around, mouth covering mine. His tongue drives past my lips, a silky conquest not to be denied. He tastes of blood and pain, of betrayal and desire.

Whimpering, I clutch his shoulder, my fingers slipping against healing flesh. Half twisted and trapped within his embrace, I'm unable to escape or deny him any punishment he deems appropriate for my transgression.

His arm braces against my back, flattening my wings to my shoulders. They quiver with the need to hide, to retract into my body once more. My spine aches, the muscles tense as he forces my wings to stay exposed.

Without waiting for me to draw it forth, more energy pours down my throat, joining the ball in my belly to create a fiery riptide that draws back within my body, my core too small to fully contain its mass. It surges outward to seek my limbs, splashes against my fingers and toes, then rolls back to my center.

My entire body trembles, my succubus senses thrown wide but unsure what to do with this amount of power. It travels up my spine, crashes through my brain, and all thought short-circuits.

Mouth softening under Tobias's, my tongue strokes against his in welcome as my arms slip around his neck. Soft hair sticks to my bloody fingers as I cradle him closer, my body becoming lax within his hold. My catalyst demon demands total control, and for once, instinct cedes to his demand.

As if he senses the change, his tight hold loosens. His arm drops from my back, allowing my wings to stretch and flutter. A soft caress against the feathers along my spine pulls forth a quiet moan. Few have ever touched my wings, and the light sift of fingers through feathers melts my bones with pleasure.

Languid, I roll within his lap and straddle his waist to give him better access.

His mouth leaves mine to find my ear. "You made a mess, little succubus."

I whine softly in apology.

A hand on the back of my head directs me to his shoulder. "Clean it up."

Panting, my mouth opens wide over his flesh, his blood bright pops of power against my tongue. The torn shirt interferes with access to his body, and I tear it further until it falls easily away. His heat stings my lips, his skin soft velvet beneath my tongue. Purring with approval, I move lower, nipping and licking at the hard planes of his abdomen.

With a hiss, the muscles contract into ridged hills, a new texture for me to taste.

I lap across the thick muscles, to the valley in the center, and follow the groove down to find the dark crevice of his bellybutton. A small pool of blood gathers there, and I hum with appreciation as I sip at its edges, little bursts of energy against the tip of my tongue. My wings stretch, the feathers spreading, and Tobias caresses the hard arcs of bone before he digs his fingers into the down near my spine once more.

Pleasure rolls through me, curving my spine and thrusting my ass into the air. The musk of his desire draws me lower, to the hard ridge of cock that strains against his slacks. Drool floods my mouth, and I reach for the buttons, desperate to drink down his power.

A hand fists in my hair to draw my head up, and black eyes stare down at me. "Did I say you could have that?"

With a whine, I strain against his hold, the tight grip on my hair adding the spice of pain to my desire. My thighs clench together in an attempt to assuage the aching emptiness of my core.

His thumb skims across my lips, and they part on a desperate pant, eager to have any part of his body inside me. But he withdraws to cup my chin. "Didn't I tell you, you would beg for me?"

A hiss of instant rejection escapes. Succubi do not *beg*.

His hold tightens, pulling me away from his body. "Are we done, then?"

Growling, I rip myself from his hold to mold my body against his in refusal. I will not be denied. My hands burn, the blood caught between my fingers and under my nails crackling to add more power. My lips and chin sizzle, slick lines down my throat sparking to add more fuel. Everywhere his blood coats my skin, it sinks inside to join the energy rolling through my body, a snare to be used against him.

The scent of sugar and sex perfumes the air, delicate lines of power that hook into his desire and pull it to the forefront. The pheromones of sex demons are better than any aphrodisiac, designed to turn our prey docile and open them to our feeding.

But instead of relaxing, he twists beneath me, a supple roll of powerful muscles. Despite the power-filled strength that floods my limbs, he breaks my hold easily.

We wrestle for dominance, hot, slippery skin and cold, hard concrete. It's not a question of whether or not we will have sex, but a battle of who holds control. In my bones, I know Tobias is the more powerful demon, but my nature demands otherwise.

My top tears and falls away as Tobias gains the upper hand and flips me onto my stomach. My nipples turn to hard, needy pebbles, my breasts pressed to the floor as his body covers my back.

I scramble against the unforgiving floor, refusing to be dominated. Succubi take. Only prey yields.

Unmoved, he reaches between us, grips the waistband of my slacks, and yanks my pants down to my knees. I buck to throw him off only for him to settle more solidly between my spread thighs. The hard ridge of his cock presses against my heat, and the more I struggle, the more I rub against him.

Instinct and desire fight within me, the desire to accept a more powerful mate at war with the need to hold the advantage.

Moaning, I shove back against his hard cock, trying to draw him in through the barrier of his slacks. My legs shake with the need to be around his waist, to hold him in place as I take my fill. I push against the ground a final time, my arms quivering, before I fall, panting, onto my stomach, my arms spread out over my head.

His bare chest settles between my wings, burning hot, and the delicious smell of ozone and embers invades my lungs, pushing away everything else until only Tobias remains.

My catalyst demon. My master.

His teeth graze my ear. "Do you submit?"

My head turns, and I nip kisses along his stubbled jaw. "Yes."

His hips roll against me, the zipper a sharp scrape of dominance against my sensitive flesh. "You want this?"

"Yes." Panting, I spread my legs wider. "Please."

His purr of satisfaction rolls through me before he reaches between our bodies once more. His knuckles tease against my slick heat as he pulls his zipper down, and a frustrated moan escapes my parched throat at the almost-caress. Then, the blunt head of his cock nudges at my entrance, and I whimper, eyes closing to block out the pantry.

He feels huge and blunt, fiery hot even to my heated skin. The pre-cum that joins my slick entrance stings and burrows in ahead of his invasion. He rubs the tip against me, teasing, and I lift my ass higher, body begging to be spread wide.

He rises onto his knees, his other hand stroking down my back. "You don't remember the first time I had you."

He slips beneath me to cup my stomach and lift me higher onto my knees. Eager, I wiggle to get a leg free of my pants to make it easier.

"You cried so prettily." One blunt finger slips between my folds to find the hard nub at my apex. He strokes over it, and my muscles clench around the tip of his cock. "Will you cry for me again?"

I reach back, clutching the loose slacks to pull him forward.

"So greedy." He rubs his tip against me once more, using it to ease me open. His hand leaves my clit to grip my hip hard and hold me in place. "It's a good thing you're a succubus, or this would never work."

Confused, my head lifts, then my mouth drops open, a low cry escaping as he slowly thrusts inside. Little bumps coat his thick shaft, and as he stretches me wide, my inner muscles burn as they give way to his invasion. He finds the end of my channel and pushes harder, forcing my body to take even more before he eases out. The nubs on his cock scrape against my inner walls, teasing my sensitivity to new heights.

"Remember my shape." Gently, he strokes the taught flesh where our bodies connect before he eases forward once more.

Head dropping, my muscles ripple around his huge cock, and I lean back into him as my body gives way, reforming itself to take him in.

He buries himself balls deep with a growl of appreciation. "Good."

Quivers of delight roll through me, his praise more satisfying than I'll ever admit. He pulls out, testing the give of my body, before thrusting forward once more, harder this time. I moan with pleasure, rocking back to meet him.

His pace increases, his hands leaving my hips now that he's sure I won't reject him. He puts them to much better use, reaching beneath me to cup my swaying breasts. Delicate and persistent, he pinches and flicks my nipples until my body hums with pleasure, and I release soft, wanton cries into the pillow of my arms.

With powerful surges, he moves between my thighs, my knees lifting from the floor with the force of each thrust. My overstimulated insides clench around him, savoring each hard ridge of his cock. I moan as he withdraws again, ass tilting more, and he pauses, half out of my body, then thrusts shallowly, his blunt head rubbing against the tight bundle of nerves within my channel that make me clench tighter around him.

Abandoning my breasts, his hands move to my ass, and he spreads my cheeks to expose my other entrance. He presses against the tight ring of muscles, forceful with determination, and I cry out again as his thumb breaches my body at the same time he thrusts all the way in.

The added penetration tightens the whole of my core, making me overfilled once more. In my ass, he pushes downward so that his next thrust rubs him across that bundle of nerves inside my channel. My back arches, the pleasure too much, and I cry out as orgasm ripples through me, my muscles clenching around his cock to hold him in place.

The world grays out around us, a shadow pantry overlaying the one around us, and his smoky voice fills my ear. "Don't try to run."

Panting, I force my tongue to form words. "What?"

In answer, he shoves me against the floor, his cock slamming to the hilt. Deep inside, he begins to swell.

My eyes widen in shock. "No, wait, pull out."

Instead, his arms clamp around my torso, locking my arms to my sides, as his teeth sink into my shoulder. His cock continues to swell inside, stretching me, before hot cum floods my channel in a rush of burning power. Ecstasy crashes down, swamping my senses, and another orgasm tightens my muscles around the knot of his cock locked within me.

He moves as much as possible, little thrusts that rub that hard ball against my most sensitive place, and I whimper and cry as another orgasm hits, this one taking me under.

NOT SANITARY

"This is why I told you to pull out," I grumble as I lay on the floor, my head in the fold of my arms.

The chill of the concrete numbs my belly and boobs while Tobias's heated body burns against my back. My wings retracted back into my body at some point, leaving no barrier between our skin. He radiates against me, a low simmer compared to the flood of energy from earlier.

I only passed out for a minute, just long enough for my body to process the onslaught of power, before discomfort pulled me from the deep sleep my body needs to absorb energy.

While I'm grateful for the short reprieve, I wish it lasted longer. At least, then, I could have slept through this indignity.

Tobias shifts and nuzzles the back of my neck,

stinging kisses trailing over the bite wound he left. The motion shifts his cock, still locked inside me, and I whimper at the pleasure of it. "Stop moving. I don't want any more orgasms."

"You're such a bad succubus," he growls into my ear, sending another buzz down to my core.

I turn my head, lifting my arms to cover my sensitive lobes. "You're never shoving that thing inside me again."

"Oh, I'm going to be inside you again," he promises as he squeezes my ass cheek. "Next time, I'll test this entrance out."

A shiver rolls down my spine, and my wings quiver in their hiding place. "Not happening."

"You like the idea."

I rear up, the back of my head knocking against his chin. "You better not get hard again."

"Sweet little succubus, I never stopped being hard." He rolls his hips to prove his point, and the shift pulls a moan from me. "See? You want me again already."

"I don't." As if to gainsay me, my muscles clench around him. His shape feels smaller, and I shove against his naked torso. "I think you can get off me, now."

"Hmm." He pulls back, and his knot locks

against my entrance. He settles back in place. "Not yet."

Bending my legs, I try to kick him in the ass. "Never again!"

His elbows settle on the floor next to my head, his full weight pressing me into the floor. "Maybe on a bed next time."

"I can't believe you did this, knowing what would happen." I succeed in getting one heel to slam against his firm ass and repeat the motion. "You could have at least warned me."

"It's not my fault you don't remember the first time." He reaches down to catch my leg and shove it outward. It opens me more fully, and he hums with satisfaction as he goes back to nuzzling my neck. "I'm about ready for round two."

Behind us, the door rattles before a quiet knock sounds. "Master, are you…well?"

My heart slams into my throat, and I choke on embarrassment. Oh, god, what if the customers heard us back here? My gaze lifts to the baking racks filled with ingredients. This was so unsanitary. I'll have to replace everything and bleach the entire room.

The door rattles again, harder. "Master?"

I elbow Tobias. "Get off me!"

With a grumble, he pulls back, stretching my edges to pop free of my body. He shifts to his side, then onto his back, shivering against the cold of the cement. He rolls his head to watch me, his eyes back to normal. Aside from the red of his lips, he looks unwounded.

Just to be sure, my hungry gaze rakes over his bare shoulder, noting his fully healed wounds, before moving lower to the clean planes of his chest and abdomen.

Somehow, his pants remain intact, the fly open to frame the beautiful length of his cock. Even at half-mast, his thickness makes me swallow. An average person would struggle with that breadth. *I* struggled with it before my body kicked into gear. The blunt head still glistens with our joining, and I lick my lips for another taste of that power.

What would he feel like on my tongue? In the back of my throat? Would I be able to take him whole? My mouth tingles with the desire to discover the texture of the little nubs that rise along his length, a darker tone than his natural skin and clearly not human.

My breath catches at the memory of them stroking my insides. At his base, his cock still swells with the hint of his knot. I would have to be careful, to hold him in my mouth. Excited at the challenge, my hand lifts, fingers out to touch him, to bring him back inside of me.

"Master? Are you alive?" Fear enters the imp's voice, and I recognize Perry.

The usual laid-back surfer persona falls away to reveal the terrified demon beneath, a being who remembers the danger of being snuffed out by a stronger demon.

"I'm fine," I call as I scramble to my feet, then stumble over the pants still around one leg.

Hopping on one foot, I yank them back on, then look around for my shirt. I spot the sleeve poking out from under a shelf, bend to grab it, then scream with frustration to find it shredded.

When I twist to glare down at Tobias, he shrugs and folds his arms behind his head. "You ruined mine. I ruined yours."

I stamp down the urge to kick his luscious form and stomp over to the rack that holds the clean chef coats, hissing over my shoulder, "Button your pants."

"You're no fun after sex." With a sigh, he rolls to his feet, followed by the metallic scrape of his zipper rising. "Where's the cuddles I keep hearing about?"

Yanking the coat on, I spin to stare at him. "This is my workplace!"

His thick brows arch. "And?"

"Cuddles happen at home!"

Expression set with determination, he closes the distance between us. "So, you'll join me tonight for cuddles?"

My mouth works as I struggle to keep up with his thought process. "No. How did you decide that?"

He leans closer, his voice a low growl that vibrates my bones. "We just had sex, so I get an IOU for cuddles later."

"I... No." My spine snaps straight. "No, you don't! We're *fighting*."

"We resolved that." He reaches out to tuck a strand of loose hair behind my ear. "You'll answer your phone next time when one of us calls."

I slap his hand away. "I did *not* agree to that! And I'm also not agreeing to be sidelined while you big, powerful men take care of my problem for me!"

He scowls and reaches past me to grip the shelf at my back, caging me in place. "You will stay away from the Hunters."

"Well, no shit, dumbass." I rise onto my toes. "That's the plan, *obviously*."

The muscles in his jaw jump as he clenches his teeth. "Then, I don't see a problem."

"The *problem* is that I need to be prepared if they *can't* be avoided," I seethe, all the warm glow of post orgasm swept away by his obliviousness. "I need to power up—"

"That's what we just did," he interrupts, and my wings razerblade against my back in agitation.

"No, that was—"

When I cut off this time, he leans down until his nose touches mine. The air between us crackles. "That was *what*, Adie?"

The air sticks in my lungs, and I sputter, "That was you—"

His breath turns to smoke. "Yes?"

My eyes narrow. "We're not talking about this right now. I need to go check on my bakery."

When I duck beneath his arm, determined to escape, he catches my hand to stop me. Surprised, I turn back to him, and a small smile curves his lips before he ducks down to drag a hot kiss across my lips.

Instinctively, my tongue darts out to catch the taste of him, burnt embers and ash, and his smile widens. "Well, at least you're not afraid of me anymore."

I blink in surprise, then lean in to breathe deep at the sweep of his neck and shoulder. The hint of forest fires still lingers there, but sweeter still is the fire that heats his skin. My own scent mingles with it, sugar and sex thick as caramel sauce, and my mouth waters for a taste.

Breath shaky, I drop back to my heels, my eyes down. "I'm sorry I attacked you."

He cups the back of my neck, fingers tangled in my hair. "I pushed you to it."

My eyes flick back to his. The burn of his power hisses between us, and my voice rumbles with the first tremor of an earthquake. "Next time I tell you to back off, you back the fuck off."

Pupils flaring wide, he takes an unsteady breath of his own before he forces his hands down to his sides. "I understand."

"Good." Spine straight, I turn and march to the door, proud to have gotten the last word.

I grip the handle and twist, then stare in dumbfounded confusion at the knob in my hand. "What the...?"

"What happened?"

I hold up the golden knob. "It broke."

He grunts, then comes to stand at my side. "Maybe you can just shove it back on?"

When I do, a metallic *ting* comes from the other side as something falls out. "*No.*"

Crouching, I stare at the broken handle, then wedge my fingers under the door to pry it open, but it sticks in place.

"Oh, no," Tobias purrs, smug satisfaction in his voice. "Whatever will we do now?"

"You know, if you're really that impatient, you can just use some of that new energy to rip the door off its hinges," Tobias drawls from his place at the desk. Asshole claimed the only chair in the room.

I pause my pacing to glare at him. "Then I'd have to pay to fix it, and I'm already going to be out a lot of money replacing all these ingredients." I sweep an arm toward the shelves for emphasis.

He spins in the chair, the chef coat he stole stretching at the seams, to stare at the tubs and bags. "Why?"

"Because we just had sex in here!" I hiss and rub my neon-blue clog over the bloody handprints on the floor. Damn things refuse to come off without cleaner.

"It's not like we did it *on* the flour." With a shrug,

he turns back to the desk. "The humans will never know."

"*I'll* know." Growling with frustration, I march back to the door and knock. "Perry, have you heard back from Jax yet?"

My fingers curl and uncurl, annoyed I left my phone locked in the drawer under the cash register and have to rely on someone else to call for help.

"No, Master." Stress fills his voice, and something nudges against my shoe.

When I peer down, his fingers wiggle under the door. I crouch and grip them for a moment in reassurance. Over the last two hours, each of the imps has come back here for similar contact, as if they don't believe I'm really okay.

What did they hear to be so worried?

With a final squeeze, I release him. "Try calling again, will you?"

"Of course, Master." His fingers disappear, and I sag against the door.

The sounds of paper turning straightens me back up again, and I turn to stare suspiciously at Tobias's broad back. "What are you looking at?"

"You're not making enough money. You should increase your prices." He turns another page. "And stop spending so much money at… What's Tam Imports?"

"That's none of your business!" I stomp over and grab the ledger out from under his hands. "How I spend money is none of your business."

He glares up at me. "Well, actually, it's very much my business. You have to have income to pay rent for your room and your portion of the dinners you agreed to purchase and make for the house."

Heat rushes to my cheeks at the reminder, and I hug the large book to my chest. "It's not your business until I can't make payments."

"Kellen said you're renting one of his properties, too." His brow lifts. "For your imps?"

My chin lifts. "Also, none of your business."

"I oversee Kellen's finances as well as Emil's and my own. Between the three of us, you have heavy financial responsibilities. Adie." Caution fills his voice, and he reaches out to cup my legs to tug me closer. "Be very careful not to overextend yourself. I…" His fingers tighten on my thighs. "Don't make me have to collect on you."

Something inside me softens at this show of concern. For all his rough edges, Tobias really does care for me in his own gruff way. I set the ledger down to twine my arms around his neck and hug him closer.

With a contented sigh, he nestles against my stomach. I stare down at his chestnut waves, only slightly disarrayed from our earlier activity, and my heart constricts at his show of vulnerability. My catalyst demon must really, *really* like me to show this level of care—

"What are you doing?" My voice comes out as a squeak of surprise.

He nuzzles my stomach again, and another button gives way. His hot tongue sneaks inside my chef coat to find bare skin. "Sex, obviously."

"Ugh!" When I shove his shoulders, his arms tighten around my waist to keep me in place as he finds my bellybutton and investigates the crevice. I bop him on the head. "Stop that!"

"But you said no snuggling at the bakery." He adds teeth, nipping at my lower stomach. "That must mean you're looking for round two right now."

"That's not what this means at all!"

The more I wiggle to free myself, the more buttons Tobias manages to open. How much practice does he have with opening clothes with his talented mouth?

His grip on me shifts, and I clutch his shoulders

as he lifts my feet from the ground. In the next instant, I find myself straddling his lap, his hard cock pressed to my core.

"We're not doing this ag—"

He catches my protest with his mouth, and power trickles into me, igniting my passion. My legs wrap around him, locking him to the chair, as I return the kiss. His growl of satisfaction rolls down my throat, straight to the growing heat between my thighs, and I rub against the hard bulge in his slacks.

Gripping his hair, I pull him back far enough to catch his gaze. "No knot this time."

His eyes narrow. "You want me inside you, you don't get to dictate how it happens."

The air crackles between us once more in a battle of wills. I doubt being with Tobias will ever be easy, but I never shy away from a challenge.

Grinning, I lower my mouth back to his to whisper against his lips, "Maybe you don't get to be inside me, then."

"Do I really have to prove my dominance again?" Embers simmer in his voice, the hint of a blaze soon to follow. He doesn't sound unhappy at the idea, though. In fact, if the increased bulge in his pants is anything to go by, he wants to dominate, to subdue.

None-too-gently, I bite his lower lip. "Every single time."

His hands shove beneath my waistband to cup my bare ass. "I look forward to it, my sweet little succubus."

As my mouth opens over his, eager for this game once more, a loud knock comes from the door, followed by Perry's happy voice. "Master, Jax has arrived, and he brought his tools!"

With a quiet groan, my head drops to Tobias's shoulder. "Tell him to go away."

"Master?" Uncertain, the knock comes again, more timidly this time. "I didn't hear that."

"She said go away! We're busy!" Tobias calls, and I bite his shoulder.

"Master?"

"Ugh!" I straighten and twist to stare at the door. "Yes, Perry, please have Jax open the door."

Tobias's hold tightens on my ass. "We're not done here."

"We're done for now." I drop my legs back to the floor. "This is me reluctantly saying back off."

He shifts me to rub over his cock, and my body trembles. "You don't mean that."

"But I said it." I hold my breath, waiting for his response.

After a moment, his hold loosens, and he pushes me off his lap. "So you did."

Bending, I cup his cheeks. "You're going to get so many cuddles later."

Embers drift across his pupils. "I am going to fuck you so hard you can't walk."

One side of my mouth kicks up. "I'm a succubus, silly. I can take all the fucking you can dish out."

CHARMED

"If this ever happens again, you can just pop the bolts out of the hinges to open the door," Jax explains as soon as the door opens.

I rush out into the freedom of the hall, gulping in breaths of sugary air to clear the sex from my lungs. "Thanks for the tip. Did you hear that Tobias?"

"I already knew." Tobias strides past Jax with a brief nod, casts one last, heated look in my direction, and takes off down the hall.

My mouth drops open in shock before I yell, "What do you mean you *knew?*"

Without response, he disappears out the side door.

Perry gloms onto my side. "Master, you're well."

"Thank you, Jax," I call from around the imp's lanky body.

A gruff rumble acknowledges me, and to

discover what I missed, I shuffle toward the kitchen, Perry attached like a barnacle.

When I check the time, I discover most of the night passed while Tobias and I were trapped. Jax didn't arrive because my imps reached him, but rather because Tally returned with all of her men for the spell casting she planned to help boost my protection.

I find her boxing up the leftover cupcakes, the front of the shop already dark through the pass-through.

Despite my protests, she helps me close down the bakery and place an order for new ingredients to be delivered tomorrow. Without comment, Jax and Slater help haul everything in the pantry to my purloined Mystery Machine out back while Xander and Reese push the tables out of the way and stack chairs on top of them.

The initial buzz of energy fades as we work, and my movements become sluggish as my body attempts to enter hibernation mode to process Tobias's energy.

The imps go into a cleaning frenzy, and soon, the bakery smells like lemons and bleach. Not the best scent to lure in customers, but it should dissipate by morning.

As they work, each finds an excuse to brush against me, some more obvious than others, and I wonder if they're trying to mask Tobias's scent on my skin. My entire body smells of him, but I don't have the heart to tell them their efforts are futile.

In the process of cashing out the register, I have to pause and stare at the money in my hands, my foggy brain unable to recall where I was at.

A hand rubs surreptitiously over my ass, and I snap back to alertness. "Okay, that's enough. No more."

"But, Master..." Kelly protests, holding his offending hands out. "He marked you, and you shouldn't smell like the catalyst demon. You should smell like—"

"Nope!" I raise a finger to cut him off. "We're not discussing what I should and shouldn't smell like."

His broad shoulders slump, and even his bushy, biker beard droops a little. When his large, brown eyes begin to glisten, guilt shoots through me. They're just following their instincts after all.

My arm drops back to my side. "Fine, you can keep doing it. But this zone"—I make a circular motion around my nether-region—"is off limits."

"But that's where the smell is the stron—"

Up comes the finger once more. "Nope!"

With a discontented whine, he shuffles forward to rub his bristly cheek against mine before returning to work.

When I glance up, I meet Reese's curious gaze, and heat floods my cheeks. Of all Tally's humans, I'm the least comfortable around Reese. He sees too much with his fae-touched eyes. The slash of brown across one pupil allows him to peer past the illusions demons use to pass as human. It makes him dangerous, though he's never been anything but kind to me.

He blinks slowly, veiling his gaze. "Do they do that a lot?"

I glance back to the cash in my hands. "Yeah, they like to scent me."

As if to accentuate my words, Martha approaches, a broom in her hands, and rolls against me as she passes.

"Like cats?" Reese asks, curiosity in his voice.

"Leave it alone," Xander mutters. "You're making her uncomfortable."

"But they didn't always do that." He sounds like a scholar fixated on his new favorite topic. "It's only recently they started. Is it because you just had sex?"

My head jerks up in time to see Xander smack Reese over the back of the head.

"Ow." He turns a hurt expression on his brother. "Why'd you do that?"

"Just because you know, doesn't mean you need to talk about it," he hisses before his perfectly normal gaze shifts to me. "Sorry. He doesn't really understand boundaries."

"It's okay. I don't mind talking about sex." I shrug and go back to the money. "It's pretty much what I'm built for, right?"

"But you restrain yourself." When I glance up again in surprise, Reese's brows furrow together. "You shouldn't. You look healthier today. Sex is good for you."

"Maybe," Xander grits out through clenched teeth, "she doesn't *want* it to just be sex."

"Humans are fragile," I mumble. My eyes shift between the two brothers. "Without restraint, I could take everything from the person I embrace."

"But Adie does not harm humans," Tally proclaims loudly as she joins us.

I hold Reese's fae gaze. "Your men are not human."

"And that is a *good* thing." Tally gives me a firm

shake. "You are grumpy for having fed so voraciously."

I cringe, remembering Tally's comments about how I'm something of a celebrity in the baku circle. Like a freaking reality TV show. "Please tell me your peeping Tom of a brother didn't tell you that."

Her mahogany eyes widen. "There are so many shadows in the pantry."

I drop my head once more. "Fuck my life."

Tally nods. "That is everyone's deepest wish."

"Oh, my god, *stop*." Groaning, I cover my face.

"Pantry is emptied," Slater rumbles as he walks through the swinging doors. "The imps are mopping up the blood, now."

Reese's lips part, and he takes a step closer. "Blood? I've never read that succubi take blood during feeding. Is that normal?" He spins back to the duffel on the floor and yanks out a thick tome. "We should update our descriptions."

"Calm down, man." With an apologetic glance for me, Slater strides around the counter. "It's not part of regular feeding. Don't write that down."

Confused, he closes the book. "But then why would there be blood?"

As Slater's voice drops in quiet explanation,

Tally squeezes my arm. "My Reese is sometimes very innocent. Do not let it bother you."

"Hey, Adie, that guy is here to pick up your staff," Jax calls from the pass-through.

"I'll be right back." I slide past Tally and into the kitchen, where the imps gather at the island, sad faces turned to me. It tugs at my heartstrings. "Oh, come on, everyone. You'll be back tomorrow."

Iris tugs on her rainbow braids. "When will we go to our new home?"

"Soon, I promise."

"Four days," Philip pipes up from the hall where he stands next to the door.

Martha's hands clasp in front of her motherly bosom. "And you will be there with us?"

I sigh, too tired for this argument. We've gone over this before. "No, I live in a different house."

"We should be with Master," Kelly rumbles and the others nod in agreement.

Philip clicks his tongue with impatience. "Let's get going, kiddos. I don't have all night."

Reluctant, they shuffle to the door and file out.

I follow behind and catch Philip's attention. "Any word from Julian?"

My cousin pulled another disappearing act, and

it has me worried. Last time he vanished, Cousin Cassandra had her talons in him.

Philip shakes his head, his boyish face unconcerned. "He'll be back when he's finished with whatever he's doing."

"You're not worried at all?"

He pushes his hair back from his face. "I've been with Julian for over a hundred years. He always bounces back."

My lips part in surprise. "Over a hundred years?"

He winks playfully and nudges my chin up. "Don't let the face fool you. I've been around since before you existed." Stepping out into the alley, he spreads his arms wide to show off his boyish body. "Anytime you want a snack, I'm just a phone call away."

My nose wrinkles with disgust. "No thanks, I'm not into children, no matter how old they may actually be."

"Hey, this"—he points to his rounded cheeks and pointed chin—"was considered a strapping adult when I took form."

I lean out the doorway. "Times have changed. So, should you!"

Middle fingers in the air, he turns and jogs after my imps.

I close the door and lock it. It's time to get our magic on.

Or whatever Tally's men have planned for tonight.

THE CARE OF WITCHES

"You'll want to stand back," Jax rumbles as soon as I step out of the kitchen.

I pause next to the display case and glance around.

Shades cover the windows to keep passersby from peeking inside, and the tables and chairs from the center of the room now sit off to the sides. Tally perches on one, her feet swinging as she watches the proceedings.

Jax walks around the room, setting out tiny votive candles that smell like cinnamon on the floor. Warm and comforting, it makes my hands itch for a mixing bowl as the sudden craving for spiced cake floods my mouth. Fall, with all its wonderful flavors, can't come soon enough.

Xander sits cross-legged in the center of the

room, his laptop propped on his folded legs and his expression focused.

Slater stands behind him, muscular arms folded across his chest and a permanent scowl on his face. It makes me wonder if I've put them in an awkward position, asking them to do magic when they're Kellen's witches. Is this considered a conflict of interest, since Kellen is supposed to be *taking care* of the Hunter situation for me?

With the floor cleared, Reese uses violet chalk to draw out a large diagram of circles and symbols around the pair. It's complicated, and the more I try to focus on it, the fuzzier it gets, until my gaze fixes on the bare floor instead of the chalk lines. It makes my head hurt and my eyes ache, and the fifth time I find myself admiring the grains in my hardwood floor, I give up and join Tally where she hovers off to one side.

"Do you know what they're doing?" I whisper as I lean against the table she perches on.

Her focus locks on the men instead of what they're doing, and she doesn't even spare me a glance. "Magic."

I roll my eyes. "No shit."

She gives me a sheepish smile. "Cinnamon candles for protection, violet chalk for insight. The symbols Reese uses are powerful, so it will be a strong spell."

Curious, I try to read the symbols again, and my eyes slide to the side. "How can you tell."

As she shrugs, the gossamer wing pattern on her back shifts. "I can't look at them. The more powerful the symbols, the more difficult it is for me to see."

Pride fills her voice, and I turn to her, curious. "How can you stand to live with them?"

Her pink brows pinch together. "What do you mean?"

I rub my bare arms where goose bumps form. "If they do this stuff at home, doesn't it make your skin itch constantly?"

"They practice in the basement. I do not go there unless there is great need." Her attention shifts back to her men. "There are wards against demons, and it is uncomfortable to venture through them."

I stare at her, nonplussed. How can she live in a house with a space designed to actively reject her? How much do her men truly care for her if they would build that kind of space within their home?

Her wings shift along her shoulders once more, though she continues to stare at Reese. "Do not be offended on my behalf. It is not asked for nor appreciated."

Shame rushes through me. I don't know anything about their relationship, so who am I to judge. "I'm sorry."

With a curt nod, her focus shifts to her left. "Brother, you should leave."

I start, then lean around her to stare at the deeper shadows beneath the table. If I focus hard enough, I can sense the disturbance there, like grit on the inside of my eyelids and the urge to yawn. I wave. "Hey, Tally's brother."

A lit votive candle slides across the floor, illuminating the underside of the table. Surprised, I glance up at Jax, who shrugs. "Dude needs to find a different hobby."

Tally's cheeks puff out. "He is just concerned. You should not chase him away like that."

Unrepentant, he holds out a blue stick lighter. "We're about ready to start. Want to light the rest of the candles, Gumball?"

With a delighted grin that flashes tiny fangs, Tally grabs the lighter and hops off the table, running to the nearest candle.

I wait until she's out of hearing distance before I

glance at Jax. "Any chance you have a ward to keep Tally's brother out of the bakery?"

He shakes his head. "Not unless you want to make it so no demon can enter."

"No, that wouldn't work."

"Didn't think so."

We stand in awkward silence for a moment, before I say, "Thank you for helping me out like this. You'll be compensated."

Restrained savagery rolls through his voice. "Making life hard for Hunters is compensation enough."

In the center of the room, Xander closes his laptop and passes it across the chalk circle to Reese, who sets it out of the way. He passes back a golden band of some kind, which Xander cradles in his cupped palms. Slater's arms unfold, his hands settling on Xander's shoulders.

Jax rolls his neck, vertebrae popping. "Looks like it's show time."

The large man moves with surprising grace as he walks around the chalked circle to position himself directly behind Xander and Slater. Reese takes up a similar position on the opposite side, facing the pair in the center.

As one, they kneel, hands out with fingers touching the outermost edge of the circle.

Across the room, Tally clicks off the lighter and hops up on another table, her feet off the ground. Concerned, I do the same. The last time I witnessed Reese and Xander performing a big spell, I sat on the opposite side of a salt line, protected from their magic.

I eye the kitchen. Should I go get some salt? Is their salt different from what I use for baking?

Before I decide, Jax and Reese do *something* and light spreads outward from their fingertips, infusing the chalked diagram with magic. The same blue glow I saw before, spreads outward from Reese's side, while red ripples out from Jax. The two magics meet in the middle, slip alongside each other, then blend into a lovely purple that makes me want to claw my eyes out.

The headache from earlier pounds against my temples, and I force myself to focus on my knees instead. Human magic isn't meant to be understood by demons, and I should just stop trying.

In my peripheral vision, the magic grows brighter, and the flames on the votive candles shift from natural yellow to bright purple. The light hangs unnaturally heavy in the air, staying close to the ground. When I glance up, everything above table height seems normal, but when I peer down, not even the glow of fluorescent lights intrude on the purple haze.

Xander speaks, his words slippery and undefined. They make my ears itch, and I resist the urge to cover them to block out his voice. I have the feeling that leaving the room is the only thing that will help, and my bones shiver a warning against stepping on the glowing floor. Concerned, I pull my legs up onto the table and hug my knees.

Next time we have a magic party, I get my own salt circle.

The spell continues for forty minutes, during which my butt goes numb from the hard table, and my headache spreads into a full body throb. When it finally ends, the lavender glow blinks out. My ears pop at the same time, and my hands fly up to rub away the pain. I work my jaw and roll my shoulders in an attempt to loosen some of the tension, but everything *hurts*.

Scratch my previous idea. No more magic for me, period, salt circle or no salt circle.

Across the room, Tally hops off her table to put out the candles. Slater helps Xander to stand, and the smaller man leans heavily against him. Reese sprawls onto his back, chest rising quickly as he stares at the ceiling, while Jax stands with an easy stretch of muscles. Of the four, Xander and Reese seem the most affected by the spell. Does that mean they're the most powerful, or do their frailer bodies just make them more susceptible to exhaustion?

After a moment, Xander straightens away from Slater's support and steps out of the circle, his sneakers scuffing the diagram in the process. He pauses for a moment next to his brother, and through some silent communication, Reese gives him a thumbs up before rolling to his feet. He walks to the duffel bag stashed under a table and pulls out a bottle of lemon cleaner and a rag. He sprays a fine mist over the floor, drops the rag onto the ground, and uses his foot to begin wiping off the design.

Xander watches him for a moment before joining me at my table. He holds out the golden circle, which I now recognize as an arm cuff. "Here, this should give you warning of any Hunters nearby."

I take it from him, and tingles rush over my fingers. "Do I just wear it?"

My skin crawls at the idea.

He nods. "Yeah, it will tingle if a magical object made from demon parts comes near you."

My eyes narrow in suspicion. "It's tingling right now."

"Yeah." He lifts a hand to the clay necklace he wears. "That's us."

I stare at the disk, which gives off the faint scent of ozone. "Something you want to tell me?"

"No." The short reply comes with a bite. "Just put on the arm band."

Reluctant, I slide the tingling band up my left arm. It stops just above my elbow, the metal a warm weight. Where it touches, my skin itches, and I want to pull it off right away. Instead, I press my hands into my thighs. "Tell me how it works."

"Those tingles you feel." He taps the band with one nail, and it rings through my bones. "When you're outside the bakery, if you feel that, a Hunter is near. The radius isn't big, but it should give you enough warning to hyper-speed out of there. Hunter's magic isn't long range. They have to be close to incapacitate you. They like to work in pairs, so the warning will be even stronger."

I flex my bicep, and the band cuts into my flesh. "Tingles mean run. Got it."

Xander lifts a shaky hand to push his hair back. "I don't suppose you have any leftover cupcakes?

Or just some sugar and a spoon? Anything will do. I'm crashing fast."

I straighten in alarm. "Why didn't you say so sooner? Of course, I have something you can eat."

He sags against the table, his eyelids fluttering down for a moment. Dark circles smudge under his eyes, and now that I look, I notice the pallor of his skin.

Before his eyes open again, I hyper-speed into the kitchen and return with a box of leftover cakes. Tossing the lid back, I grab one of the mini bumblebee cupcakes, pop open his mouth, and shove one in.

He chokes in surprise, eyes flying open, before the sweetness registers on his tongue. I hold up another, which he takes with a look of alarm, as if afraid I'll keep shoving them into his face. Which is tempting.

I glance past his shoulder to the other men, who all show signs of exhaustion, and my wings rustle against my spine with the need to feed them.

"Tally," I bark, and the little baku demon bounces to alertness. "Your men need sugar. Grab another box of cakes."

With a salute, she runs into the kitchen.

Slater shakes his head. "I really don't—"

"You"—I point at him with one sharp talon—"will eat your sugar like a good boy. I will not get in trouble with Kellen for damaging his witches."

His mouth snaps closed, and I turn back to Xander, who shoves another cake into his mouth, eyes wide as he chews.

Sighing, I lift another cake and put it into his empty hands. Who knew witches were so delicate?

FOGGED IN

"Thank you for your help tonight." I shove another box of leftover cupcakes into Xander's hands, despite the frosting that already stains his lips from too many treats.

Guilt pushes at me for not having fed him and Reese when they exorcised the house I rented for my imps. Mentally, I make a note to stock up on sugary treats next time I ask them to perform any magic. Not that I plan to ask them for more help. I will not abuse Kellen's witches.

Xander stares down at the box, a little green in the face, but doesn't offer a protest. "Of course. Anything for Tally's friend."

"Or Kellen's woman," Slater adds as he heads for the side door. "Can't fail him again."

"You didn't fail him last time." I push hair back

from my face with a shaky hand. As I help put the tables back in order, fatigue wears on me more and more. Tobias's energy rolls in my stomach, dragging at my bones and pulling me to sleep. "There's no way you could have stood up to Domnall."

He cuts me a hard stare. "You know that doesn't mean anything."

I meet his gaze squarely. "Kellen will never hear from me what happened that night."

He gives a tight nod. "And I will do anything within my power to help when you ask."

Jax clasps the other man's shoulder. "We all will."

Reese joins us, his large duffel slung over his shoulder. "Adie, do you know you have a hairy gnome in your kitchen?"

I stare at him blankly, my tired brain unable to process the words.

Face falling, he darts an uncertain glance back into the kitchen. "Is there *not* a gnome in your kitchen?"

"That is Vova," Tally announces as she comes up behind him. "Vova is a Domovoi, not a gnome." She turns to me. "And he is impatient for us to leave. I have set out his offering, but he will not take it while we remain."

"Thank you, Tally." I glance at the men. "Thank all of you for coming so late. Or so early?" I scrub a hand over my face. "Either way, thank you."

With a smattering of goodbyes, the men tromp out into the dark alley. Slater goes last, holding the door for Tally.

She stops to squeeze my arm. "Go home. You need to digest."

"I will," I promise.

With a smile, she skips forward and links her arm through Slater's. The hard man softens, tucking her close to his side as they follow the others. I hover at the door, my hand lifting to rub at my tingling bicep. The farther away the witches get from the bakery, the less the arm cuff nips at me.

By the time they reach the alley and disappear around the corner, the irritation vanishes altogether. When Xander said it had a short range, he wasn't kidding. But any warning is better than none.

Cool wind funnels down the alley, and, with a shiver, I pull up the zipper on my hoodie before I step out and lock the door. My steps lead me in the opposite direction the others took, to the van that waits in the back parking lot, where the contents of my pantry now fill the back.

What am I going to do with all this flour and

sugar? The small cupboard the guys gave me at the house won't store all of it. Wracking my tired thoughts, I come to a decision and climb into the van.

The drive to the imps' new house only takes ten minutes, and I back into the broken driveway. Clearing the house of its haunting didn't fix as much of the dilapidation as I hoped, and I scheduled an inspector to confirm that the house was sturdy and that the imps won't fall through the floor. I need to find them furniture, too, before they move in.

So much to do, and so little time.

For a moment, I lean my head back and close my eyes, breathing in the unique silence that comes at four in the morning. But when gray shapes begin to flit across my eyelids, I force them open once more. No time for sleep yet.

Keys in hand, I climb out of the van and open the back, then hoist a large bag of flour onto my shoulder before I walk up the porch. The steps still creak, and I skirt around the center where a bottomless pit used to reside. Despite Reese and Xander's reassurance, I can't bring myself to trust the magically mended boards yet.

The ugly lion head knocker glares at me, its ruby eyes baleful in the glow cast by the streetlights.

I glare back at it as I open the door. "Better get used to seeing me, buddy. I'm your new renter."

The metal knocker bangs loudly as I shove open the door, and I eye the lion once more for signs of life before I step inside. The foyer is everything I remember, with grand chandelier and a sweeping staircase. I take the archway to the left, past a formal parlor, and into the kitchen, setting the first bag of flour on the empty counter.

Unloading the rest of the ingredients takes little time, but my energy levels continue to wane. If I don't find my nest soon, I'll end up curled on the floor as my body shuts down.

In that moment, the drive back across town feels like too much. Too much time. Too much focus to navigate city streets. Just too much. I need my bed *now*, not twenty minutes from now.

I lock up the house once more, make sure the van is locked, then spindle energy out into my limbs. Even hyper-speed takes effort, but it brings me to my front porch in five minutes and barely makes a dent in the energy I took from Tobias.

Knees weak, I sag against the front door and fumble in my pocket for the keys. Sleep drags at my eyelids, color washing from the world.

Somehow, I make it inside and stumble to the

stairs. By the time I reach the top of the first landing, I'm crawling, and the steep path to my attic bedroom undoes me. I can't do it. My legs and arms shake, and I curl over my knees, forehead to the cool ground.

To my left, Emil's door creaks open. The hardwood floor vibrates with heavy steps, before warm, moist air snuffles at my hair.

"Go away, Tac," I mumble. "I'm sleeping."

His large, wedge-shaped head bumps against me, and I roll onto my side, then my back as he continues to prod at me. Unable to fight him off, I sprawl at the base of my stairs, one wrist knocking against the bottom step to my room while the other dangles off the landing. I blink blearily up into his saucer-sized, green eyes. Tufted ears swivel before he leans down to snuffle over my stomach.

Weak, I lift a hand to push him away, but my arm barely makes it an inch off the floor before it falls to my side.

He sniffs higher, lets out a low rumble of displeasure when he reaches the arm with the spelled cuff on it, then snorts loudly into my face. When I remain unresponsive, he circles my prone body for a moment before dagger-sized teeth close gently over my calves.

The ceiling shifts as Tac drags me down the short hall to Emil's room, and my butt bumps up onto the plush carpet at the doorway. Instantly, warmth envelops me from the fireplace. It casts golden light over his soft, white furniture, cozy and inviting.

We reach the edge of Emil's bed, and Tac backs onto it, dragging me up.

"Tac, what are you doing?" Emil demands, sleep heavy in his voice.

Tac drops my legs, and the bed bounces as he stomps around, driving Emil from beneath his mound of blankets. His rumpled, white hair appears first, followed by bare shoulders as the comforters puddle around his waist.

When the ice demon's frosty gaze lands on me, he blinks once in surprise before sitting up. "Adie, do you have any idea what time it is?"

"Blame the stupid cat." I curl onto my side once more, weakly lifting my arms over my head in the semblance of a cave. "I was just trying to sleep."

Tac rumbles and shoves me with his giant head, uncurling me once more.

Emil pushes the covers back, glorious in his frosty nudity, and crawls to my side. He bends closer, hair soft against my cheek, and inhales. "You've fed."

"Mmm," mumbling unintelligibly, my eyes drift shut.

His fingers drift snowflakes across my lips, and they part. Another deep breath, and relief fills his voice. "You fed from Tobias."

Head rolling, I catch the pad of his thumb and suckle the ice from his nails. It helps to ease the fire that roils in my belly, and I roll closer to him.

A cool hand smooths the hair back from my face. "You need to rest."

Nodding, I let his thumb slip from my mouth.

Gentle hands tug at my clothes, and I let myself be undressed without resistance. Emil lifts me into the center of the bed before his cold body curls around mine, and the blankets cocoon us in darkness. The bed shifts, and Tac's weight settles over our legs, a low chainsaw rumble vibrating the mattress.

With a sigh of relief, sleep claims me.

Gray fog rolls across the back of my eyelids, hinting at the shape of unformed buildings, the edges soft and billowy as they begin to take shape before dissipating. Dreamland. Closer than it's been since I abandoned it for the human plane.

Did my feeding earlier finally give me the push to return to the place of my birth?

Excited, I move toward Dreamland, but no matter how long I walk, Dreamland stays just out of reach, refusing to take form.

A quiet rustle causes the bank of gray clouds on my right to surge upward. With a flinch of surprise, I spin toward it. I'm not used to Dreamland shifting so much, and other demons who travel here don't physically move the landscape, we simply pass through it.

I squint as the fog clears in places, shifting to combine with the clouds around it. A sudden flash of red burns against my vision in the otherwise monotone world, and hope surges.

"Julian?" The heavy air dampens my voice, cutting off my call before it travels an arm's length away. The red begins to fade, and I step off the path to follow. "Julian, is that you? Why have you disappeared again?"

Another rustle comes from my right, and fog swamps me. I freeze in place for a moment, before my wings slip free and gently beat back the gray. When my vision clears, I search for any sign of red, but find none.

While gorging on Tobias's energy got me closer

to Dreamland, I still need more power before I can fully cross the between the two planes.

Resigned, I turn back the way I came only to find my path obscured. I spin slowly, searching for a landmark, but the ever-changing landscape makes finding one impossible. My heart slams with sudden panic. Every other time I've visited Dreamland since taking form on the human plane, one of my cousins led me there and back.

This is my first venture here alone, and with dawning horror, I realize I don't know how to reconnect with my physical body where it rests snuggled within Emil's embrace.

MONSTER IN THE MIST

The gray fog of Dreamland swirls around me. It doesn't matter how much I backtrack the way I think I came from; the landscape changes from one breath to the next, eddies of gray creating new, twisted paths. All I know is, I'm no closer to the city, I have no clue how to return to my body, and I'm on my own.

Another bank of clouds bursts upward, and a flash of red catches my attention from the corner of my eye. Hours ago, I determined the crimson streak definitely wasn't my cousin Julian, lost here with me.

Whatever creature lives in this in-between place is here to make sure I stay.

I turn slowly, a gradual shuffle of feet and twist of hips to disrupt the fog as little as possible. Sure enough, a thick zigzag of ropes now covers the path

I just traversed. As I watch, the ropes puff out a gray mist that links together to form a larger cloud until it becomes indistinguishable from the gray around it.

My heart flutters in panic.

The nightmare haunting at the imp's house never scared me. If it somehow damaged my corporeal body, I could heal easily. But in Dreamland, things are different. I'm not a demon wearing a human suit. I'm *me*, exposed and vulnerable.

And the more I wander, the closer the red creature in the mist ventures. It could be a lost baku, starved and unable to reach human nightmares to feed from. Or a succubus, like me. The latter presents more danger. Baku can't feed from beings unless they sleep. But a fellow succubus, hard up for energy, will devour anything it can get its talons into.

My knees tremble as I force myself back the way I came, breaking through the new barrier. It brushes cold tendrils over my bare thighs, dragging hungrily at my skin. It clings and leaves gray splotches, like cotton candy from a cone, behind as I pull free. More clings to the back of my knees, and I brush it away, my stomach an uneasy fist against my spine.

If I remain here too long, will I eventually be cocooned in the stuff?

An image of spiders with prey trapped in their webs flashes through my mind. How long will I be trapped before someone thinks to search for me? Will anyone bother?

A quiet chitter reaches my ears, and I spin once more, unable to pinpoint the muffled noise. Did it come from ahead or behind? Am I walking into a trap? But staying still feels equally dangerous.

The chitter comes again, definitely from behind, and I turn back, then force my legs into motion again.

I grip my elbows tight. "Hey, Librarian? How about an assist right about now?"

The fog deadens my voice, and no telltale tingle or flash of light open around me.

My shoulders slump. "Sure, always on your schedule, huh?"

The bank of clouds to my immediate left shoots into the air, and I stumble back from it with a startled yelp.

This time, I catch the mottled tentacles before they vanish. Black with lighter gray spots to blend into the environment. Thin ropes of fog drift from small spikes on the undersides. I wrack my brain for any demon that fits that description. While many sport tentacles in their native form, I can't recall any that generate fog, or even webbing, for that matter. That's science-fiction, horror movie type stuff, not the real world of demons and humans.

I stop my blind search and drag in a deep breath. Wandering will get me nowhere. There has to be a knack to this. How do my cousins always move so easily from the demon place to the human plane? It's been a while since one of them came to take me hunting, and the last time I visited Dreamland with Landon, I blindly followed him without paying attention to my surroundings.

It makes me want to give the impatient me a good kick in the ass.

Pausing, I close my eyes to block out my surroundings and focus on my corporeal form. I currently lie in Emil's bed, snuggled up with my ice demon, my belly full of Tobias's energy. Tac lies on our feet, the monster kitty's weight solid and reassuring.

In the distance, a low rumble reaches me, like the beginnings of a landslide. The air chills in response, and when I open my eyes, my breath forms new fog. My bones ring like a tuning fork, and when I take my next step forward, the vibration grows. Around me, the entire landscape shakes, the ground rolling to make each step more difficult. Ice crystals form lacy nets in the air and crunch as I break through them.

My men are angry, and their heightened emotions draw me back to them.

Behind me, the ice clouds crackle and break in a scurry of movement. My wings rustle, a warning of danger. I quicken my pace into a run, the ice growing heavier with every step.

The ground rumbles and a sheet of ice breaks off and sheers across my path, its edges razor sharp. I leap over, and a glow of light flickers in the shadows, a pop of blue that flickers and almost vanishes before it surges back to life once more.

As I near, it takes shape, a tattered rope that pulses with a familiar energy. I grasp the end, hissing when it sinks beneath my skin, burrows along my bones and through my guts to find the core of energy that creates my existence.

All at once, I see the path back to my body and surge toward it.

Another crash sounds and I peer back, curiosity damning me.

In the landscape of icy fog, a dark shape rises. Tentacles lash the ground in anger as it blinks a hundred red eyes. Around it, smaller versions swarm, little pops of red blinking in and out. The creature rises higher until it towers above, and one thick tentacle lifts, then slaps down toward me.

Frantic, I turn back to the rope and grasp it tightly, allowing it to hurtle me back to my waiting body.

~

My eyes snap open to gray, and fear slams through me before I realize I made it back to the human plane. The gray is the shadow of Emil's comforters.

Next, the angry voices register. Emil and Tobias.

The ice demon's body still rests against mine, but now his muscles turn to frozen stone. Frost forms where our bodies touch.

Beneath me, the bed shakes with Tobias's anger. "I have an IOU. It's my night."

Ice cracks through Emil's voice. "I am not aware of any *schedule*, and I won't turn her away when she comes to me in need."

"What need could she have possibly had for you?" The weight of a mudslide slides over us, suffocating. "I filled her to bursting earlier."

"And then left her to find her way home

alone?" The temperature drops even more, and I shiver. In answer, Emil's hand curls over my shoulder in an icy caress meant to reassure. "You *know* succubi need a safe place to digest their meals when they gorge, but you abandoned her? And what were you doing feeding her at the *bakery* in the first place?"

Despite the chill, Emil's obvious concern warms me, and I snuggle closer to him.

Tobias ignores the last question to address the first. "She's a capable adult, able to know her limits. If she needed to go home as soon as she fed, she would have."

Aw, Tobias believes in me. My toes curl at the revelation. He's going to get so many snuggl—

Oh, fuck. I gave him an IOU for snuggle time when I got home from work. While it wasn't official, it was vocalized and accepted. But instead of going to him, instincts drove me to my own room, to the safety of my nest. I just lost the power to fully make it there, and Tac brought me to Emil instead.

I need to make this right.

Pushing away Emil's hand, I struggle to find the edge of the comforter and free my head. Hair covers my eyes, and I shove back the blue tipped strands to gaze at Tobias. The catalyst demon fills Emil's doorway, his toes at the edge of the soft white carpet. He still wears his business suit from earlier.

Did he wait up all night for me to come to him?

Guilt pushes me farther out from under the bedding. "Tobias, I'm so sorry. Everything took longer than expected, and then I was just *so* tired, and—"

Emil touches my arm, freezing my words. "Where are you going?"

I glance back at him in surprise. "To Tobias?'

The pale blue of his eyes fades to white. "After I protected your body for the last two hours?"

"I—" I twist to stare at Tobias, who waits impatiently. "But, I need to—"

"You were completely defenseless." Ice cracks in the air behind me. "Even when Tobias arrived, you didn't wake. Helpless, if not for me."

My back stiffens at that, and I spin back to Emil. "Now, wait just a minute. I'm not *helpless*."

"Like a baby turtle with its belly exposed." His lips peel back in a dark smile. "What's a hungry hawk to do when faced with such a treat?"

"Strike without hesitation," Tobias says, and the air shifts as he crosses Emil's threshold.

The ice demon's attention shifts past me. "I didn't invite you into my sanctum."

"You never uninvited me after the last time." Tobias *tsks* quietly. "An oversight on your part."

"One I will rectify." The bed dips behind me, and Emil lets out a warning growl. "Tobias—"

"We're at an impasse," he purrs, and it shakes through my bones. "This is the most expedient resolution."

"You are not welcome in my bed," Emil growls, and where our bodies touch, my skin grows numb from the cold.

"Yet here I am." Heat engulfs my other side, and Tobias's hand slides along my hip. "We've shared before."

Ice cracks on Emil's lips as he speaks. "I'm not in the mood to share."

The two demons glare at each other over my head in a silent battle of wills. The air between them begins to shift, a mini cyclone in the making.

"Okay, hold on, both of you." I wave my arms to dispel the storm before it takes hold. "I never agreed to be shared. Especially between *you two*."

Now, Emil's frozen gaze shifts to me. "Why not between *us two*? Is there someone else you would rather share with?"

Reaching up, I boop him on the nose. "Don't get your panties in a twist."

When he catches my hand, frost forms a shackle around my wrist. "Do not mock me."

"Yes," Tobias rumbles, his breath fiery against my bare shoulder. "Why not us?"

My wings rustle in agitation. "Hey, now, Emil doesn't want to share, either. Why are you guys getting offended that I'm in agreement?"

"Because I know why Emil objects." Burning hands cage my ribs, cracking the thin layer of ice there. "Why do you?"

"Yes, Ms. Pond, why?" Emil reaches out to paint snowflakes over my collarbones. New ice for every layer Tobias's heat melts.

My body groans in protest, my bones shivering with a warning of the danger of hot and cold. The last time these two turned me into an Adie Sandwich, their combined energies rattled me, too close to pain for my taste.

"You guys are too much together." I wiggle to dislodge their hands, but they cage me in on both sides. "I'll break."

"You'll heal." Emil's fingers slide down my chest to build tiny snow drifts on my aching nipples.

Tobias reaches around to spread a burning palm over my lower stomach, heating my core as he whispers into my ear, "Imagine how good Emil will feel, sliding into all this warmth. I can keep my hand here the entire time, keeping you melted for him."

Emil growls again, low and throaty with desire. When my gaze lifts to his face, pale pink tints his milky skin. How quickly my ice demon loses to the draw of warmth.

"And when you're filled with him"—Tobias's other hand drifts down to cup one of my ass cheeks, squeezing the plump flesh—"I'll fill you, too. Imagine the power to be gained by feeding from both of us at the same time."

His voice strokes along my body, his words a siren's song of promises. Panting, I let Tobias push me forward, closer to Emil, and my ice demon cups my cheeks, drawing my lips toward his. There's a reason to resist, to not give in to this moment, but my brain short circuits as I gasp and pull Emil's breath into my lungs.

Across the room, a thunderstorm floods the entrance in the form of an enraged Kellen. "Adie, you have some explaining to do!"

It breaks the spell Tobias wove around us, and Emil shoves the other demon off his bed.

He lands with a pained curse as I twist to gape at Kellen. "What?"

He shakes a fist through the door, lightning

zipping across his knuckles. "Where's my Mystery Machine?"

"Oh." My eyes widen in realization, and I yank the blankets up to my chin for some semblance of protection. "Yeah, about that…"

"And what the fuck is this supposed to be?" He shakes his fist again, and now, I spot the blue and orange nose of a toy van poking from the top.

"That's a Mystery Machine."

At the time, I thought it would be funny to leave the toy replica in the empty parking place. Thanks to Landon's past obsession with cartoons, I have an entire box of Scooby Doo related items. I *also* thought I'd get the van back before anyone noticed it was missing.

Too bad my sorry ass left it abandoned at my unhaunted house.

"*This* is *not* a Mystery Machine." He opens his palm to display the tiny thing. "This is obviously a Chevrolet. The Mystery Machine is a Volkswagen!"

I scoot closer to the edge of the bed. "Well, actually, there are a few different versions—"

"You borrowed a Volkswagen!" he roars. "This is not equivalent!"

In response, I yank the blanket over my head.

Kellen continues to rage, despite my awesome

stealth tactics. "If there is *one* scratch on my van, I am going to use that luscious ass of yours to buff it out. *Where* is my Mystery Machine? The *real* one?"

"At my other house."

"Excuse me?" Kellen's voice drops to a low rumble of thunder. "I hope I didn't hear you right, so please repeat."

I peek out of the covers. "At my other house."

His lightning-kissed gaze shoots to Emil. "*Please* let me enter your room so I can turn that devious little succubus over my knee and—"

I yank the cover back over my head and snuggle down in the fluff of Emil's pillows, tuning out Kellen's rage. He can't come in here; I'm *totally* safe for now.

That is, until Tobias yanks the covers off me. I stare up at the treacherous demon in shock. He glances to Emil. "Sharing time is over."

"Get her, Tobias," Kellen crows from the hall.

Emil grumbles a protest and rolls off the opposite side of his bed, dragging a fluffy pink bathrobe over his body.

Hurriedly, I scramble after him toward safety.

A hot hand clamps around my ankle, yanking me back.

Flailing, I grab the bottom sheet and hold on tight. "No, this isn't fair. I'm in the safe zone!"

The sheet slips, popping free on one corner, and the entire bedding set comes off as Tobias drags me from the bed.

Emil glares down at the mess—me tangled in the sheets, blankets, and pillows—and tightens the sash on his ridiculously soft bathrobe. "Everyone, get out! Entrance to my room is revoked!"

Around us, the air thickens. The sheet tangles tighter around my body and drags me toward the door. Tobias tries to dodge and trips instead. Together, we roll across the carpet and out into the hall.

Kellen hugs the wall to prevent himself from being bowled over. Through the opening, Tac peeks from his hiding place behind Emil, his ears twitching, before the door slams shut in our faces.

I blow hair from my eyes. "Well, look what you did now."

"What *I* did?" Tobias picks himself up and brushes off his knees. "*You're* the one who was being childish."

"Okay, look, you neanderthal." I struggle to my feet and throw one edge of my stolen sheet over my shoulder like a majestic toga. "You need to stop trying to drag me places. You're not living in caves anymore."

Offended, he rears back. "I never *once* lived in a *cave*."

"Well, actually, there was that time in the middle ages—" Kellen shuts up when Tobias's angry gaze shifts to him.

"What time is it, anyway?"

The two men stare at me blankly for a moment, before Kellen checks his watch. "Six thirty-four."

That explains why neither Tobias or Emil are at work yet. Kellen must have gotten home late to only just realize the van was missing from the garage.

Which reminds me…

Before either of them remembers their original argument, I flood my limbs with energy and hyper-speed up to the safety of my bedroom.

No, there will *not* be any spanking today!

(UN)SNEAKY

I lock myself in my room and ignore the angry growls as Tobias and Kellen pace outside my door. After I dress, I grab the book the Librarian gave me from my nightstand and settle onto the foot of my bed to flip through the brittle pages.

Being stuck under the leg of Landon's table as a support for an undetermined number of years didn't do it any favors. Dirt flakes from the cover as I flip through it, skimming over text in search of pictures. Strange markings line the gutters, hatches and squiggles that remind me of the marks Xander uses for human magic.

Unlike what Tally's witch boys write out, I can actually focus on these.

I trace a finger over the drawings, curious what they could mean. Are these the ones I should avoid over other ones? Should I show the book to Reese, or is that a super bad idea?

Flipping to another page, I find a drawing of a demon. The giant bat wings and cloven hooves are a dead giveaway. The creature clasps a screaming human close, mouth open to display pointed fangs. Wavy lines connect their mouths, and at the demon's feet lay the brittle husks of other humans.

I squint at the animalistic brow. So that's He Who Devours, huh? The big bad I'm supposed to align myself with in order to survive?

Closing the book, I set it aside and venture back to the door, then crouch to peer under the narrow gap at the bottom. The hall outside my room appears empty, but I wait until five minutes past when Tobias and Emil leave for work before I sneak out of the house.

I don't appreciate Tobias waking me up so early, though his and Emil's anger helped me find my way back to my body. If not for that, I might have been stuck in Dreamland a lot longer. Or trapped by that monster that hid in the mist.

What was that? I've never heard of a creature like that in Dreamland.

Shivering, I hug my elbows close to my body as I hyper-speed toward the bakery. I need to swing by to accept delivery of the new dried goods. While replacing all the flour and sugar came as an unexpected setback, I can't feel too negative about it since it brought me and Tobias closer.

All three of the guys have shown, in one way or another, that they like me, and it warms my little demon heart. I never would have guessed, when all of this began, that our deal could lead to a caring relationship.

The delivery truck arrives right on time, and the nice men even bring in the goods and load them into the newly sanitized pantry. I sign off, then look around the bakery. Hunters aside, things are really looking up for me right now.

I still have hours before I need to start the first batch of cupcakes. Recently, my kitchen demon, Vova, has started the cakes before I come in, but it hasn't been long enough to rely on his help. He's still too new to the bakery, and I worry another, quieter kitchen will lure him away.

With time to kill, I pull out my phone and dial Philip.

He answers on the fourth ring, his voice groggy. "Boss, that you?"

"No, it's Adie." His reminder of my missing cousin pops a hole in my happiness, but I shake it off. Philip said Julian will return when he wants to and not to worry. "I thought I'd come by today and take the imps out shopping."

"M'kay. Just ring when you arrive, and I'll let you in." The line goes dead once more.

Locking the bakery up, I hyper-speed back across town toward the imps' new house. With only days left to get them settled, we need to go buy basic necessities. A few of the rooms come with furniture, but they'll still need bedding and pillows, and some clothes for when they want to go out on their own.

Mired in thought, I don't sense the demon until it's too late.

As soon as I come to a stop in the driveway, a golden-skinned arm shoots out from next to the van and latches onto my arm. "Gotcha."

A startled shriek escapes.

Wincing, Kellen releases me. "Shush, you'll wake the neighbors."

"Don't *do* that!" I swat at him. "Don't you know there are Hunters out here trying to kidnap me?"

"Do *you* know?" His lifts red eyebrows. "You're zipping around town without a care in the world, not letting any of us know where you are. How are we supposed to protect you like this?"

Inwardly, I cringe at my own actions. "Well, I

guess I was more concerned about protecting my ass from *you* to really think about it."

His lips part in surprise. "Whoa, look who's being honest this morning?"

Now, I frown at him. "It's not *that* unusual."

"You like to evade topics a lot." His head tilts to the side. "While you're feeling chatty, why don't you tell me again about the night Domnall attacked you. Because no matter how many times I run it through my head, something's not lining up with the order of events."

The blood drains from my face. The unexpectedness of the question leaves me floundering for a reply as I struggle to remember what I said last time. "I was at the bakery… and Domnall pulled me into the alley—"

"Why were you near the alley?"

"I—"

"How long after Slater left did you go into the alley?"

"Why are you—"

"You're lying to me. You lied to Emil. You attacked Tobias." He leans close, his voice an angry whisper, "I like you Adie, more than I should, and you make life fun, but you're endangering my family."

Refusing to be intimidated, I rise onto my tiptoes and shove back. "You and the others are hiding information from me, which endangers *my* life. Your threats are too black-and-white to leave room for anything but subterfuge. If I lie, it's for a good reason!"

He reaches out to grasp my arm, unerringly finding the magic cuff hidden beneath my zip-up hoodie. "And this? You think none of us noticed this *magic* in the house? You stink of it."

Anger spikes through me. "If you guys let me in on the game plan for how to deal with the Hunters, I wouldn't need to seek alternative protection!"

He growls in frustration. "You don't need to know. You just need to stay safe."

"There!" I jab a finger at his face. "Right there is why I don't tell you guys everything! You're treating me like a child."

"Because you *are* a child!" he roars, and thunder claps overhead. "If you fed more, if you held onto your energy better instead of zipping all over town, you wouldn't be a walking target right now."

I stiffen in his hold. How did things shift so suddenly between us? I thought, of the three, Kellen was the gentlest, the most easy going. But the enraged god who now towers over me shakes my bones with the primal need to flee, to find shelter to wait out a storm that could destroy the city.

Staring down at me, his expression softens, and he rakes a frustrated hand through his fiery-red hair. "I'm sorry, it's just…I don't want you hurt, and sneaking out of the house was the height of stu—"

He cuts off, leaving the sentence unfinished, but it hurts all the same. Maybe I should have let one of them know I was leaving, but it's not like they arranged to escort me around or anything. At least, not that I'm aware of. Who knows what testosterone driven plan they came up with while keeping me out of the loop.

I drop back to my heels, feeling suddenly small when only moments before, I felt invincible. This sudden weakness makes my skin itch. My hands clench into fists, fingernails lengthening into talons against my palms.

Wings razorblading against my spine, I growl, "Be very careful with your next words, storm demon."

Kellen gently clasps my arms. "Adie, honey, I'm sorry. You're not stupid. You're clever and keep me on my toes. It's just, sometimes, your impulsiveness endangers you."

Spine stiff, I refuse to yield to the comfort he

offers. Like a storm, he blows hot, then cools fast, and my emotions can't keep up with him.

"You're right, though, this is a two-way street of trust, and we're failing on both sides." His thumbs rub circles on my elbows as he thinks for a moment. "Tonight, can you get off work early?"

I lift my chin in defiance. "It's my night to close."

"Can you switch with Tally? Or have one of the imps close? Maybe…" He squints as he searches for a name. "Martha? Or Kelly?"

Some of the angry hurt eases. He's paid attention to me and mine, enough to know the names of my imps and which ones are most capable of supervising the store.

Reluctant, I nod. "I'll see what I can do."

"Good." He tugs my stiff body against his chest in a hug that sends tingles down my front. "It's time we have a household meeting."

"Past time," I mutter into his chest.

"And about the Mystery Machine." Pushing me back, he reaches out to pat the side of the van affectionately. "You stole it to cart your imps around?"

Lips tight, I nod.

"How about I add a rental fee for it, and you can

keep using it?" He winces. "Just, try not to wreck it."

My eyes narrow on him. "One hundred a month."

"That's robbery."

I lift my chin. "You're a giant asshole."

"You're using my guilt against me."

"Damn straight I am. You called me a child and stupid. It's going to take more than a *van* to make that up."

"It's not a van. It's a Mystery Machine."

"It's a Volkswagen Bus." I sniff. "Not even a proper Chevrolet."

"You're killing me. This is how I die."

"You'll survive." I stick out my hand.

Reluctant, he clasps my fingers. "Fine."

I grip him tighter and yank him down to my level. "And you'll pay for the gas."

"The hell I will."

"Yes." I bare my teeth at him. "The hell you *will*."

A spark zaps between our palms, our deal bound and sealed, and he yanks his hand free. "That was a dirty trick."

I shrug and rub my stinging palm against my leg. "You're old enough to choose your words more wisely."

Unable to help himself, he smiles in appreciation. "I knew there was a reason we chose you."

I scoff. "You didn't *choose* me. You stumbled over me by accident and were too lazy to find a different succubus."

"Hmm." He gives me a strange look, before turning to the van. "How about I give you a ride to the bakery so I can make sure you're safe inside your wards?"

Chagrined, I stuff my hands into my pockets. "I wasn't planning to go in just yet."

He frowns. "Then why did you leave the house so early?"

"I'm going to pick up my imps and take them shopping."

He shakes his head in disbelief. "You really have no sense of self-preservation, do you?"

"I have my warning system." I touch the hidden armband, which has stayed quiet so far. "And I'll be in a public place, surrounded by people."

He rubs the back of his neck, then turns to open the driver's side door. "Fine. Get in. I'll go *shopping* with you."

Instantly, I perk up. "Yeah?"

"Yeah." He waves for me to go around to the other side. "Hop in."

Zipping past him, I plant myself in the driver's seat. "*You* get in. This is *my* van."

∽

Kellen eyes the entrance of the building where Julian rents office space and shudders. "I'll wait here while you go in."

One hand still on the wheel, I turn in the seat to stare at him. "What happened to escorting me around for my protection?"

"I can see the elevators from here. If I go up there, I'll be the one in need of protection." He shudders again. "I'm pretty sure that cousin of yours told all his strippers to hit on me whenever possible."

My fingers clench around the steering wheel. "You don't say."

"So much coconut body oil."

"I'll have a word with him about that." Whenever I see him next. Which, for his own health, better be a while from now. Shoving open my door, I swing my legs out. "I'll be right back."

I feel Kellen's gaze on me as I hurry around the

front of the van and into the building. As I wait for the elevator, I call Philip to let him know I arrived. By the time I make it up to Julian's office, the sleepy demon slouches in the open doorway.

He gives me a tired nod, with none of his usual attempts at sexiness. "Hey, Adie."

"Hey, sorry to wake you." When he moves to one side, I step into the large office. Cubicles on either side of the room create an aisle down the center that leads to Julian's office. When I glance in that direction, I find the frosted glass door shut tight and the lights off. "Any word from Julian?"

"Not yet." Scrubbing a hand over his face, Philip strides down the walkway and stops in front of one cubicle, rapping sharply on the temporary wall. "Up and at 'em, kiddos. Your ride's here."

Iris's rainbow head appears first, sleepy blue eyes blinking at me. "Master?"

Now, I feel doubly guilty. I should have planned this better so they had more time to prepare. "Hey, I thought we could go shopping today, and I can show you the new house."

Kelly's head appears next, his brushy beard flying in every direction. "Master's house?"

"Yes, the one I'm renting for you guys."

On the opposite side of the aisle, a blond imp appears, plump lips parted in a yawn. "A house?"

Philip frowns at her. "Go back to sleep, Jazabel. This has nothing to do with you."

"They get a whole house?" She aims a sexy pout at Philip. "I want a house."

"Fuck my life," Philip mutters and turns his annoyed attention on me. "See what you're doing? Hurry up and get them out of here before *everyone* wants a house."

Jazabel's focus shifts to me. "Are there beds?"

My brows furrow. "Yeah, of course."

She grips the edge of the cubicle. "How many imps per bed?"

Philip points at me. "Don't you dare answer that."

For the moment, I turn away from the sexy imp to face Philip. "Hey, you said you've been with Julian for a while, right? Which means you're pretty old?"

His arms fold over his chest, his expression now suspicious. "Yeah, in a manner of speaking."

"You ever heard of a demon called He Who Devours?"

His expression clears into a blank mask. "Why would you ask that?"

"The Librarian told me to call him up, but..." I shrug helplessly.

"Yeah, I've heard of him." He taps his chin in thought. "He went by Dorantes back in the day, but I'm sure he's changed it since then. He'd have to with the way humans like to track stuff these days."

Hope blooms in my chest. "Any idea where I can find him?"

Philip shakes his head. "No, he travels around a lot. Why don't you ask those demons of yours? They ran together for a while. Like a freaking club. That whole *destruction* thing they have going, you know?"

"Yeah, I know. They're being tight-lipped about it, though."

"Then maybe you should take their lead." He reaches out to pat my shoulder in sympathy. "Those guys are old as they come. They know their way around when it comes to people like He Who Devours."

I raise my eyebrows at him. "You ever meet the Librarian?"

He gives a full body shiver. "Terrifying hag."

"Who do you trust more on this kind of thing?"

Philip's gaze trips past me to the open door, and I glance over my shoulder to check for the telltale sparks of a portal before I remember she doesn't really need doorways to listen in on people.

"You know what?" Philip's voice drops into a sexy purr. "I'm just a low-level imp, ready to bang whenever you need a top off. That's all I know or care about."

I roll my eyes. "Still not happening."

"Then get out of my office." His smile holds a hint of feralness before he raps once more on the cubicle, hard enough to shake the entire row. "Get a move on!"

Scurrying comes from the other side.

Curious, I peek over the edge to find Martha helping Jesse into a slinky black top while Perry yanks on his pants. The five imps bump around and fall over each other in the limited space allocated to them. A u-shaped desk divides the cubicle into an upper and lower. Blankets with thin pillows line the top of the desks, and a matching set rests beneath on the floor.

I turn back to Philip. "That's barbaric."

Around the room, more blond heads appear, kohl-rimmed eyes fixed on us. Glitter sparkles from a few, while others glisten with the ever-present coconut oil.

Philip's voice drops as he leans closer. "This is a

halfway home to train them up, so they can venture out into the real world. In their natural form, they sleep in the cracks under beds and nightstands and hide in dryer vents. This is the Hilton as far as they're concerned."

"This is less than a tenement. How does forcing them to live like this prepare them for the human world? Are you expecting them to live in boxes once their contract is up?"

"Some of them do. Some don't make it that far." Angry now, he points to the ones who peek out. "When I offered my first contract to get onto the human plane, I would have murdered any other imp for this kind of hospitality. Julian helped show me a better way of life. We do the best we can to give them a job that's marketable and can be used in any city they want to move to."

"By turning them into strippers," I say drily.

"We offer catering experience, too." He rolls his shoulders to push back his angry outburst, and the usual, boyish mask slides back into place. "Food and sex sell, no matter what year it is or where we live."

My imps stumble out into the aisle, fussing with their stripper clothes, so out of place on their non-stripper bodies. They stand out in comparison to the other imps. Kelly, the large biker with tattoos and facial hair. Iris, with her rainbow hair and androgynous body. Martha, all soft curves and a matronly bob of white hair. Perry, blond and lanky, with a surfer vibe. And small Jesse, still soft and gray as it struggles to pick a form.

Julian's misfit castoffs who he sold to me for practically nothing, so they wouldn't interfere with his business.

I'm proud of them for rebelling, for refusing to accept what was pushed on them. And no way will they be returning to this place tonight.

Shrugging out of my zip up, I wave to them. "Come on, we're getting out of here."

They scamper forward, brushing against my sides with soft coos of, "Master."

I hug them back. "You guys ever been to a mall?"

They shake their heads.

"Well, you are in for a treat!" I drape my sweatshirt around Jesse's shoulders and pull up the hood to hide its gray face and too large eyes, then glance back to Philip, who watches us with a hint of longing in his eyes. "You know, if you ever want to get off the sex menu and learn how to bake cupcakes…"

"You're kidding, right? Julian would murder

me. And then you for luring me away." He throws back his head to laugh. "No, I'm good where I am."

"If you say so." As we walk to the door, a headband on the stripper rack catches my eyes, and I snatch it up.

"Hey, that costs two dollars!" Philip calls after us.

Glancing back, I meet Jazabel's eyes. "No bed share, two to a room, fully stocked kitchen, and form of your choice."

Philip swears as a loud chitter starts up, and I slam the office door shut with an evil sense of satisfaction. Can't wait for Julian to come back to *that* mess.

I'll definitely be the first person he calls, now.

KITTY DISGUISE

"You really think that's going to work?" Kellen asks as he watches me fit the cat ear headband onto Jesse's head over the hoodie.

We stand in the open, slider door on the passenger side, with the imps still huddled on their seats.

"Yeah, humans will just think Jesse is a kid dressed up as a cat." I fuss with the headband a little more to make sure it won't come off easily. "How's that feel? Is it pinching anywhere?"

Jesse lifts long-fingered hands to caress the fuzzy ears and chirps happily.

"Okay, then, I think we're ready." I glance around at the rest of the imps to make sure I have their attention. "There's going to be a lot of humans in here, but it's the middle of a workday, so it shouldn't be overwhelming. Think a busy day at the bakery."

In unison, they give solemn nods.

"We're going to work in the buddy system. Martha and Kelly, you stay with each other at all times. Iris, you're with Perry. Which leaves Jesse with me and Kellen." Turning, I point past the other parked cars to the modern art fountain in the plaza. "See that fountain?"

Again, they nod.

"If you're separated, you come straight there and wait. One of us will find you." Kellen nudges my hip, and I push him away with a sigh. "One more thing. You are *not* allowed to steal anything on this trip. That's against human law. You'll get in trouble, then you won't be allowed to come live at the new house."

They exchange uncertain glances, which I totally agree with. Mischief imps aren't known for their ability to resist shiny objects. Or the random sock. Or car keys.

Then, inspiration strikes. "If you can resist the urge for four hours"—I hold up four fingers for emphasis—"each of you will get a prize. And I'm not talking sparkle balls, here. I'm talking something *big* and *extra* shiny."

Eyes wide, they lean their heads together and chitter with excitement.

I clap my hands to regain their attention. "So, are we all ready?"

They all rush for the exit, and I lift Jesse free before my careful disguise gets crushed in the mass exodus. Dutiful, they form up in pairs and link hands. Not weird at all. Kelly can totally be a son escorting his mom around, and Perry and Iris could be dating.

A soft, slender palm creeps into mine, and I look down at Jesse, who smiles up at me with pointed canines. Crap, it's taking the cat thing a little too literally. I lean back to check and make sure a tail didn't sprout, too, and sigh with relief.

Kellen tugs on the van door to shut it, then runs around to double-check we locked all the doors before he jogs back to my side.

I glance up at him. "Ready?"

His shoulders pull back as he stares at the mall. "As I'll ever be."

∻

The first shop we visit, we replace all the stripper clothes with normal attire fitting their chosen forms.

Kelly manages to find a leather vest for five dollars that he almost stuffs under his mesh shirt before remembering the rule about stealing and adds it to our cart instead.

Iris, unsurprisingly, ends up with a stack of tie-dyed t-shirts and embroidered, bell-bottom pants.

Martha has to be talked out of buying nothing but aprons.

Perry just shrugs and lets me and Kellen pick out all his clothes.

Jesse surprises me by wandering into the kids' section and chirping happily at a sundress with llamas on it. It worries me at first, afraid I'll soon end up with a pet llama, but the imp seems equally thrilled with a sweatshirt featuring a giant, eight-bit hamburger.

In the home decor department, they select flannel sheet sets for the coming fall and matching comforters. The imps hold every item as if it's a treasure, always checking for approval before they add each piece to our cart. Kellen has to leave my side to fetch a second shopping basket and lets Martha push it around the store.

When I reach for a box of casserole dishes, Kellen touches my arm. "You sure that's a good idea?"

"They've gotten comfortable using the ovens at the bakery." I crouch to grab a set of sheet pans, too, and push them into his arms. "They'll need to cook for themselves if they're going to be self-sufficient."

"I guess." He turns to shove the items onto the undercarriage of one of the carts. "I just hope you bought fire insurance for the house."

"It withstood a cult; it can withstand imps."

"Master!" Iris calls as she rushes up to me, clutching a jar of glitter. "Look!"

"It was only a matter of time," Kellen whispers.

Iris shakes the jar and little flecks of purple trickle out. Glitter, the modern-day plague. Once it infiltrates the house, it will never be exterminated.

"That *is* exciting." I reach out and pry it from her hands. "But how about we look at lampshades for now? Did you see the one with fringe on it?"

Iris reluctantly shifts her attention to the aisle of lamps. With her back turned, I stuff the jar of glitter behind a box of frying pans.

Standing, I glance around the store and realize we're missing an imp. "Hey, where's Jesse?"

Kellen twists to glance back toward the clothing section, where Martha and Kelly test how many pillows they can stack in the already towering cart and shakes his head. "I don't see Jesse."

I catch a flash of cat ears bouncing along a rack of clothes, the imp too short to be visible. Pointing, I scoot past our cart to run after the small imp. Jesse is the one I feared losing the most, and I still lost track of the imp.

When I reach the aisle, I freeze. A human child, maybe six or seven, walks next to Jesse in an awkward sideways dance as her arms wave through the air. I search the row for a parent and spot her mother farther down the aisle, checking the tags on winter coats.

Steps hurried, I rush to intercept. The kid might not care about Jesse's odd appearance, but the mom will.

"And I have *four* cats." The little girl holds up four fingers. "Princess Marshmallow is all white except for a black spot on her nose." As she points at her own nose, her eyes cross, and she giggles. "Princy is spotted. Spotted cats are the prettiest. He has orange and white and black and only one ear because he had to defend Princess Marshmallow from an evil dragon!"

Jesse nods, attention held rapt by the child.

I stop next to them and grasp Jesse's shoulder. "Hey, didn't I tell you not to run off?"

Jesse's head tips back, and the imp gives me a

pointy-toothed smile. "Master, this is Olivia. She has four cats."

"So I heard." I nod at the wide-eyed child. "Thank you for playing with Jesse, but we really need to go now."

"Are you Jesse's mom?" Her hands move to her hips. "You don't look like her mom."

I force a smile. "Jesse's adopted."

Confusion clear on her face, her mouth works over the unfamiliar word before she squints at me. "What's adopted?"

I stare down at her for a second, taken aback by the question. What are they teaching children these days that she doesn't know what adoption means? "Well, it's like you with your cats. You adopted them from somewhere else, but they're your family, right?"

"We *bought* our cats." She taps one foot. "You didn't *buy* Jesse. That's illegal."

Shows what she knows. I did, in fact, buy Jesse.

I force a smile for her as I steer Jesse back toward the group. "It was nice to meet you, Olivia."

The little girl spins to face her mom, shouting, "Mom! I want to adopt a Jesse!"

I quicken our steps to put distance between us,

and Jesse peers up at me. "Master, I would like a cat. Olivia says they are soft and like to purr."

Dismayed, I pat its head. "Cats are a big responsibility. They have to be fed, and you have to clean their litter boxes."

"I would like a spotted one," Jesse insists. "Olivia said spots are pretty."

As we near Kellen, I mouth, *Help me*.

He straightens in alarm, his blue gaze sweeping the store for a sign of danger as he strides to meet us. "What's going on?"

"I want a cat." Jesse turns liquid brown eyes on Kellen. "Do you have a cat?"

"Uh." Brows lifted, he glances at me, and I shake my head frantically. "No, *I* don't."

Jesse reaches up to stroke the fuzzy ears on its head. "I will name my cat Left Sock."

Unsure what else to say, I pat Jesse's head again. "I'll think about it. But we need to get you all settled at your new home first, and you'll need to show you can be responsible."

"Responsible." Jesse's long fingers drop to its gray cheeks, pressing at its soft, malleable flesh. "Is Olivia responsible? Olivia has *four* cats."

Alarm shoots through me. Oh, god, all I need is for one of my imps to take on the form of a seven-year-old. The paperwork nightmare. Public schooling.

"No, Olivia is *not* responsible," I say firmly. "Olivia has her mom to help look after the cats. She won't be able to take care of them herself until she can get a job and pay for litter and kibbles."

Jesse blinks up at me. "I have a job."

"You *do*. But if you looked like Olivia, it would be illegal for you to work at the bakery." I crouch to be on level with the small imp. "Olivia is a *child*, and children have to go to school with other children. They can't work until they're older."

Jesse's gaze shifts behind me, to where the other imps congregate, and its soft shoulders sag. "Older."

Giving it a gentle squeeze, I stand. "Okay, everyone, I think we're done for the day."

As the others complain and shuffle their way toward the front of the store, Kellen slips up beside me. "You're very kind to them."

I cut him a sideways glance. "That doesn't make me weak."

"I didn't say it did." He strokes my back, lingering over the space between my shoulder blades where my wings hide. "I think I get why you don't go back to Dreamland. You really don't want to hurt humans, even when you have your instincts under control. You see them as more than food, right?"

I turn to Kellen in surprise. "No, I don't go to Dreamland because I *can't*."

Now, it's his turn to look surprised. "What?"

"I thought you knew. Everyone else seems to. And Tobias has made enough comments."

"No." Kellen draws out the word. "No, I didn't know. I assumed you went corporeal early. I mean, I've seen your wings, they're not fully formed, but not being able to access Dreamland? What were you doing for food before we found you?"

"My cousins took me along for hunts sometimes, or I skimmed, like I did at your club." I shrug. "It was working."

"Why weren't we informed about this?" he mutters under his breath.

"Informed?" I frown at him. "Who would inform you? You could have just read my history book before signing me on as your household succubus."

His focus shifts to the cash registers as he takes a place in line behind Martha and Kelly's towering cart. "I don't like the Library."

"It's not so bad once you get used to the hag."

The corners of his mouth tighten. "Then we haven't been to the same Library."

The room does like to shift motifs a lot, which makes me wonder what form it takes when Kellen visits. Before I can ask, Kellen strides forward to show the others how to load their selection onto the conveyor belt. The bored cashier runs the items over the scanner, one by one, and stuffs them into bulging bags to be collected on the opposite side. More items go onto the belt, and I catch sight of the jar of glitter.

How the hell did Iris find that again?

Before I can stop her, though, the cashier grabs it, swipes it over the scanner, and chucks it into a bag.

If we were going to have glitter in the house, I should have just left the haunting in place. It would have been less horrifying.

At last, the cashier rings up our total. I almost have a heart attack, but Kellen calmly pulls out his wallet and passes the cashier a stack of cash. I keep my lips sealed. If he still feels guilty enough for yelling at me to pay for my stuff, I'm not going to complain. In fact, I'll milk it as long as possible. I just wish I threw in some stuff for myself while we were looking.

Out in the plaza, Kellen tells us to wait at the fountain while he runs our purchases to the van.

With my hand linked with Jesse's once more, I direct the other imps to check out the food options that edge the large area. They disperse in a buzz of excited chitters, and I walk Jesse over to the first option, a burger and hot dog place. The giant corn dog on the menu makes my mouth water.

I'd love to wrap my lips around one of those.

Checking to see if Jesse shows interest, I find the imp focused on the teenager behind the counter instead. The guy looks to be about eighteen, fresh out of high school, with pimpled skin and greasy hair. His tall, lanky body hints at future muscle once he fully grows into himself. Gaze serious, Jesse touches its cheek once more.

I walk us down to the next food option. Mexican. The taquitos look equally tasty, the slender, deep fried rolled tortillas a temptation for my taste buds.

Tension fills Jesse's body as it observes the dark-skinned young woman behind the counter. She wears her brown hair pulled up into a high ponytail, her brown eyes sparkling as she takes orders. She's soft and round in the hips, with full thighs, and narrow in the chest. When she goes to the soda machine to fill a cup, she hops off the stool she stands on, instantly losing six inches in height.

When I make a move toward the next place, a stand that sells chocolate dipped bananas on a stick, Jesse resists.

Ah, it's finally time.

I search the plaza, catch Kelly's attention, and wave him over. The large imp crosses the distance quickly, and together, we form a barrier to hide Jesse from view.

The other imps slowly drift over to join us, curious to discover what Jesse finally chose for its form. Kellen jogs back from the van and veers over to us, his brows raised in question. I lift a finger to my lips and point down at Jesse, though he can't see the small imp through the others who crowd around us.

It only takes a couple of minutes before quiet coos of appreciation erupt. I stare down at Jesse in confusion. Its form remains the same, *maybe* an inch taller, but it could also be slouching. The others pat Jesse's shoulders in approval.

Confused, I crouch to peek under the hood. Jesse's gray skin now holds a nutty-brown glow, while its large eyes scaled back to a more human size and tilt up at the corners. The soft, round cheeks look more defined, youthful, but on their way to maturity. Passably human.

I check the chest area and find small, barely visible breasts. With a work ID, Jesse can pass as a small eighteen-year-old, though driving is out. Even with a phone book, she won't be able to see over the steering wheel, and reaching the pedals is out of the question.

Jesse reaches up to stroke her new cheeks with shortened, human-looking fingers. "Responsible?"

I pat her head. "Legal to work."

She grins, displaying sharp canines. Well, I guess mostly human is as good as we're going to get. Humans sometimes have fangs, right? Cosplay? Are vampires and werewolves still in fashion?

Jessie catches my hands, brown eyes pleading. "Cat?"

"We'll talk after you're settled at the new house." With one last pat on the head, I stand. "Okay, who's hungry?"

Five hands fly into the air, and I point at Kellen. "Food's on him."

(UN)GUARDED

After the shopping trip, we swing by the house to drop everything off, and the imps take a quick tour of the house, claiming their bedrooms, before we all head into work.

I offer to drop Kellen off at his club down the street, but he waves the offer away. "It's not that far. I can stretch my legs."

"If you're sure." The imps run ahead of us down the alley, excited to get to work, and we hang back at the van. "Thank you for going with us today. I had fun."

"Too bad none of the furniture stores had Tobias's replacement chair." He reaches out to tug on the end of my braid. "We'll just have to go shopping again."

Warmth fills my chest. "Yeah, I suppose we will."

"Maybe without the kids next time." He leans closer, his voice a low purr that heats my core. "You have no idea how much watching you eat that corn dog affected me. You're evil."

"Well, I *am* a demon." I peek back at the alley to make sure it's empty. Lunch didn't assuage the desire for something warm and thick in my mouth. Slowly, I drag Kellen into the back of the van and close the door. "Actually, I really wanted to fill my mouth with something else."

"Yeah?" He doesn't resist as I push him onto the center seat. "I'm listening."

Kneeling between his parted thighs, I grab his belt and yank it open. His hard cock already presses against his fly, and he shifts lower on the seat to give me better access. "This isn't repayment of some kind for buying all that stuff, is it?"

I pause with my fingers on his zipper to glare up at him. "No, that was your guilt for being an asshole. Now, shut up and let me suck your cock in peace."

"Ah, I love that mouth of yours." His hand covers mine over his hard dick. "But, you know, if you ever *do* want me to pay for—"

"Finish that sentence, and I'll bite it off instead."

"I'm talking loans, sweetie. You need help, Tobias and Emil aren't your only option." He strokes my cheek. "I'm worried about the rate you're bleeding money by taking on these imps."

"Whoa, you really know how to kill a mood." Pushing up from his knees, I slump onto the seat next to him, lean my head back, and close my eyes. "What I *really* need is someone to read me the freaking succubus manual. I asked Tally, but she said it's not possible."

"You have a manual?" Then his head whips around. "Wait. You can't *read*?"

I scowl at him "I can *read*. Just not our own language."

"We *really* need that household meeting." He lurches to the side and opens the door. "Make sure to come home early tonight."

As he buckles his belt, I follow him out. "When I know for sure, I'll message you."

"See that you do." Spinning, he grips my cheeks and plants a searing kiss on my parted lips. "And I want an IOU for that blow job."

My tongue flicks out to catch the taste of him. "Then, you better improve your seduction skills, because that right there was *lame*."

In response, Kellen spins me around, slaps me on the ass, and orders, "Get to work, woman."

Laughing, I trot toward the alley. "That's more like it!"

"Bring me home some cake!"

I lift a hand in acknowledgment.

"Lemon!"

"You'll get what you get!"

"Stingy!"

Still laughing, I grab the door handle and yank it open. Warm air floods out, smelling of butter and sugar and carrying the caress of happiness. It swirls around me in a welcoming embrace before it sinks beneath my skin, adding to the ball of energy already in my core.

With a grateful sigh, I step into the hall and freeze.

The cuff on my arm, silent since yesterday, flares to life with a skin-crawling tingle.

Someone with dark magic invaded my sanctum.

Spindling energy out to my limbs, I walk slowly down the short hallway, hands loose at my sides. Excited chitters fill the kitchen as the imps prepare to open the bakery. Iris and Perry pull cooled trays of cupcakes from the racks and move them to the decorating station, while Jesse scurries around with the display plates, sliding them onto the counter one at a time.

Through the pass-through, I see Kelly giving the tables a fresh wipe down while Martha preps the espresso station.

Everyone has a job, and no one seems concerned.

As I walk to the swinging door and push it open, the tingling grows worse, and I resist the urge to rip the armband off as I sweep the room for the intruder. Instead, I spot Xander in the booth in the corner that Tally's men claim while they stay with her at work. His laptop sits open on the table, and he hunches over it, typing away.

Tally turns from the cash register, a broad smile on her face. "Good afternoon!"

The tension eases from my shoulder, and I rub my left arm in an attempt to calm the tingles set off my Tally's and Xander's presence. "Oh, hey, Tally. I didn't expect you in so early."

"I was nervous about the new delivery and whether Vova would feel comfortable enough to start the first batch of cakes after the change." She leans forward to whisper, "We need to have another talk with him about wearing the hairnet."

Silent, I nod. Convincing the domovoi demon of

the necessity of wearing the hairnet is an ongoing struggle. The ancient hearth demon just doesn't grasp modern hygiene. But I'll forever be grateful for his protection and for beginning the cakes before the rest of us arrive for the day. It cuts down cost and reduces the number of hours someone needs to be in the shop.

"Hey, I was going to call you. Do you think we could switch closing tonight? Kellen wants to have a house meeting tonight while Emil and Tobias are awake." I rush to add, "I'll come back at closing to pick up the imps."

Her pink brows furrow together. "What happened to Philip?"

"He was going to stop driving them back and forth soon anyway." I skirt around the revelation of how the imps live, unsure if it would offend Tally or if she would find it perfectly normal.

There's just no way I can let them go back to that, and I'm ashamed I never peeked into the cubicles before. When I saw them the first time, I pictured cots set up like little living units and didn't want to intrude on their limited privacy. Shame on me for my assumptions.

Without elaborating, I say, "I figured they could start living at their new house starting tonight."

She nods, accepting the explanation. "I'm fine with that. Xander was complaining about working so early in the day. Perhaps I can convince him to go see a movie."

"That sounds fun."

Her mahogany eyes brighten. "There's a new Slasher on Diamond Pond out."

"Oh, that sounds…exciting?"

"I've seen every one since they began releasing in the nineties." She claps her hands together. "My brother took me to the first one. Mitchel Marham is a true villain to be feared. So many nightmares involve him."

"Well, you guys have fun with that." I resist the urge to shudder. Slasher movies aren't the way I'd like to spend my afternoon. There's enough darkness in the world without making up more monsters to fear.

Excited, Tally hurries around the counter and over to Xander's table, where she bounces on her toes until the young man sighs and closes his laptop with an unintelligible grumble. He slides his computer into his satchel and stands, motioning Tally to the door.

The two leave, and I return to the kitchen,

grabbing a spare hairnet from the basket by the door.

~

At six o'clock, the armband flares to irritating life once more as Tally returns. Roses fill her cheeks, and she spends a solid fifteen minutes explaining, in graphic detail, her favorite murder scenes from the movie.

At last, we do the hand-off, and I let the imps know I'll return for them at two in the morning to take them to their new house.

Walking back to the office, I remove my chef coat, throw it into the laundry basket, then shrug into the hoodie I reclaimed from Jesse when the imp changed at the house earlier. I send Kellen a text to let him know I'm on my way, then grab the box of lemon cupcakes I set aside for him. Into it, I add a couple of blue roses for Emil and some unfrosted hummingbird cakes for Tobias, who dislikes sweets.

With it tucked under one arm, I walk out of the bakery and into the cool evening air. The days continue to grow shorter, and the breeze that sweeps down the alley brings with it the metallic approach of autumn. I can't wait for the first snow, and my mind whirs with plans for hot chocolate cupcakes with toasted-marshmallow topping.

I pause outside of the door to take a deep breath, and the tingles on the armband increase. I rub it against my side and move down the alley, wishing there was a way for the guys to make it so Tally didn't set the damn thing off. Her presence makes its effectiveness at the shop moot, but it will still be good for when she's not around. The thing is irritating enough that I can't ignore it.

The tingles grow worse, and I chafe the band against my side harder. Maybe I just shouldn't wear it when Tally's around. I can keep it in my pocket or something.

A shadow passes over me, and I freeze, head jerking up. A large figure blocks the entrance to the alley.

Behind him, the setting sun makes it difficult to decipher his features, but the wind shifts direction and brings with it the tang of ozone and destroyed forests.

Shocked, the box of cakes drops from my hands, and I stumble back as the man steps forward.

Golden eyes glint from the dark shadows across

his face. "Adeline Boo Pond. Just the succubus I was looking for."

My hand lifts to my throat, the taste of ash clogging my airway. "Domnall."

TRAPPED

The box hits the ground, little cupcakes tumbling out to smear the alley with blue and yellow frosting, but I don't have time to worry about Kellen's disappointment at the ruined desserts. All my focus goes to the demon who blocks my way to the parking lot.

Domnall.

My fingernails lengthen into talons, while my legs shake with the need to bolt. The urge to fight or flee war with each other, freezing me in place.

His head tilts to the side. "I should correct that. I wasn't really *looking* for you. You're not exactly hard to find." He steps forward, his hand trailing over the brick wall of my bakery. "The succubus who caters to *humans*."

The sneer in his tone jolts me into motion, and I stumble back. For all my bravado with the guys, I'm not ready for this confrontation. I need more time to plot, to lure him into a trap of my creation, not be ambushed unaware right next to my place of business.

Unconcerned by my slow retreat, Domnall continues forward. "I would have come sooner, except that you made Kellen rather upset with me." Sharp nails scrape against the bricks, sending a shiver down my spine. "Which, of course, brought Emil and Tobias against me."

My retreat stops, the revelation of their protectiveness emboldening me to stay and fight.

He *tsks* quietly, and the smell of burning forests grows stronger, filling the air in the narrow alley with an acrid smog. "If I'd known they'd throw such a snit over their latest pet, I would have gone somewhere else."

My hands curl into fists, talons biting into my palms to add a tinge of copper to the air. "I'm no one's pet."

"So you say." He shrugs. "But don't fool yourself. You're a necessary parasite in their home. It's the deal they made to stay on this plane. If you fail to live up to your contract, or you cause them too much annoyance, they'll easily replace you."

The words ring in my head with truth.

Domnall believes what he says, and it peppers holes in the fragile bud of confidence that's been growing from my relationship with Emil, Tobias, and Kellen.

My wings shiver in their hiding place against my spine, small, unformed, and weak. My already shaky determination flees. Today is not the day I fight Domnall.

Energy floods my limbs, and I spin to flee.

Another dark figure steps into the alley from the street, and I freeze once more, corned between two enemies.

Then the light catches on pink tinted white curls, and confusion leaves me breathless. "Julian?"

"There you are!" He skips forward, his long black duster billowing behind him like a cape. "Tally said you already left. I thought we missed you!"

"We?" I peer over my shoulder and find Domnall too close for comfort. Skittering forward, I latch onto Julian's arm. "You're with Domnall? I told you to *avoid* him! He's evil!"

"Well, aren't we all, dear?" Julian pats my hand in reassurance. "After your frantic call, I just *had* to see this terrifying demon for myself, and who do I find but my old hunting buddy!"

"Hunting bud—" My mouth gapes for a moment

before I snap it closed. "Julian, where have you *been*? I've been worried, and poor Philip—"

He waves away my concern. "Philip's a capable imp. He can take care of the business for a few weeks."

"*Weeks*." I can't seem to pull in enough oxygen, and dizziness swamps my head.

"If we're talking about as big of an infestation as I think we are, we'll need at *least* that long to roust them all out!" He rubs his hands together as he vibrates with excitement. "I've missed this *so* much."

"You were always an excellent partner, Jules," Domnall purrs, and I flinch to find him right in front of us. "I've missed you. Give up this working thing and join me for a few centuries of fun."

Julian wags his finger playfully. "Now, you. Don't tempt me. I have a good thing going right now. This is just a mini vacation."

"Julian," I hiss to regain his attention. My heart beats erratically, ready to burst from all the emotional highs and lows. "What's going on?"

He turns his head to study me, and at this distance, I make out the faint rim of pink around his blue contacts. "Philip called and told me you were looking for He Who Devours."

"You talked to Philip?" I fume for a moment.

Philip obviously had the ability to reach my cousin at any point and hid it from me. Then his words process, and I rise onto my toes in excitement. "Wait, do you know where I can find He Who Devours?"

"Um, yeah." He reaches up to pat my head as if I'm slow, then points to Domnall. "He's right in front of you."

Domnall thrusts out his hand. "At your service, Adeline Boo Pond."

∽

I fling open the front door and barely pause to kick off my clogs before storming into the living room. "Kellen, you have some explaining to do!"

It gives me a brief sense of déjà vu, a role reversal from this morning, but I shake it off to glare at the three demons ensconced in their padded seats without a care in the world. Tobias lowers his tablet to raise an eyebrow at me. Emil reclines on the long couch with his feet up, unconcerned, and Tac raises his head from the floor, tufted ears swiveling to attention.

Kellen's lightning-kissed gaze settles on me. "Yes, I believe that's what this meeting is about?"

"Not that!" The crackle of burning wood brushes my back, and I point without looking. "*That*! Explain that!"

"You're a rude child, aren't you?" Domnall growls, and I skitter farther inside to put distance between us.

The men in the room straighten with matching scowls, and Kellen's voice drops to the low rumble of thunder. "Domnall. Didn't I warn you what would happen if you approached Adie again?"

"Yes, old friend, but I'm here at the bidding of a power greater than you."

"Knockie, knockie!" Julian calls before the front door slams shut, and he bounces into the room. His eyes light up as they land on Kellen, and he skips forward. "Kellen, long time no—"

His words cut off as I grab him by the back of the collar. "No."

"Oh, come on. There's three of them." He makes grabby hands at Kellen. "Share a little."

"No," I growl again before propelling him toward my floral couch stationed in front of the fireplace. "Sit."

"You really are no fun." He pouts and sprawls on the middle cushion, legs spread wide.

For the first time, I fully take in his outfit, so at

odds with his usual attire. Instead of his standard, red-pleather short-shorts, he wears baggy black pants stuffed into combat boots that lace halfway up his calves. A tight black t-shirt shows off his slender muscles and tucks into his pants, held in place with a black leather belt. The edges of a red button-up peek out of his ankle-length, black-leather duster. Gel slicks back his soft curls into an unmoving helmet, making his cheekbones appear sharper in comparison.

"Julian, are you dressed like Spik—"

He points at me. "Not another word!" Then he sniffs with disdain. "If anything, that wannabe vampire looked like me. I rocked this outfit decades before television even existed."

"And you did it so well," Domnall purrs. "Of course they'd steal your look."

The vain incubus preens under the praise. "Flattery will get you everywhere."

"Except back at my side." Domnall stalks closer, voice persuasive. "Remember all the murdering? How much fun we had?"

"Enough!" The floor shakes with Tobias's anger, and I hop onto the cushion next to Julian, cuddling against his side. "You are not welcome here, Domnall. Leave."

"No can do." Uncowed, Domnall turns to the couch Emil sits on and waves his hand. "Make some room. We need to talk."

Emil's lip curls back in a snarl. "Sit on the floor."

"Seriously?" Expression resigned, he turns to the flower couch. "What has you all in a tizzy? It can't possibly be over this whole power dump issue."

Tac rolls to his feet, wings spreading wide to block Domnall from joining me and Julian. I can't see his face past the black feathers that block my view, but Tac's chainsaw growl of warning fills the room.

Domnall's voice turns faint with betrayal. "You, too, Tac?"

"You're not welcome here." Kellen leans forward, elbows on his knees. Lightning dances between his fingers and the air grows heavy with ozone. "And you're not currently powerful enough to say otherwise."

"Yet here I stand." When I peek over Tac's wing, I find Domnall in the center of the room, arms spread wide. "We need to put aside our differences for now. There are bigger problems in town, and your little succubus is at the center of them."

Black bleeds over Tobias's eyes, masking out the

white until an abyss stares back. "We're taking care of that."

"That's not your *job*." Domnall pounds a fist against his chest. "You're venturing into *my* territory. The Hunters are *mine*."

Next to me, Julian shivers with delight, and I look at him, aghast.

He shrugs, unapologetic. "I *do* miss the sport."

Back in the day, Julian took witch hunting seriously, until the higher-ups put a stop to such practices for fear it would expose us to the humans. Since meeting Tally's men, the idea rolls my stomach. How many of the eradicated witches were truly bad, and how many were like Xander and Reese, and to a lesser degree, Slater and Jax? How many innocent lives were lost?

Annoyed by whatever he reads from my expression, Julian's eyes narrow. "Don't look at me like that. They were all bad people who harmed one of ours first."

But how does he know that? What proof was offered? Even among humans, it's well known that innocent people were burned at the stake because some spoiled human didn't get their way and pointed a finger in the other direction. Demons could easily do the same.

Disquieted, I tug on Tac's wing until the giant cat monster lowers it. Sitting in front of me, he scoots back until his heavy, kitty butt rests on the tops of my feet. I lean forward to stroke his soft, black fur in thanks for his protection, and he rumbles quietly in return.

The men eye each other in an uneasy standoff. If they really did encroach on Domnall's territory somehow, which I'm unsure of since Kellen owns most of this city, then it's a serious allegation. Possibly even finable in demon court.

When the silence stretches too long, I raise my hand. Julian sighs with disgust, but it gains the attention I desired. "What territory?"

Domnall raises an eyebrow, as if I should have figured it out by now. "Why, the witches, of course."

My brow furrows. "Which witches?"

An evil smile spreads across his face. "*All* the witches. I'm judge, jury, and executioner."

DREAMING

I shiver at the words and use all of my willpower not to look at Kellen.

Are Tally's witch boys in danger from Domnall? They're not evil, but will he care? Julian lounges at my side, completely unconcerned. But why would he be?

While he knows about Reese, he doesn't care about the fae-touched human. He doesn't know the sweetness he shows toward Tally every time he comes into my shop, or the help and consideration he and his roommates have shown me, both with the imps' haunted house and protecting me from those who wish me harm.

Tension stiffens my muscles at the sudden memory of Xander at the entrance to the alley, laptop in hand as he and Slater tried to banish Domnall back to the demon dimension. They hurt him then, distracted him long enough for me to get us to safety. Does the demon remember? Does he hold a grudge against them?

My reasons to take him out just grew by four. Five if I include Tally. Who knows what happens to her if her witches disappear?

My hand fists in Tac's fur for support as I straighten. "I think we should hear Domnall out." Three shocked expressions whip toward me, and I force myself to appear relaxed. "As he said, a greater being sent him here." I meet Kellen's and Tobias's gazes before shifting my focus across the room to Emil. "Unless one of you would like to gainsay the Librarian?"

The three exchange silent glances, a flurry of communication filling the space between them. Their eyes narrow in unison and shift to Domnall.

Tobias, the appointed speaker, stands and offers Domnall his vacated chair. "Have a seat, brother. We'll hear you out."

"About time." Domnall plops down and kicks his feet up, hands folded over his stomach as his golden eyes take in the room. "I like what you've done with the place. I haven't been here since since your last succubus... What was her name?"

"It doesn't matter," Emil bites out as he pulls back his legs for Tobias to sit opposite him.

I twitch a little at that, and Julian lets out a discontented mew at the brushoff of one of our cousins. Horrible taste and annoying personality aside, she's still a demon whose name should be remembered.

As if sensing my unhappiness, Emil's white lashes flutter, but his attention stays fixed on Domnall. "Say what you need to say and leave. It's late."

"You've become a bunch of old spinsters," Domnall scoffs, flicking a hand in Tac's direction. "Cat included."

"If that's all you have to say—" Kellen begins.

"Fine, I get it. Domnall did bad." He slaps his own hand. "Can we move on now?"

"That's what we're all waiting for you to do, asshole," I snap from the safety of Tac's shadow. "The Librarian seems to think I need your help against the Hunters."

His dark eyebrows lift. "Well, yes, I think that's pretty obvious, don't you?"

Now that panic doesn't drive my actions, I allow my senses to open to him. He's surprisingly difficult to find in a room filled with destruction demons.

Even with storm season on the way out, Kellen overshadows him by quite a bit.

It's true then; he doesn't regenerate power the way my demons do. Which means his power source must come from something not elemental or internal. Something more difficult to access.

I stroke the soft down between Tac's wings. "Honestly, since you"—I search my brain for a nice way to phrase it—"offloaded all your power the last time we met, you don't seem fully capable at the moment."

Julian gives an offended gasp, while Kellen coughs back a laugh.

Domnall's feet thud back to the floor as he leans forward to focus his intense, gold eyes on me. "Oh, believe me. I'm more than capable. When it comes to witches, I'm your only safeguard."

I tilt my head to the side, long, white hair slithering over my shoulder. "Because you do…what exactly?"

"I'm He Who Devours, pet." He bares his teeth, which look sharper now. "What do you *think* I do?"

"I'm guessing *devour*? I've honestly never heard of you." I turn to Julian. "You never mentioned Domnall in your witch-hunting stories."

Julian whips around to hiss at me. "Watch yourself."

But Domnall hears the truth in my words, even as they create a lie. Julian mentioned a partner in the past, though I always pictured more of a sidekick-like character from comic books. But he never put a name to him. I take vicious joy in needling both men.

Domnall's golden eyes narrow for a moment before he rolls his shoulders, shrugging it off. "So, the way I see it, we need to set you up as bait, draw out the Hunters, and take care of them in one fell swoop."

"Not happening!" Kellen thunders.

The floor shakes with Tobias's, "No."

Ice crackles in Emil's throat. "Absolutely not."

I grip Tac's fur tighter, causing the beast's wings to flutter. "Fine. When and where?"

"Now, wait just a minute —"

I hold up a hand to cut Tobias off. "You can yell at me later."

The air in the room turns heavy, pressing down on my shoulders as if it can hold me there by will alone, but my demons fall silent.

I nod to Domnall. "What's the plan?"

"Well, at least one of you sees reason." Domnall

claps his hands together, ignoring the three glowering destruction demons. "They've already set a few traps around town in the places you frequent. The easiest one is in the parking lot of your bakery. With the waxing moon, Sunday night will be ideal for them. The type of spell they use for entrapment works best then. We'll create an opening that they'll be hard pressed not to jump on."

I tense at the bomb he just dropped. A spell in my parking lot? How did I not know this? With the way demon minds shy away from human magic, it must make things easier for the Hunters. How many other spells have I walked past and not realized? My fancy new armband never alerted me to them, either. Because they're not active at the moment? I would need to ask Xander about that.

Pushing those concerns to the back of my mind, I nod at Domnall in agreement. While I don't like to bring danger to my place of business, there's no reason to drag this out by luring them to a different location.

Julian bounces on his cushion. "This is going to be so much fun."

Unlike my cousin, the idea of delivering the Hunters to Domnall rolls my stomach. I haven't harmed a human in a long time, and so far, these

Hunters have only graffitied my building. Can I bring myself to actually destroy them? Because I can't pretend we'll be doing anything less.

The picture from the demon book about Hunters flashes through my memory, of Domnall draining the life of a Hunter, and the husks that already lay at his feet. Dead.

I push the thoughts to the back of my mind as well, hardening my heart. "How do we get them there?"

"After the bakery closes, walk over to Kellen's club, Fulcrum. It's not out of character, so it shouldn't make them suspicious. Hang out there for an hour, then walk back to the bakery. Julian and I—"

"And us," Kellen cuts in. "We'll be there."

Domnall waves a hand. "Fine, as long as you stay hidden. We need Adeline to look vulnerable, which means being alone."

Kellen rumbles at the idea but gives a tight nod.

"The Hunters will be watching Adeline, so when they see she's alone, they'll call in reinforcements. We'll keep in contact by cell phone, which will make you look distracted." He catches my eye, his expression serious. "They'll have weapons of power to circle you. With the spells already in place, the trap will go into effect quickly."

I flinch at the reminder.

Domnall nods in sympathy, an expression I thought him incapable of. "Human magic is tricky, which is why the greater-demons appointed me to this position. I can *see* it; understand what it does."

A shiver rolls through me, and I wiggle my feet farther under Tac's butt for comfort. "What do the spells in my parking lot do?"

"They'll drain your power, bring you down to the human level." He leans closer without leaving his chair and sniffs the air. "You smell pretty weak as is. You should go into Dreamland the next few nights and really gorge. Stock up as much as possible. It will tax their spells, and they won't be able to attack until you're drained. That gives us more time to get into position and take them by surprise."

Worried now, I bite my lip. "How important is it that I power up?"

Domnall's brow furrows, and Julian snorts. "Adie can't go into Dreamland."

Emil's head snaps toward me, while Tobias looks unsurprised, as if hearing I haven't fixed my issue by now is just a given. Kellen just leans back in his chair with an air of resignation.

Guess he didn't tell the others the reason for our house meeting tonight.

Domnall frowns. "I don't understand."

"It's a long story." Julian pats my knee. "But she's working on fixing it, right, dear? And in the meantime, look at the smorgasbord she's surrounded herself with!"

Emil shifts into a sitting position, one leg dropping to the floor. "But you've been working on that. Weren't you in Dreamland this morning? Isn't that why you didn't immediately wake up?"

Now Tobias scowls. "Why would she be in Dreamland when she just fed? She was obviously still digesting."

Emil and Tobias eye each other, and I'm reminded of their argument this morning, the air between them crackles with tension. Then the two demons turn their focus to me, and I wiggle under their accusation.

Sure, blame the poor succubus.

Julian shifts to study me as well, then shakes his head. "Nope, not ready for Dreamland yet."

With a disgusted sigh, Domnall flops back in his

chair. "Why are we bothering to save this succubus?" he asks the room in general. "Better to destroy the corporeal form so she can fix whatever's wrong."

Julian whips around to hiss, "Never say that again."

Domnall shrugs, unconcerned. "It's just facts. No reason to get bent out of shape over it."

My cousin thrusts to his feet and points at the door. "Go wait on the porch. You're done here."

With a stony expression, Domnall rises from the chair and marches stiffly to the door, slamming it shut with enough force to shake the house.

I stare at Julian in awe. Where Domnall ignored the threats of my higher-level demons, my sassy cousin made him leave with minimal effort.

Julian flops back down on the couch and throws an arm around me. "The nerve. Talking about destroying such a delightful form when you're doing fine on your own."

Some of my annoyance toward him fades, and I press into his side. For all his talk, my cousin really does care.

A throat clears, and I glance over to find Emil and Tobias waiting expectantly. My mind blanks. What were we talking about? Oh, Dreamland or digesting.

I straighten once more. "Both. I think. I'm not really sure."

Julian reaches out to stroke my hair, his tone holding the patience of a parent whose child is making up stories. "No, dear, you're not quite strong enough to go back to Dreamland on your own."

Annoyance back to full force, I smack his hand away. "I know what Dreamland looks like, enough to know whether or not I was there."

"So you *were* there?" Kellen leans forward in his chair. "But this morning, you told me you couldn't return."

Unsure how to describe it, I pull my feet out from under Tac and lift them onto the couch to wrap my arms around my knees. The memory of that in-between place fogs my memory in gray and drags back the terror brought on when that creature rose out of the mist and almost squashed me.

My breath stutters, and I take a moment to push down my instinctive fear. "Tobias gave me enough energy to allow me to…I don't know…reach the outskirts of Dreamland? I could see the city, but I couldn't get to it, if that makes sense?"

Beside me, Julian stills, not even his chest rising with breath.

"Adie, honey, there's no outskirts," Kellen says

softly, his gaze filled with sympathy. "It overlays the human world, so unless you were in the ocean or something…"

My eyes narrow on him. Dreamland is for the demons who feed through dreams, like succubi and baku. Not for storm gods. "Because you've spent how much time there?"

"I've been around enough succubi to have a pretty good idea."

I twitch at the reminder.

When Tobias and Emil nod in agreement, I turn to Julian, who stares straight ahead, his shoulders stiff. "Tell them."

His eyelashes flutter. "You're probably just confused and were having normal dreams. Too much power all at once can make you see things that aren't there."

I rear back in surprise. While his words don't hold the bitterness of a lie, they ring hollow. Sensing subterfuge, Kellen, Tobias, and Emil turn their focus to Julian.

Julian runs his palms down his thighs before he pushes to his feet. "Well, I better get going. Can't expect to keep Domnall waiting forever."

"Julian!" I leap to my feet and land on something soft. Tac yelps and leaps forward, yanking his tail from beneath my heels and sending me back to the couch.

My cousin uses the distraction to make it to the wall that separates the living room from the front door. "I'll see you all on Sunday!"

"Julian, I know the difference between dreaming and Dreamland!" I yell as I struggle to my feet. "There were creatures there that built webs! They tried to trap me!"

The front door opens, and my shoulders sag at his unhelpfulness.

But when it doesn't immediately shut, hope replaces my disappointment. "Julian?"

From the other side of the wall, his boots scuff against the hardwood floor. "I hope you were dreaming, Adie. But maybe you should give Landon a call, just to be safe."

And with that, he slams the door shut.

ASK SOMEONE ELSE

The echo of the door still rings through the room when three sets of angry eyes swing back to where I sit on my floral couch.

My wings shiver with warning, and I bounce to my feet before they box me in. "Well, good house meeting, everyone. Glad we did *that*. Who wants hot chocolate? Tea?"

"Sit." The single word comes from Tobias with the weight of an avalanche, and my legs collapse.

"Stay." At Emil's command, Tac swings around and slams his wedge-shaped head onto my lap like an anchor. His nose shoves against my stomach, moist breaths warming my skin.

"Talk." The crackle of Kellen's voice drives into my gut, pulling confessions up my throat to roll down my tongue.

I clench my teeth and bare them at the three men. "This is not okay."

"No, you bringing that demon home with you is what's not okay." Tobias thrusts to his feet to pace across the room. "Two days ago, you were so terrified of him that even the reminder of his scent had you running in the opposite direction. And now you're... What? Friends? Everything's *forgiven*?"

"No, everything's *not* forgiven." I shove at Tac's head, not liking being trapped.

With a snort, he presses down harder, and one tufted ear swivels forward in silent reproach.

I shift my glare from the soft spot between Tac's eyes to Tobias. "No, I haven't forgiven Domnall. I can barely stand being near him. But thanks to your —" I cut off, unsure I want to bring up the near disaster of Tobias pushing me past my limits at the bakery. "But thanks to your assistance, I can tolerate him for now. What I'd like to know is why everyone here knew who He Who Devours was and didn't tell me!"

"Because he terrified you, honey." Kellen stands and walks over to the couch to capture my hands. Static tingles between us, little nips that burrow down to my bones and zings to my core. Gaze soft, he squeezes my fingers. "How could we expect you to work with him after what happened? You needed time, and we're fully capable of taking care of a couple Hunters."

My insides turn to mush at his obvious concern.

"And you're not powerful enough to deal with this, anyway." Emil's cold logic douses my mushy emotions in a bucket of ice water. "Now, what's this about you not being able to get into Dreamland? I thought you got all those books from the Library to fix that, and you just didn't want to harm humans, now. Like a succubus version of vegetarianism, or something."

"Well, I *don't* want to harm humans." Reluctant, I pull my hands free of Kellen, who then makes himself comfortable by perching on the arm of my sofa. "But the only way I can return to Dreamland right now is if one of my cousins takes me. Though, I got pretty close this morning."

"Yes, the outskirts." Tobias pauses in front of his chair and wrinkles his nose with distaste before returning to Emil's couch. Guess he doesn't like the way Domnall smells, either.

I cross my arms. "I don't care what you think you know. *I* know where I was while asleep."

Tobias nods slowly, the muscle in his jaw ticking. "After Julian's reaction, I'm not doubting you."

I bristle at the comment. "Yeah, because believing me on my own is too farfetched."

Kellen slaps a hand over his face and groans into his palm. "And *this* is why we needed a house meeting."

My chin lifts. "Because you guys don't trust me."

"And you don't trust us," Emil points out, voice cool. "This is a two-way street."

"More like a one-way street into a brick wall," I mutter. When stony silence greets me, I let out a huff. "Look, I know you're all *ancient*, and you've been living together for a while, yeah?"

They exchange glances and nod in unison.

"So all of you know how the others think and react." They exchange another series of glances, and I point between them. "See? Like that. You don't even have to talk out loud. You just understand each other."

Emil frowns. "And this bothers you?"

"It doesn't *bother* me." I pet Tac's large nose, and his chainsaw purr rattles my bones. "I think it must be really nice to have people you can rely on without question. But it makes it difficult when you're all on the same page and I'm on the opposite side, you know? And when it comes to something that directly involves *me*, well..." My focus shifts between them. "You're not my mentor, you're not my bosses, and you're certainly not my owners."

Kellen drops down onto the cushion next to me, making mine bounce. "Adie, we don't think we own you."

"I'm your contracted succubus." My eyes sting, Domnall's words still knocking around inside my head, burning at my self-confidence. "How else could you possibly think of me? If I annoy you, or piss you off, you can just replace me."

"Did Domnall tell you that?" Emil growls with stunning accuracy.

"Someone needs to send him back to the demon plane," Tobias bites off. "This kind of bullshit is why he was banned from our territory to begin with."

"Honey." Kellen's fingers on my chin pull my head around. "Domnall's twisted in the head. There's no two ways around that. He likes to mess with people, tear down their self-confidence. Ask Julian sometime why they separated to begin with."

Anger spikes through me, and my eyes narrow. "He hurt Julian?"

Sadness fills Kellen's eyes. "You should ask him."

"Why is everyone always telling me to ask someone else?" I shove at Tac hard enough that he rears back with a snort of disgust. "Why can't anyone just give me an answer?"

Kellen catches my wrist before I can leap to my feet. "Because I can't. Not on this. All I know is that when Julian arrived and asked for some space to start up a business, he didn't look good."

"We'd separated from Domnall a few centuries before he started running with your cousin," Emil adds. "But we know how he used others of your kind."

Tobias's black eyes flick away from me, the muscle in his jaw jumping, the knuckles of the hand he rests on the couch arm turns white with pressure. "He doesn't have to wait so long to offload the power he drains from witches. He doesn't have to be harmful to other demons."

Rage boils in my blood. "And you guys just let him keep doing it?"

If they'd stepped up sooner, I wouldn't have had to go through Domnall's power dump. I wouldn't know what it feels like to suffocate on ashes, to burn from the inside out, to be left coated in filth that can never fully be scrubbed away.

Kellen strokes my cheek. "We're sorry, Adie."

"Sorry?" I jerk free of him. "*Sorry*? You're saying he does what he did to me to someone else every time he hunts down a witch? How many succubi and incubi has he hurt over the centuries? Why didn't you *stop* him?"

Bitterness fills Tobias's voice. "We filed complaints, but the higher-ups don't care."

"You filed *complaints*?" Staring at him in disbelief, I scramble to my feet to put distance between us. "*Complaints*? And that absolves you of everything?"

Unable to look at them, I turn and march for the stairs, ready to pack my stuff and leave, contract be damned. I can't stay here anymore. Not knowing they could have stopped Domnall and stood by instead.

Lightning fast, Kellen blocks my escape, his arms braced on either side of the stairwell. "Adie, you don't understand."

"What's to understand?" I rise onto my toes, shoulders thrown back. "The three of you are way stronger than Domnall. Don't tell me you can't take him down if you wanted to!"

"But we *can't*." Frost prickles my back a moment before Emil's hands land on my shoulders, shoving me back to my heels. "It's forbidden."

Annoyed, I glare over my shoulder at him. "Well, yeah, I don't expect you to destroy his core, but you could send him back to—"

Tobias appears behind Emil. "No, Adie. We're forbidden from fighting him, *period*. The most we can do is block him from our territory to protect those who live inside our borders."

My lips part in confusion. "But…why?"

Emil's hands slip down my shoulders to grip my biceps in icy shackles. "Think about it. We're *destruction* demons. We're more powerful than Domnall, but he's not weak. Especially if he's hunted recently. If we fought—"

My shoulders slump in defeat. "Cities would be destroyed, and humans would know about us."

When he leans forward to rub his cheek against mine, my skin numbs, my anger melting away. With a shiver, I nuzzle him back and inhale his frosty, sweet scent. The adrenaline brought on by our fight vanishes to leave lassitude in its wake. It makes me want to curl up in my ice demon's embrace and sleep for a millennium.

"Stop it." Static crackles through my body,

jolting me back to alertness as Kellen tugs me away from Emil. "We're not done talking."

"Haven't we talked enough?" Tobias steps around Emil to yank me out of Kellen's hold. His hot hands melt away the last of the ice in my body with the gentle insistence of a fireplace on a winter night. "I say it's time for bed. And Adie gave me an IOU for snuggles."

"Now, wait a minute," Emil growls, his hands landing on my arms above Tobias's, the instant cold freezing my bones and making them crackle, on the verge of pain. "You disrupted *my* snuggles this morning with your *tantrum*—"

"Whoa, guys." Kellen holds up his hands to disrupt the imminent fight. "She's not a piece of rope to play tug-of-war with."

Relieved at least one of them can be reasonable, I smile at him. "Thank you, Kellen, I—"

"Besides"—his hands land on my shoulders, tiny lightning bolts burrowing down to make my already brittle bones vibrate—"you heard Domnall. Adie doesn't need snuggles right now, she needs to power up, which means—"

Frost creeps up my arms as Emil's grip tights. "I hold more power than you right now."

"I'm *always* powerful." Lava slides down my arm.

"There's a storm coming, I *need*—"

"*Shut up, all of you!*" Spindling power out to my limbs, I break free of the three demons and stumble back to my couch, my body achy and ready to collapse from too many conflicting powers. I collapse face down on the cushions. "None of you get to decide whose bed I sleep in." Lifting a heavy arm, I wave in their direction. "*My* choice. Not yours."

A moist nose prods my cheek, followed by a blast of hot air.

Turning my head, I narrow my eyes on Tac. As if I'll forget he trapped me earlier. "No, *you* don't get snuggles, either, you traitor."

Saucer-sized green eyes blink at me.

"No, you won't win me over with compliments."

His left ear swivels, and my heart melts.

"Oh, you big romantic, you." I scrub my palm up his snout. "Fine, but only because you're so sweet."

"Did the demon cat just win over us?" Kellen asks in disbelief.

Tobias nods. "Yeah, I think he did."

Emil stretches his arms over his head in a lean ripple of muscle. "Looks like I win."

The other two turn to him, and Kellen's eyebrows lift. "Say what?"

"Well, Tac sleeps in my room, so..."

"Oh, but we were rejected from Emil's room," I coo at Tac, who snuffles in agreement. "I can't go where I'm not wanted, so you'll sleep with me tonight, right, you big, beautiful, fluffy pillow?"

Kellen claps Emil on the shoulder. "You shot yourself in the foot with that one."

"Shut up." Emil takes a step toward me. "I can re-invite—"

I scratch Tac's nose. "We can play kitty cave. What do you think?"

One giant paw thumps onto the couch above my head, and Tac's wings flare as he rises above me.

"No!" Rolling to my back, I fling my arms up to ward him off. "Not *now*!"

The couch wobbles as he gets his back paws onto the edge, and the others laugh as I scramble over one padded arm before Tac plops down in my spot.

Rising to my feet, I bop him between the ears. "No snuggles for you, either, then!"

In answer, his eyes close as a contented rumble fills the room.

It finds an echo in my stomach, and I rub it. "I'm hungry."

"It *is* dinner time." Kellen turns toward the kitchen. "Last at the island cooks!"

I make it to the kitchen last, but only because I let them win. We all know I can beat them in speed if I want, but I have a craving for chicken Parmesan tonight. If one of them wins, it will be frozen dinners or donuts for sure.

Tobias, Emil, and Kellen take their preferred stools at the island, opposite the stovetop. A large kitchen table waits off to the right, where the remnants of Tac's destroyed Tiffany lamp litter the floor. For some reason, they never sit there. It makes me wonder if they've always preferred the island or if this is a new phenomenon since I started to actually use the kitchen for its true purpose.

Their avid interest makes me feel like one of those celebrity chefs as I fill a pot with water, turn the oven on, and put the skillet on to heat up. I pause in the process of unwrapping chicken to peek up at them. "How come you don't own a TV?"

Tobias frowns. "Why would we?"

I roll my eyes. "For entertainment?"

"Do we look like we need entertainment?"

I eye them, lined up like my own personal audience. "Yeah, sometimes."

Emil shrugs. "We've lived most of our lives without modern technology."

I move the chicken from the butcher paper to the cutting mat. "But you embrace cell phones and tablets and cars."

Tobias *tsks* quietly. "We're not heathens."

"It's a lost battle with those two." Kellen leans his elbows on the counter and cups his chin, batting his lashes at me. "But I have a TV in my room if you want to watch something."

"You do?" I consider what I've seen of Kellen's room. "Where? I don't remember seeing one."

"Ah, Adie, you sweet little peeping Tom." He wags a finger at me. "You can't see everything while staring through your shutter at me."

I snort back a laugh. "I see enough."

With Kellen's room directly across from mine in the opposite tower, our windows offer me a perfect view of him walking around naked while he gets ready for work. I've had a lot of chances to study that perfect, golden ass of his. His room, not so much.

When I moved out of my mentor's house, I never bought myself a TV, not wanting the added expense or the noise. Landon's constant video game playing killed my desire to own one. But now I miss it sometimes, especially at night when I come home after everyone else is already asleep.

I peek at Kellen. "What size TV?"

He grins like the cat who just caught the canary. "Come to my room to find out."

Emil shifts on his seat and eyes Kellen, but the other demon ignores him.

"Hmm, we'll see." Covering the chicken with plastic wrap, I pull out the meat mallet and hammer the breasts to an even thickness.

It feels good, and I slam the hammer down with more force than strictly necessary.

"Um, Adie?" I glance up to find Kellen's eyes wide. "How flat are you going to make those?"

My gaze drops back to the mat and the flattened chicken. "I'm going to stuff them with mozzarella, so pretty thin. Why?"

"Oh, okay. For a second there, I thought maybe you were working through some aggression."

I twirl the hammer in my hand. "Am I making you nervous, Kellen?"

"Nope!" But he inches a little away from the counter.

Quietly, I slice up the cheese, fold each breast

around a thick piece and season them, then get out two bowls. I set up the egg and breadcrumb stations, before checking the temperature of the pan. It feels about right, so I lightly dust the chicken breasts with flour.

At last, I break the silence. "So, about Sunday—"

"I'm against it." Tobias interrupts. "It's too dangerous."

"Yes, I know." Olive oil and butter go into the skillet, and I dredge the first piece of chicken through the waiting bowls before sliding it into the hot pan. It pops and sizzles, the room filling with the delicious aroma of Italian seasonings. "I don't trust Domnall to protect me. His real goal is the Hunters. I'm just the bait. Once he has them where he wants them, I'm obsolete."

The men relax, and Emil nods. "I'm glad you see things our way."

"That's not what I said." Another piece of chicken goes into the pan. "I'm going through with the plan. I want this finished and Domnall gone."

"Adie," Kellen groans.

"No." This time, it's my turn to cut them off. "I trust you guys, but I won't have you infringing on Domnall's rights on my behalf."

"We can work around that," Tobias protests.

"But there's no reason to." I finish loading the skillet before planting my hands on the counter to hide the fine tremor that rolls through me. The entire plan scares me. It's too undefined and relies too much on assumptions. "This is happening, so we need to figure out a way to minimize the danger. While Domnall's busy with the Hunters, you three will protect me."

(UN)SAFE

At nine-thirty Sunday morning, I park in Tally's driveway, my palms sweaty against the wheel.

The rest of the week flew by, D-Day arriving way faster than I expected. While I didn't spend the time in between boinking the guys' brains out to stockpile energy, I *did* relent and snuggle with them each night to skim the power they naturally release. They argued, but it made no sense to reduce their effectiveness when we all knew that, no matter what, I would be the weakest link.

With the bakery on shorter hours for Sunday, I offered Tally the day off, but she refused, reminding me I needed a way to get the imps out of the bakery once we closed.

Instead, she offered to bring them home after work, seeing as they live a couple houses down from her. It helped ease some of the tension that rode me all week.

Everyone confirmed the Hunters wouldn't be interested in my imps, but I find that hard to believe. They're a minor power demon, practically bottom of the barrel as far as demon hierarchy goes, but the ability the morph their shape seems like an enviable power in my book. Being stuck with only one form since coming to the human plane gave me a new appreciation for the fluidity I enjoyed in Dreamland.

When Tally doesn't come bouncing out of the house at my arrival, I shut off the Mystery Machine and climb out.

I pause next to it, glancing down the block to the dark lines of the imps' house. If I could figure out how to run the bakery by myself, I would. I hate to put anyone in danger. But we all agreed that today needed to look like any other day at Boo's Boutique Bakery.

Which means the imps need to be there.

I walk up the wooden steps and across the porch to the front door. An ugly lion head knocker greets me, so much like the one at the imps' house that it makes me wonder if a cult used to live here, too.

Maybe the whole block was a cult. A lot of suburbia feels rather cultish.

Hesitant, I grip the gold ring and let it fall against the plate. The metal thump echoes in the foyer beyond before silence resumes. The lion's red eyes flare for a moment before dimming once more, and a shiver rolls down my spine. Reese likes the knockers, but I find them creepy.

Tingles come to life in the band around my arm, an early warning system that human magic approaches. A moment later, the door swings open, and Reese gives a distracted nod before he turns and heads back down the hall past the curved staircase.

Bones shivery, I stick a toe over the threshold. When I find no resistance, I step inside, glancing around curiously. The house's layout is a mirror image of the imps' house, but painted in warm, masculine tones, with comfortable furniture and plenty of light.

Almost too much light.

I squint at the crystal chandelier overhead and the lamps on the walls and tables, every one of them turned on despite the sunshine that streams through the windows. Even the sideboard has a small nightlight under it to banish the shadows.

Are they trying to keep Tally's nosy brother out?

Xander's voice drifts from deeper in the house. "We're in the kitchen!"

Closing the front door, I follow Reese's path past the stairs and down the brightly lit hall to where it opens into a large kitchen. Rustic chic, with distressed white cabinets and light-gray, marble countertops. A large wooden table with wrought iron bolts sits in the center, acting as a sort of island, and copper pots hang from an iron rack overhead. The smell of coffee and something burnt fills the room, and I hesitate at the entry.

Slater leans against the table, sipping from a white speckled mug. Dressed in tight, black clothes, with his closely cropped dark hair and thick gauges in his ears, he somehow manages to look at home. Next to him, Jax perches on one corner, his feet swinging, equally comfortable in a blue t-shirt and worn flannel with the sleeves pushed up to his elbows. Reese and Xander stand behind the table, Xander with his arms braced wide as he stares down at the laptop open in front of him, and Reese at his elbow, staring into a patch of shadow between a kitchen cart and the stainless-steel fridge. A small smile quirks his lips, and he nods to something only he can see.

The four of them, so different from each other, somehow form a cohesive whole, as if linked together on a level beyond friendship. And as they glance up at me in unison, I feel like an outsider, an intruder in a sacred place. My eyes drop to the floor, where someone carved a deep groove into the wooden planks and filled it with gold. It curves around the table and disappears from view, but I have no doubt it completes a full circle of protection.

My gaze focuses on it easily, which means it's not currently active, but with all four witches present, it would take little to empower it.

Xander lifts a hand to beckon me closer. "Adie, come in. Would you like some coffee?"

A few more steps bring me into the kitchen, but I stop with my toes at the edge of the circle. My wings shiver with warning. A power I don't understand lives here, and I can't bring myself to cross the golden line. Odd items litter the tabletop. Bundles of herbs that sting my nose; pale, flat stones; feathers; and even a small, animal skull.

Nervous, I lick my lips and glance around for Tally, not finding the pink haired demon. "No, no coffee, but thank you."

Reese glances at the kitchen cart again, his attention snared once more by the shadows.

Slater shifts and sets his mug down. His deep voice comes out like gravel as his gaze fixes on me. "Are you *sure* you don't want us there tonight? We can help."

With a shiver, I rub my tingling arm, chafing at the metal band beneath my hoodie, and glance around once more. "It's not a good idea for you to be near the bakery right now. You saw what Domnall is capable of."

"Which is why we're worried." Xander closes his laptop. "He *hurt* you. You could have died. Why would you now trust he'll keep you safe?"

"It would have only destroyed my corporeal form." But the words coat my tongue with bitter ash. I don't actually know if Domnall's power dump would have just destroyed my corporeal form. It felt like everything inside me burned, even the core of energy that makes me a succubus.

But their concern warms me. We're on the edge of friendship, shared experiences bonding us together. It feels like they want to help me for my own sake and not just because I'm Tally's friend.

Xander's hands glide over the smooth surface of his laptop. "I've been researching the marks in the alley, and I think we can help counteract their effect, at least temporarily."

I shake my head, my braid whacking me in the back. "No, I don't want you near the bakery until this is finished." My gaze sweeps the room to take in the others. "Any of you."

Worried about Domnall, I asked Tally to keep her witches away from the bakery for the time being. They weren't happy with the request, especially after Xander checked out the parking lot and confirmed what Domnall said about it being set up as a trap. He wanted to remove the spell work, but we convinced him to leave it in place. We can't let the Hunters know we're onto them, or they'll move the ambush to somewhere less advantageous.

Xander's lips tighten, but he gives a stiff nod. "We agreed to stay out of it for now. None of us want to be on that demon's radar. We have something else to help protect you."

Reese finally leaves off staring at the shadows, sifts through the items on the counter, then lifts out four pale-gray disks. A hint of ozone comes from them, and curiosity pulls me closer to the counter. Tingles rush up my legs, and I cast a suspicious glance down at the golden circle that surrounds us, but I already committed, so I step up to the edge of the table. The smell of ozone grows stronger as Reese extends the disks.

I reach out, hands cupped together, and he sets them gently in the basin of my palms. The disks tingle, adding to the irritating warning of my armband, and I resist the urge to drop them. Instead, I pull them closer to study the gray ovals.

Each sports a hole on one end, and I frown, then juggle them into my left hand to lift one and inspect it. The smooth surface on either side gives me no hint as to what I hold. It doesn't even make my eyes slide sideways like most human magic.

With a frown, I glance up at Xander. "Am I missing something here? Is there a symbol I just can't focus on?"

"No, this is kind of a combo thing." Uncertain, his eyes flicker to Reese for a moment, while Slater and Jax turn motionless beside me, holding their breath.

Reese blinks at him in response, as if not understanding his obvious concern, before he fixes his mismatched eyes on me. "This is demon and human magic." He weaves his fingers together. "Together, they're stronger."

I roll the disk between my fingers. "There's no demon magic here."

"Well, obviously. We're not demons. Besides, it has to be personalized." Reese circles the table to come to my side. "The human magic is on the inside, which is why you're able to focus on the disks. Xander inscribed it, and I formed the pendants." His eyes twinkle. "If we let Xander mold the clay, everything would be lumpy."

"I'm a software designer, not an artist," Xander grumbles.

"Okay." I lift the disk to my nose, sniff, then sneeze at the scent of clay. It reminds me of the scent that clings to Tally and the guys, without the hint of demonic ozone. My gaze shifts to the cord around Reese's neck that disappears beneath the collar of his shirt.

Seeing my interest, Reese hooks a finger in the cord and drags his pendant out. The smell of clay and ozone increases as the disk falls heavy against his chest. When he makes a move to lift it, Jax rumbles with discontent.

Slater shushes him. "She's Tally's friend and already proven more than once her willingness to keep secrets."

"It's forbidden magic," Jax protests, but he stays perched on the edge of the table. "She should be made aware of the danger of such knowledge. Given a choice on whether to hold this secret."

Reese hesitates, hand over his pendant, and

glances back to his brother before his gaze shifts to the shadowed corner. "We are alone for now. Aren is keeping the others away."

Aren? That's Tally's brother, right? I think I remember her mentioning him by name.

Before I can voice the question, Xander nods. "Jax is right. We shouldn't give you something like this without your full knowledge. Especially since it won't be just you taking the risk. It will also be Emil, Tobias, and Kellen."

My hands open, dropping the disks to the wooden tabletop. Reese winces as they clatter and bounce around but makes no move to reclaim them. I don't want anything to do with magic that will harm my demons.

"It's easier to show and then explain." Reese lifts his pendant to show me one side.

Unlike the blank ones they gave me, his contains an etching, a swirly shape that reminds me of cotton candy. Someone carved it into the clay, and rusty red stains the deep grooves. For a moment, it shifts and rolls like fog, stretching to cover the entire disk before curling back in on itself. With the motion comes a sense of brightness, a flash of pink happiness that reminds me of Tally.

I lift a finger to touch the demon glyph, and

bubbles pop against my skin. Amazed, I pull my hand back and meet Reese's eyes. "Is this Tally's glyph?"

He nods happily, then flips the pendant over.

When I glance down, my eyes instantly shift to the side. "I thought you said the human magic was on the inside?"

"The spell is." Xander leans on his hands, arms spread wide. "What you're not seeing right now is Reese's witch's mark."

As Reese tucks his pendant away, I turn to Xander in surprise. "You have marks like demons do?"

"Kind of?" He rolls his shoulders. "It's part of gaining power over our magic. We each went through a trial, and at the end, once we proved our control over magic, we received our..." His brows furrow together as he struggles to find the right word.

"Our second name," Slater supplies on a gravelly rumble. "They're sacred, linked to our power, and should only be shared with those we trust."

Understanding, I prod the blank disks on the counter. "And what do they do?"

Reese's hand covers mine, drawing my attention back to him. "Baku are not allowed corporeal form.

They are strictly beings of dreams. For Tally to be here, she needed a link." A blush stains his cheeks. "I could touch her through the barrier of our worlds and bring her to the human plane, but once we separated, she would be pulled back. Xander, too. But not Slater or Jax."

Jax kicks his heels against the table leg. "We're not as powerful."

"You're powerful in different ways." Xander's words hold the pattern of a frequent argument, and Reese's nod backs up his statement.

"Anyway"—Jax hops down from his perch and folds his arms over his chest—"Reese and Xander figured out a way to combine our magic with demon magic to help Tally hold her form here." He lifts a hand to touch the pendant hidden under his shirt. "We're linked, our power bridging the planes so that she can stay here with us."

My wings rustle against my back as my mind whirls. Yes, I can see why this type of magic would be forbidden. Demons could snatch witches and bypass the entire process of demon politics, taking corporeal form willy-nilly and flooding the human plane. There's a *reason* for the way things are, and if demons could break the rules easily, staying hidden among the humans would become impossible.

Then my mind veers off on a different path. What if this magic could be reversed to allow humans into the demon plane?

I shove the pendants back across the table. "You shouldn't play with this type of magic. It's too dangerous."

Xander gently pushes the disks back. "You need this, Adie. If something goes wrong, this can be the difference of whether or not you stay on the human plane."

I shake my head, braid whipping against my back. "I'll just be sent back to Dreamland. This is too dangerous."

Xander's eyes soften. "Hunters don't send demons back to the demon plane, Adie. They bind you to your body, then tear you apart. If something goes wrong tonight, that's it for you. Even if you're willing to take the risk, what about your imps? Who will protect them? And Tobias, Emil, and Kellen will be left without a succubus again."

My hands shake where they cup the disks. "The imps will be freed. And my demons can just find a new succubus to take care of them."

Reese's hand settles on my shoulder, startlingly warm through my hoodie. "Are you okay with that?"

Wings rustling with unhappiness, I stare down at the pendants.

If my imps are freed with my death, will they be okay? Will they be able to find jobs in the human world? Kelly might be able to gain work as a handyman, but he's still mostly untrained. And the others could maybe find jobs at a coffee shop.

But there's so much paperwork involved in integrating into the human world, paperwork I haven't bothered to set in place because I have time before I need to worry about that kind of stuff. How arrogant I've been, taking time for granted. Long life does not equal immortality.

And *am* I okay with the idea of the guys signing a contract with another succubus? My mind balks at the very thought. No. They're *mine*. No one else will touch them. The possessiveness goes beyond a basic protectiveness of my food source. It's not just their energy I want to keep for myself. It's everything about the men. Even Tac is mine.

Slowly, my fingers curl around the disks, tingles sharp against my palms. "Tell me what I need to do."

CHANGE OF PLANS

Tally shifts from one foot to the other. "Are you *sure* you don't want me to stay?"

Behind her, my imps cluster in a tight group, chittering to each other. Not wanting to worry them, I stayed quiet about tonight's plan, but they sense the tension in the air. They'd been especially touchy today, to the point I hid in the kitchen to avoid being pawed at in front of my customers. Not even an entire bag of sparkle balls and pinwheels could make them smile.

Now Tally stands as a barrier between us because we both agree that, with the current mood in the bakery, if they can reach me, they'll refuse to leave.

And I need them gone. I can't be worrying about them when I face the Hunters tonight.

Jesse, in front of the group, clutches her glitter-baby. It's an obnoxiously large-eyed, stuffed cat covered in rainbow glitter fabric that she chose as her prize for being good during our shopping trip earlier in the week.

I force a smile for their benefit, which does nothing to ease their worry, and face Tally with my shoulders thrown back in an attempt to exude a confidence I don't feel. "Yes, I'll be fine."

"You have your...necklaces?"

When I picked Tally up this morning, Xander invited me inside, and the witchy boys gifted me with new protection charms.

Tally had arrived at the tail end of Xander's explanation on how to link me to my guys, full of apologies for taking longer than expected to get ready.

They had hunched their shoulders guiltily, making me wonder if they'd hoped to hide the pendants from her. I don't know why they would have bothered except for the dozens of worried glances Tally cast me on the drive to the bakery.

Does she not like the idea I'll have them? Or just that they tried to go behind her back to give them to me?

"I have them." I pat my pocket, where the clay disks rattle together.

At my first break, I got out a metal thermometer and used its sharp point to dig my glyph into one side of each of the disks. Once I added a drop of my blood to each, I became conscious of them in an uneasy way, like part of my awareness now resided in my pocket. An uncomfortable feeling, and one I find distracting at a time I need to be alert.

Tally bites her plump, lower lip, sharp little teeth worrying at the delicate flesh for a moment of indecision. "If they do not want to wear them, just give me a call. Reese, Xander, Jax, and Slater will take their place."

I reach out to grip her shoulder in reassurance. It costs her to make the offer and warms me to know she would lend me her men for something so intimate. But I have no desire to share that much of myself with her witches. Even planning to do so with Emil, Tobias, and Kellen makes me shiver with an odd mixture of apprehension and excitement.

I meet her mahogany eyes. "I appreciate the offer. But I will not ask that of you or your men. You've all done enough for me already."

Relief washes over her face, followed instantly by self-recrimination, before her voice drops to a whisper. "Perhaps the imps?"

"Perhaps." I agree with zero intent to follow that

thought to action. I'm their protector, not the other way around. Whatever tonight's outcome, I will not endanger more of my people. I glance at them again. "If anything happens, contact Philip. I've made arrangements as best I could with such short notice."

She gives a jerky nod, her large eyes brightening with unshed tears. "I will do my best."

An answering sting fills my eyes, and I blink quickly before releasing her. "Look at us, getting all emotional. For all we know, nothing will even happen tonight."

She sniffles loudly. "I am not sure if I should hope for that or not."

"My fingers are crossed for a swift resolution." I hold up my hands, middle and index fingers crossed, and Tally does the same. "Okay, get out of here. I'm going to finish closing up and then get myself over to Fulcrum as planned."

With a tight nod, Tally turns and spreads her arms out to herd the imps toward the door. They shuffle away, casting reluctant looks back at me. I wave, smile wide on my face, until the door closes. As soon as the latch catches, I slump against the kitchen island to give myself a few minutes of quiet reprieve. I have no confidence in our plan where it comes to Domnall. If things go sideways, I don't want my guys in harm's way, either.

My hand slips into my pant pocket to grip the disks, fingers finding the indents where my glyph now rests. I stroke my fingertip over the gentle curve and shiver as I feel a secondary stroke against the energy at my core. This feels dangerous, too. I should have asked more questions, demanded to know what would happen were these to fall into the wrong hands. I want more time to test these out, not throw them into the mix on a day already rife with too many possibilities for failure.

In my back pocket, my phone buzzes, and I reach to pull it out, warmth filling my chest when I find Kellen's name on the screen. Swiping to unlock the screen, I read his message.

Kellen: Everything ready, sexy?

My thumbs fly over the screen.

Adie: On my way now.

Kellen: You bringing me something sweet?

Adie: Lemon cupcakes?

Kellen: I was thinking your ass, but I'll accept cupcakes, too.

Laughing, I tuck the phone away and shrug out of my chef coat. Once I drop it in the laundry bin, I walk to the pantry. Goose bumps rise on my arms, but I resist the urge to slip into my hoodie, leaving it draped over the back of the desk chair. I don't want my wings encumbered if I need to move fast. Small as they are, they'll still give me an added advantage if If need to flee upward.

From the shelf, I grab the empty bakery box, my prop for heading over to Fulcrum. It's not unusual for me to take the staff treats when I visit Kellen, and I hope Domnall's right that the Hunters are watching, see I'm alone and vulnerable, and strike.

With a deep breath to brace myself, I step out of the side door and into the alley. My heart pounds hard, and a fine tremor shakes my hands. Humans pass the entrance on one side, where the narrow passage opens onto the main street. In the opposite direction, the parking lot waits, with only a few cars. I turn toward the humans and the iffy protection they offer when my phone buzzes again.

Juggling the box to one hand, I dig it out, expecting to find Kellen messaging me again, but instead, Philip's name flashes on the screen. Irritated at the demon for his subterfuge regarding my cousin's vanishing act, I almost send him to voicemail, but worry stays me. What if this is about Julian? Or my imps? My heart slams into my throat. Could something have gone wrong with Tally?

Quickly, I press accept and lift the phone to my ear. "Yes?"

"Oh, good, you answered!" Far from worried, Philip sounds excited. "Change of plans. Head directly to the parking lot."

My brain scrambles to process this change in plans. If Philip wants me in the parking lot, it means the Hunters are near, so I need to play this up. "Oh, hey, yeah I was just on my way to the club for a late dinner. Do you have a meeting?"

Philip's voice drops to a whisper. "Something alerted them that you're alone. Maybe Tally leaving with the imps. They're already in place, so there's no need to draw them out."

"Okay." I clear my throat to hide the tremor. "What time should I expect you home?"

A long pause follows before he huffs. "Girl, I have no idea what you're trying to ask. You're horrible at this."

I bite my lip, but my brain blanks. I can't come up with a way to ask how many Hunters there are, or if Kellen, Tobias, and Emil were alerted already and are on their way. My text conversation with Kellen *just* happened. And he obviously expects me at the club. Did someone contact him about the change in plans?

Blood rushes through my veins. "Maybe I'll just swing by to drop off the cupcakes? Your doorman can put them in your office."

"Don't chicken out now." His firm tone does nothing to soothe my anxiety. "Julian and Domnall are in place and waiting. Now's your moment."

I force out a brittle laugh. "Well, if you don't hurry, Emil and Tobias will eat all the cakes. You know how possessive they get."

Another long pause. "Okay, I think I get that one. And, yeah, Domnall called them. They'll be there soon."

I swallow down the lump in my throat. Do I trust that Domnall actually followed through on that promise? He didn't want them in the way.

"Well, I'll see you when you get home, then!" I hang up before he tries to reassure me again and text Kellen.

Adie: SOS Bakery

Shoving my phone back into my pocket, I turn and force my legs to carry me toward the parking lot. With the end of summer, the days have grown shorter, and the sun already dips below the horizon. My eyes search out the slender sliver of the moon, but it hasn't yet risen. Will the Hunters still attack without the moon in the right place? Didn't Domnall say that was part of their spell?

I drag in a deep breath and hug the empty cake box to my chest for the flimsy barrier it offers. My clogs scrape against the concrete, and I force my steps to stay even as I approach the parking lot. Xander tried to point to where the different parts of the spells were inscribed on the brick buildings that edge the small lot, and one is on either side of the opening.

As I near, the band around my arm flares to life, a million fire ants eating into my flesh. My wings razerblade against my spine in warning as I walk into the parking lot, and a greasy film coats my skin. It drags at my strength, barbed hooks slicing into the energy at my core and dragging it down my legs, toward my feet. The sensation leaves me light-headed, and I sway for a moment, the cake box falling from my hands.

Instinct takes over, and my wings burst from my back as I spin on one heel and run for the alley, only to slam into an invisible barrier.

Pain flares at every point of contact as I bounce off and land hard on my ass. Pain flares up my spine, and I scrape at my skin, trying to push the slime away.

A dark figure steps into the alley, and for a moment, I'm shocked at how *average* he looks. No dark cloaks for this witch. Instead, he wears acid-washed jeans, converse, and a dark t-shirt tucked into his waistband. Light-brown hair falls gently around a face that would blend into any crowd for its sheer ordinariness.

Another figure joins him, an elderly woman, and recognition sparks. I remember her coming into the bakery, said something cryptic about someone stepping on my grave. She'd been friendly, but now she stares at me with cold disgust. From beneath her padded housecoat, she pulls a thin stick with little white beads on it. She rattles it at me, her mouth moving to shape words that my ears refuse to hear.

But I feel their intent as the slime thickens, weighing me down. With effort, I push back to my feet, my wings flapping to give me balance, and I turn to the parking lot exit, only to find a third figure there. He holds something round in his hands and shakes it in tandem with the older woman's words.

My focus zeros in on it at the same time my gorge rises. He holds a skull, bleached white with empty eye sockets. Small horns still protrude from the cheekbones, with larger ones on the forehead. A lava demon, perhaps, or one of the rock trolls.

I swing back to the two in the alley. "Why are you doing this? I've done nothing to you!"

"Slattern whore." The man spits on the ground. "Devil temptress."

I reel back from the vehemence in his voice, and the older woman steps forward, shaking her stick harder. The white beads bang against the wood, a rattle that echoes in my blood and bones, and the drag of energy increases, the power ripping from my core.

Breaths frantic, I search the parking lot for an ally. Where's Domnall and Julian? Philip said they were here, what are they waiting for?

My hand drops to my pocket, to the three disks inside, and the draw of power slows, diverting to the pendants.

The old woman frowns, the winkles in her face deep, and she turns to the man. "She's fighting it."

"No shit," I growl through clenched teeth.

"I thought you said she was weak," the man snaps back, ignoring me.

"That's what we were told." She shakes the stick again, and I focus on the beads.

No, the knuckle bones. One of my people. Torn apart and used against me.

Anger turns my vision red, energy flooding my limbs, and I hyper-speed toward the pair. Their eyes widen, fear and uncertainty bright on their faces in the moment before I slam up against the barrier and bounce off once more.

The woman lets out a creaking laugh. "You see? She's weak, just like they said."

He licks his lips. "Do you see her wings? We won't be able to make much from such small feathers."

"Better small feathers than no feathers at all."

I pick myself back up, focusing on the wall to their right, to the places where my eyes refuse to focus. Damn, Domnall. Damn, Julian, too. There's only three of them, how long are they going to stand around before they take action?

As if on cue, a scream splits the air from the parking lot exit, swiftly cut off in a liquid gargle. The two in front of me flinch, and I rush toward them once more, scrambling up the side of the building until I find the place where my skin burns. Talons extended, I tear into the brick, ripping mortar, clay, and sand away. The hooks in my gut loosen, and with a crow of victory, I launch across the opening to the opposite side, ripping apart the symbols of entrapment.

The slimy barrier weakens but doesn't fall. More symbols mark the parking lot, but they're not enough. Even a weak succubus like me won't fall to these humans.

Clutching a large chunk of brick in one fist, I give the two Hunters a toothy smile. "You're going to die here."

The man grabs the old woman's arm. "We should go. This isn't what we were promised."

She shakes free of him. "Don't be a coward. It's only one succubus."

"Yes, stay and play." Spindling energy out, I throw the brick at them. It hurtles through the air, slams into the invisible barrier, and sticks in mid-air.

The man pales, staring from it to me as he shakes his head. "I'm not dying here. Not for a handful of tiny feathers."

"Oh, I don't know. They don't look so small to me," Julian drawls as he steps into the alley behind them. "Feathers like those go for a pretty penny on the black market."

I hiss a warning at my cousin.

Julian waves a bloody hand in dismissal. "Don't worry, dear. Your feathers are safe."

"Took you long enough." I drop back to the ground to press against the barrier. It gives a little beneath my push, the spell compromised. I stare past the Hunters to my cousin. "Hurry up."

"This is what's wrong with the youth of today. So impatient." Julian catches the old woman's eyes. "You know what I'm talking about, right? They just have no concept of theatrics."

"Don't talk to me as if we're equal, devil spawn." She lifts her stick, shaking it at Julian. "Get ye back to hell."

Julian throws his head back as he laughs. "Oh, goodness, no. Not equal in any way. You're a babe in the cradle compared to me." He reaches into his coat and pulls out a gun. Calm as can be, he levels it on the man and pulls the trigger.

Shocked, I watch the man fall to the ground before the muffled pop even registers. I don't know what I expected, but not this calm execution.

Julian swings the gun toward the woman, and a smooth, ash-filled voice fills the alley. "Now, pet, don't take all my fun."

Some emotion flickers across Julian's face a moment before his expression smooths out, and he tucks the weapon away, a broad smile spreading over his face as he swings around. "I would never *dream* of it, darling. I saved the powerful one for you."

Domnall swoops forward, gold eyes bright as they fix on the old lady. She shakes her stick harder, a spell slipping from her lips, but Domnall brushes it aside like an annoying gnat. His strong arms curve forward, almost gentle, as he embraces her, and her unintelligible words take new form in a frantic prayer.

My gut tightens as Domnall's head dips toward hers, and I force myself to watch as his mouth opens impossibly wide, his jaw unhinging. It's nothing like the picture in the book.

I clench my teeth against the bile that floods my mouth as he devours her. When he finishes, only a shriveled husk remains inside her clothes. His arms open once more, and the wind catches what I can only assume is skin, blowing it away.

With her death, the barrier falls completely, and I stagger forward. "Is it done?"

Eyes heavy with satiation, Domnall wipes the back of his hand over his mouth. "No, there were only three here. I've felt more than that in town."

Shivering, I hug my elbows as I scoot around the fallen man. "What about him?"

"There's still some power to be gained here."

Domnall crouches over him, lifting the limp body by the collar as his mouth opens once more.

With a shudder, I hurry toward my cousin, unwilling to watch Domnall devour another Hunter. Once was enough to give me nightmares.

As I join him, Julian turns toward the street side of the alley. "Philip, did you find anything?"

The youthful imp bounds into the alley, his soft cheeks flushed from running. "Sorry, boss, they got away."

Julian nods. "How many were there?"

"A handful at most." His steps slow as he gazes past us, his face paling. "Whoa, that's really…"

"Never mind that." Julian lifts a hand to draw Philip's attention back to him. "Which way did they go? Maybe we can still—"

Philip jerks, confusion crossing his face as he stares down at the bloody blade that protrudes from his chest. His body jerks again as it yanks out, then swings through the air in a whistle of sharp metal.

Energy floods my limbs, and I spring forward, arms out, but I'm too late as the sword cuts cleanly through Philip's neck. His head flies forward, and instinct brings my hands up to catch it as his body falls sideways to reveal another Hunter, sword already whistling in a return arch toward me.

CLEANUP

Time slows.

Behind me, Julian's bellow of rage floods the alley.

In front of me, the Hunter's sword swings down, ready to separate my head from my shoulders the same way it just did to poor Philip.

Sticky warmth flows down my front and coats my arms as I clutch his head to my chest. The smell of copper fills the air, thick enough to block out anything else.

I should move. Power still floods my limbs, allowing me to take in every detail as the sword arcs downward. But I stay glued to the spot, stuck in place by Philip's blood, by my inability to protect him.

My breath freezes in front of my face in a plume of white that crystallizes mid-air. I stare at it in confusion for one frantic heartbeat before ice floods the alley. It spreads like wildfire, deafening with the shriek of ice forming and shattering only to reform again. It splashes up the walls and across the ground in a curving tidal wave that swamps the Hunter.

The sword freezes, its sharp edge a stinging kiss against my neck.

Shocked, I stare at the Hunter, now an ice statue, before I stumble back a step, out of the way of danger even if my sense of self-preservation came too late.

As fast as it arrived, the ice melts, the alley now sweltering with the warmth of a midsummer day. Heat dries out my skin, tightening it against my bones like a sauna, and salty sweat beads on my upper lip. The Hunter's body falls to the ground, landing halfway across Philip's decapitated form, to reveal Tobias and Emil at the end of the alley.

Snowflakes spiral around Emil, his frozen white eyes fixed on the fallen Hunter. Ice crystals glitter across his cheekbones, and blue tints his lips. A god of winter, come down from his icy kingdom to blanket the world in frozen death.

Tobias stands beside him, a dark contrast to his icy beauty. The air shimmers around Tobias, his tanned skin glowing with banked fires. Black eyes that reflect dying stars shift from the Hunter to me, and the ground rumbles beneath my feet. Here is a demon who destroys worlds, who pulls meteors off orbit to smash into our planet, who rips open the earth and spits lava into the sky.

My legs collapse, and for the third time tonight, I land hard on my ass. Philip's head bounces in my lap, far heavier than a head should be. Reminded of the imp, I glance down. He still looks confused, his boyish face frozen in time, his soft lips parted as if to ask a question. I brush back his hair, and the fine strands stick to my bloody fingers.

How could he be so happy and now be gone?

Hand shaking, I touch his cheek. Soft against my fingertip, it still holds the warmth of life, and my breath catches, hopeful his eyes will spark with life, that his lips will fold into his clever smile. But his face remains the same, the spark of life that fueled him gone.

My fault. *My fault.*

The words pound against my temples with every beat of my heart. The Hunters came here for me. No one else should have been in danger. How did this happen?

The ground beneath me shakes again, then

groans as the cement cracks open, the bodies descending into the earth.

No, Philip, shouldn't be buried with his killer. Frantic, I cradle his head in one arm and lurch forward on my knees to grab his ankle before he disappears.

A hand touches my shoulder. "Adie, what are you doing?"

I drag Philip's body out of the hole. "He shouldn't be buried with the Hunter!"

A warm hand smooths back my hair, bringing with it a rush of static. "Honey, Philip's not going to care what happens to this body."

"It's not right." I release the ankle and grab Philip's belt, pulling him onto my lap. His head and body should be together, in a better place than this dirty alley.

"Okay, we understand." Kellen kneels in front of me, his arms out. "Let me take his body. We can bury it in our backyard, okay? We can plant some tulip bulbs so there will be flowers in the spring."

Sniffling back my tears, I nod and let Kellen take the body. As he stands, Tobias appears next to him, his hand out. "Come on, I'll help, too."

Shaky now, I reluctantly pass him Philip's head.

His eyes widen in surprise, but he accepts it without comment.

Emil comes next, his steps creaking as he holds onto the ice. He stares down at me with whited-out eyes for a moment before his hand slowly extends.

Yes, I want the comfort of my ice demon right now. I need this pain to go away, to numb the horror of my part in Philip's demise.

"What's she so hysterical about?" Domnall demands.

An angry hush comes from my cousin.

"What?" Domnall drawls. "It's just an imp. They're a dime a dozen."

Rage clouds my vision in red. How dare he. He's equally complicit in this. If he hadn't hurried the plan, if he'd given the Hunters more time to gather—

The hard hilt of the Hunter's sword fills my palm, and I hyper-speed toward Domnall. This ends *now*.

In a blur of motion, Julian rams me into the wall, grabbing the hand with the sword and slamming it against the bricks. Hard clay gives with our impact, and sharp corners cut into my back.

I shove against him, but Julian has centuries on me and holds me in place without effort.

His power presses against mine. "Adie, stop."

I hiss in defiance.

His power pushes harder until the air squeezes from my lungs. I wheeze, mouth gaping, and he leans in, his mouth next to my ear. "This is not the moment."

Gray dots my vision, and my thoughts flounder. What does he mean, *not the moment*? His friend just died! How can he not want revenge?

My mouth gapes, lips forming the demand I lack the oxygen to make.

Julian gently kisses my temple before he takes the sword from my hand. Tucking it inside his long, leather jacket, he steps back.

The others remain where they stood, our fight over before they even registered it began. Emil still stands with his hand outstretched, his brow furrows in confusion to find the space in front of him empty. Kellen and Tobias wait beside him, their arms filled with parts of Philip.

They search the alley, locating me and Julian halfway between them and Domnall.

Domnall's golden eyes narrow in suspicion. "What happened just now?"

As the rage that drove me dissipates, the demon's power pulses strongly, increased threefold by the Hunters he devoured. He's more powerful now than the first time I met him.

I would have come up against that and been squashed like a gnat on a windshield.

"We need to take care of the other bodies." Julian glances back over his shoulder. "A little assistance, Tobias? That trick with the ground opening is *very* convenient."

Still looking suspicious, Domnall checks the corners of his mouth with two fingers, as if afraid he left some Hunter residue on him. "Yeah, makes clean up easier, not having to hide the corpses."

Julian saunters up to his side. "Need a kiss, dear?"

Domnall cracks an evil smile. "No, I'll hold onto the power a little longer."

"You do like to stockpile it, don't you?" Julian links his arm with Domnall's like a couple on a date instead of a murder spree. "Come on, let's go fetch that one from the other side of the parking lot so we can make a nice pile of bodies."

"I do like to see them stacked up." Domnall glances back at the now smooth ground where the fourth Hunter disappeared beneath the cement. "Pity about that one. I might have been able to pull something out of it."

As the two men disappear into the parking lot, my hand clenches around the memory of my stolen sword. Domnall will only gain more strength as this fight continues. I need to be there when he's weak once more. Which means after he's dumped his stolen power. Being the recipient of that almost killed me last time.

How many witches had he drained to be that powerful? One, two? I shudder. No way I can take that and still be able to fight him.

That thought brings up a new concern. How does Domnall plan to offload all that power once this is over? Does he expect me and Julian to take it? Julian just offered. At least, I think that's what he was doing. But will he offer when there's more? My gut clenches at the thought.

Kellen, Emil, and Tobias stop in front of me. They make a macabre tableau, true demons from human imagination, complete with blood splatter and body parts. But Kellen and Tobias hold Philip's two halves with respect, honoring the imp in death. Were he here, he'd be delighted; I just know it.

My eyes sting with fresh tears. How long before Philip regains enough of himself to take form on the demon plane? How long will he have to wait to return here? The line for imps to cross the two worlds is long. They're fast breeders, and finding a sponsor is first come, first served.

Emil disrupts my thoughts. "Adie, are you ready to go home?"

With a jerky nod, I push away from the building. "Yeah, I'm ready."

"I'll pull the car around to the back. Can't have the humans seeing this." He reaches into Tobias's suit pocket and withdraws the keys, then turns and jogs toward the street.

While we wait, Tobias studies me. "What happened here?"

Tired, I rub a hand across my forehead and cooling blood sloughs off. It rolls down my nose like jello, hangs from the tip for a heartbeat, then plops to the ground. I stare at it for a moment, then at my hands. Red smears them and coats my tank top and the thighs of my slacks. It brings with it the disturbing realization that I'm sticky with Philip's blood. While we weren't necessarily friends, I liked the imp. And there's no reason he should have died here tonight.

I extend my arms, spreading my fingers to watch the blood form webs between them.

Concern fills Kellen's voice. "Adie, honey? You okay?"

"No." I bring my fingers together, then spread them again, watching the webs reform.

Beneath the copper tang of blood, I catch the baby powder scent of imp. Despite the way the blood congeals, it doesn't feel cold. Instead, it blankets me in a layer of warmth, as if Philip's trying to let me know that he doesn't blame me for his death. Philip still lived when his blood sprayed over me, in that brief second between life and death, which means power still lives in his blood. Disconnected from his core, it didn't return with him to the demon plane.

Kellen ducks in front of my face, his gaze worried. "Adie?

I throw my senses wide, letting go of that part of myself that stops me from feeding on every human I pass. A flood of emotion swamps me, worry and anger from Tobias and Kellen, a lingering sadness from Julian, triumph and greed from Domnall. Past them, the humans who go about their everyday lives, the boredom, tedium, excitement, joy, and pain. All the complex feelings of life. They ghost across my skin, a buffet for the taking.

Philip's blood shimmers and sinks beneath my flesh, curling around my bones in a gentle embrace before sinking into my core. For a moment, the world shifts. In the alley, pebbles I never noticed before take on a shine that makes my fingers itch to snatch them up and stuff them in my pocket. The sweetness emanating from the bakery brings drool to my mouth. I covet the treats within, wanting to hoard them all to myself.

Is this how imps see the world? No wonder they distract so easily.

Then the moment passes, and I blink Kellen and Tobias back into view. Apprehension fills their eyes, and I lift a clean hand to tuck a loose strand of hair behind my ear before I reach out to take Philip's head back into my arms. Tobias releases it with a visible sigh of relief and scrubs his hands against his suit.

I can't blame him for it. Philip's head now feels like a block of ice, no power here to give it life. Even so, I hold him carefully. He won't be disrespected in death. His passing back to the demon plane wasn't planned, so he will be mourned properly.

I stroke his hair in farewell. Until we meet again, here or on the other side.

Wheels crunch in the parking lot, and the nose of Tobias's expensive sports car comes into view.

Domnall and Julian follow close behind, an emaciated body slung between them. They drop it on top of the other body, and I see now what a body drained of power after death looks like. It's not as complete a devouring as the old woman, who Domnall took alive. This one's skin shrivels tight to the bones, the mouth and eyes gaping holes in the face. I've only seen this before in documentaries of mummies.

"Be a dear, pet, and fetch that piece over there?" Domnall points down the alley, and I turn to see the sheath of the old woman's skin caught against the bricks. "If we're disposing of the bodies, we might as well be thorough."

Julian skips forward and pinches it up between his thumb and forefinger. "Why's this always left?"

"It's the bits that are already dead in the body." Domnall smacks his lips. "The younger the witch, the less there's left behind."

I shudder and clutch Philip's head closer for comfort. Why does he know that? He's only supposed to devour bad witches, which implies time enough for them to grow up to *be* bad.

Julian drops the dried-out bit on top of the pile, and both demons look at Tobias expectantly.

With a scowl for them, the ground rumbles, then splits in two, the bodies sinking below the surface swiftly. When it shifts back together, only a thin crack in the cement shows where they now lay.

In the parking lot, Emil toots the horn with impatience, and Tobias's hand spreads over my back. "Come on. Let's go home."

"What, so soon?" Domnall's hands move to his hips. "I thought we'd all go back to Fulcrum and have some celebratory drinks."

Kellen moves to walk ahead of us, his steps fast with anger. "Fulcrum's closed for the night."

"What? Why?" Domnall checks his watch. "We still have most of the night ahead of us."

"Someone changed our plans," Kellen bites off. "I told the staff to kick everyone out and close the place down."

Domnall claps his hands. "Even better! No smelly humans to stink the place up!"

As we near, Tobias smoothly steps behind me, moving me to the place closer to the wall and farther from Domnall. "We're going home."

"You're all a bunch of spoilsports." Domnall grabs the back of Julian's neck, yanking him roughly against his side. "You'll celebrate with me, won't you, pet?"

Julian grins up at him. "Where else would I go?"

Disappointment rolls through me. How can he be so cavalier? He lost one of his own tonight.

Julian's gaze flickers toward me, an inscrutable expression in his eyes, before they move away, and he points toward the street. "Shall we?"

Domnall claps him on the shoulder. "Show me the best place in town."

"Nothing but the best for you."

We don't stop to watch them leave, heading instead in the opposite direction to the waiting car. Emil pops the trunk, and Kellen casts me a hesitant glance before he folds Philip's body into it. I follow to deposit the head inside as well. As I do, I note the rubber lining and what looks like the plug for a drain.

Who knew my demons were so gangster?

We climb into the car, Kellen and I squeezed into the almost non-existent backseat with Tobias in the front.

As Emil shifts into drive, Tobias twists around to study me once more. "What happened tonight?"

"Domnall moved up the timetable." My head turns toward Kellen. "He said he informed you."

Lightning skitters across his pupils. "No, he did not."

I nod, expecting that answer. "He lied. And

someone told the Hunters where to find me. One of them said as much before she was taken out."

The air in the car grows heavy.

I turn to face forward. "I only have two questions. Did Julian know Domnall lied? And who set me up?"

(UN)CLEAN

For the rest of the drive home, heavy silence fills the car.

When Emil backs the car into the driveway, he bypasses the garage and continues into the backyard. Busy with work and uninterested in gardening, I haven't spent any time out here. As the wheels bump onto the grass, I twist to peer out the rear window.

The large, brick house forms a wall blocking the street on one side while a line of trees blocks the other side, hiding the backyard from nosy neighbors. A tall, brick wall, with wrought iron spikes on the top, peeks out in the narrow space between the garage and the trees. Does it circle the entire yard? The neighbors on either side own mini mansions, too, with the distance between houses providing a privacy all its own.

It piques my curiosity, but not enough to explore right now. Maybe after I have a chance to go to the garden store and buy those tulip bulbs Kellen mentioned.

I peek at him from the corner of my eye. Will he go with me? I enjoyed shopping with him last time.

He catches my glance and leans close enough to allow sparks to jump from his arm to mine. "What are you plotting?"

I bite my lip, stupidly embarrassed. "Will you go with me tomorrow to buy flowers?"

His hand catches mine, static crackling between out linked fingers. "I'd be happy to."

Tobias clears his throat. "We can have some delivered. It's not safe to go out until the Hunters are caught."

I narrow my eyes on the back of his head. "I'm not going to stay in hiding. I have a business to run."

"That's different from traipsing around out in public." The scent of lava fills the small space of the car. "The bakery is a controllable environment. One of us will escort you to and from work from now on."

Instead of anger, my tension eases, and I release Kellen's hand to touch Tobias's shoulder. "What happened tonight isn't your fault."

"No, it's not." The car bumps to a stop, and he jerks away from my touch to fling open the door. "It's yours for giving in to that asinine plan in the first place. We never should have agreed to let you do it."

I twitch at that. They don't *let* me do anything. I'm my own demon. But I've learned enough about Tobias to recognize he's angry at himself and the situation. I'm just the easiest target to vent his frustration on right now.

That doesn't make it better, but it also comforts me to know the thought of losing me drove him to this state.

Kellen squeezes my knee, then pushes the seat forward, climbing out to help Tobias. I follow, and Emil pops the trunk.

While Kellen and I gather Philip, Tobias stomps around the yard, as if unsure where he wants to plant the body. Emil leaves the engine idling and joins Tobias. The two put their heads together and decide on a place close the tree line. Tulips will look good there in the spring, and it's far enough out of the way that a lawn mower can easily avoid them.

I cradle Philip's head while Kellen lifts out the body. By the time we walk over, a shallow grave already waits in front of Tobias and Emil.

As I set the head at one end, I position it so Philip can see the sky one last time.

Kellen lowers the body, making sure to place the neck stump directly under the head to make Philip whole once more. "Do you want to say any final words?"

I really didn't know Philip that well, but I fold my hands in front of myself, the way I've seen humans do at funerals on TV. "Philip was a hardworking imp, always ready with a smile. His absence will be felt."

When I step back, Tobias takes that as his signal, and the ground rumbles, the body lowering as earth falls in around the edges. When it stops, a flat rectangle of dirt remains. Little clumps of grass poke through in some places, untidy in an otherwise immaculate space.

I glance at Emil, expecting him to fuss, but all he does is shake his head and mutter about buying seeds before he shoves the keys into Tobias's hands with a curt, "Park the car."

He then spins on one heel, grabs my hand, and pulls me toward the house.

Surprised, I trip after him, checking over my shoulder for the others.

Tobias stomps to the car, while Kellen shoos me on.

We find the path that leads back to the house, and Emil's stride lengthens.

Concerned by his icy silence, I double my pace to keep up. "Emil, what—"

He lifts a hand to cut me off, and worry slices through me. He hadn't reacted in the alleyway. I took his silence for indifference, but now, I recognize the anger that crackles inside him. It paints frost across his nape and shimmers in his white hair. With each of his steps, it creaks like shifting glaciers.

I let him drag me up the porch and into the house, not even pausing to take off our shoes before we're up the stairs. Instead of veering left at the landing, he pulls me into the bathroom, the space tight for two people.

The door knocks against the cast iron tub before he tugs me close enough to close it. Ice coats my front in an instant, and he releases my hand to yank at my tank top. Slivers of ice fall to the floor, and I lift my arms over my head to let him take it off before he rips it. Without looking, he throws it into the trash, then reaches for my pants.

As he kneels, I touch his shoulders, the cold of his body burning my fingertips. "Emil, it's okay. I'm not hurt."

His voice crackles. "You were covered in blood."

I lift one foot, then the other, stepping out of my clogs and pant legs in the same motion. "None of it was mine."

"I can still smell it on you." He shoves his face against my stomach, and I shiver at the chill of his breath. "It's still here."

"Okay, I got it." Stroking his hair with one hand, I reach out with the other to turn on the water. I want to wash the night's events off, anyway, and if this will help calm my ice demon, I'll gladly comply. "I'm going to wash myself squeaky clean, okay?"

He glances up the length of my body, his white lashes a veil for his frozen eyes.

I test the water, find it warm, and trail wet fingers across his cheek. The drops freeze, and I swipe them away with my thumb. "Hey, why don't you get in the shower with me? We can warm you up a little."

His lashes flutter again, a quick dart of eyes to the shower and back. "It's not hot enough."

"Okay." I turn off the cold spigot. "How's that?"

Uncertainty fills his voice. "You'll burn yourself."

"Not if you're with me." I urge him to his feet and get to work on his clothes, pushing his suit jacket off before undoing the buttons one-by-one.

Even in his current state, he won't like me ruining his shirt.

I hang both items on the hooks attached to the door, then mirror his previous actions as I kneel at his feet. Steam fills the small bathroom, freezing in a fractal-patterned cloud around us, only to melt and refreeze in a different pattern.

Taking off his loafers, I set them aside and work on his pants.

Every inch of creamy skin I uncover shimmers with frost. He needs to let this power go, or I'll have to take it from him. We can't risk an early winter settling over the city. Not when fall hasn't yet taken root.

Rising to stand in front of him, I grasp his hands and step into the shower. He follows without hesitation, and I turn to put him directly beneath the spray of water. Steam hisses up from his back, and a full body shudder rolls through him. I reach past his shoulders to cup the water, and it stings, a burn of a different kind than Emil's ice.

I bite back a hiss and smooth my heated palms over Emil's chest, melting away the frost. More forms, and I repeat the process, determined to warm him.

Cold hands cup my waist, and my head lifts. Soft blue bleeds into his eyes, chasing away the white storm, and another shudder rolls through him.

"That's right, let it go." I rub warm water over his cheeks and smile as more blue appears, a lake thawing after a brutal winter. On my tiptoes, I lean forward to nudge my nose against his. "There are those beautiful blues."

He blinks slowly, a languid sweep of white lashes, and shifts at glacial speed until his front presses fully against me, his lips a snowflake's breadth from mine. "We're here to wash you, Ms. Pond."

"So we are."

Eyes still on his, my legs spread as I crouch just far enough to grab the body wash from the edge of the tub. It slides my body down his front, his cock slipping between my breasts, before I rise once more. Now, pink stains his cheeks, his lips parted on a shaky breath. His cock hardens to nudge against my lower stomach, a reward for my efforts.

But instead of closing the distance between us,

he reaches back, turns the cold water on until the water becomes a more tolerable temperature, then shifts to place me beneath the stream. He takes the body wash bottle and shoves me deeper beneath the spray.

I sputter as water streams into my mouth and blow a wet raspberry at him.

He ignores my childish act and calmly lifts the bath poof in his hand to squirt a generous glob of soap onto it.

Okay, washing me can be sexy, too.

Wet enough, I step forward expectantly. He sets the poof against my shoulder.

Yeah, this can work.

With brisk motions, he sets to scrubbing hard enough that it feels like he takes off the top few layers of skin.

Not sexy at all.

With a shriek, I try to dance out of his reach, but the bathtub really isn't large enough to escape. He catches me with ease. I shove his arm away as the poof nears once more. The soap turns my body slick, and I end up spun around, head half under the water, my back against his chest, and his cock hard against my ass.

Furious, I wiggle and squirm, unable to escape. "Emil, you can't be serious!"

He tightens his hold. "I'm always serious. Now, hold still while I clean you, Ms. Pond."

SECRETS TOLD

By the time Emil lets me out of the shower, every inch of my skin glows rosy pink, even the bottom of my feet. He then proceeds to brush my hair, braid it into a twist that keeps it off my neck, and rubs a sweet, coconut oil all over my body.

I'd love to say this led to sex, but that would be a lie.

Instead, he swaddles me in his personal robe, muttering under his breath about masking Philip's residual scent.

The bathrobe's fluffy pink sleeves cover my hands, and the hem drags on the floor. I prop my fists on my hips and glare at the ridiculous man. "Are you done?"

He reaches out to fuss with the collar, pulling it tighter at my throat. "For now."

Suspicious, I inch away from him. "What's that mean?"

He follows my retreat. "I am re-invoking your invitation to my bedroom."

I perk up, gaze skimming down his deliciously nude body and the semi-hard length of his cock. It never quite settled during our shower. He enjoyed my wiggling, even if I *was* trying to escape. "Oh? Can we go there now?"

His attention shifts from me to the clothes strewn over the floor.

"Seriously?" With one palm on his chest, I push him back a step, then crouch to gather the clothes in my arms. "You are one fussy-ass demon, you know that?"

"Ms. Pond." Quiet reprimand fills his voice, but it holds a layer of warmth. He enjoys needling me way too much, and I should enjoy it a little less.

"You know, we could solve a lot of problems by putting a hamper in here." With his trousers in my arms, I grab the leg of my slacks and stand.

Something hard hits the floor, followed by three more clunks, and we both look down at the pale-gray disks as they bounce across the tiles and under the pedestal sink.

"What are these?" Frowning, Emil bends to pick them up.

Oh, crap. I totally forgot about the extra protection Tally's witches gave me. "Wait, I'll get them."

I drop the clothes in my rush to grab the pendants, but Emil scoops them up first.

A low growl fills the room. "Witch's magic? Did you obtain these from the Hunters?"

His fist closes around them, knuckles turning white, and I clutch his wrist before he destroys them. "Wait, they're mine! Don't hurt them!"

His glacier-blue eyes dart to mine, and snow flurries across his pupil. "More human magic? Why do you have these?" He reaches out to tap the metal band around my bicep, and it rings a vibration into my bones. "Isn't it enough that you have this? You're a demon, Adeline, you should not play with human magic."

"They helped me." I pry his fist open and scoop the clay disks up, examining them for damage. They look intact, and I carefully tuck them into my pocket.

"Explain." Then he lifts a hand. "Wait. Let's go downstairs first."

Inside the bathrobe sleeves, my hands curl into fists. "Why?"

"It will save having to explain twice." He reaches past me to pull open the bathroom door, knocking me in the ass in the process.

With a huff, I press up against his front to make room. "You know, not everything has to turn into a house meeting."

He glances down at me. "The last time I allowed you to convince me of that, you had just been attacked by Domnall."

Since I can't argue that, I ignore it and jut my chin out. "This is different."

"Then, you can explain how." He nudges me around. "Downstairs."

"Fine." It's not like I planned to hide the witches' gift from them anyway. I just planned to broach it with Kellen first, in case the others somehow didn't know about his little coven.

As I step out into the hall, my toes curl against the cold wooden floor. I desperately want slippers or cozy socks. I pause at the foot of the stairs that leads up to my room, but Emil's hand on my shoulder directs me downward.

When his hand remains in place, I glance back

with eyebrows lifted. "Shouldn't you put on some clothes?"

He peers down at himself, as if only just noticing his nudity, then frowns at me.

I sigh. "I'll meet you in the kitchen, you nag."

The corner of his lips twitches up, almost too fast for me to catch his amusement, before he backsteps onto the landing and heads for his room.

"Grab me some socks, too!" I call after him.

I find the others in the kitchen. Kellen stands at the island, a box of donuts open in front of him, while Tobias paces. Angry energy still vibrates from him, and he barely acknowledges my presence with a tick in his jaw muscle before he spins away to stomp toward the kitchen table. I wave at Tac when I spot him under it, cuddled up with the now disfigured toy knight I gave him. It looks like it's now missing one arm, and teeth marks dot his helmet.

Seeing my opportunity, I hurry over to Kellen's side.

"Well, don't you look snuggly." Kellen throws an arm around my waist and pulls me closer. "If you're very nice, I will let you have the plain cake doughnut."

I wrinkle my nose. "That's the throwaway doughnut and not worth bargaining for."

"Hush, you. That's Tobias's favorite."

I rise onto my tiptoes and lower my voice to a bare whisper. "Kellen, I have an important question for you."

"Hmm?" He glances down at me, curiosity sparkling in his eyes. Or maybe that's just the lightning. "What's that?"

I lick my lips and wait for Tobias to stomp past once more before breathing, "Do the others know about your witches?"

Kellen's eyes shift to Tobias. "Why?"

"Because they gave me something, and Emil found it. Now, he wants info."

Tobias stomps up to the counter. "What are you two whispering about?"

I kiss Kellen's cheek, drop back to my heels, and snatch up the plain cake doughnut. "Kellen said I can have this one for dinner."

"I'm not sure a cheek kiss is considered *you being very nice* to me," Kellen mutters under his breath.

I smile. "You should be more specific."

Tobias eyes the pink cardboard box. Frosting or sugar smother the rest of doughnuts, and rainbow sprinkles dot a few. "We are *not* having doughnuts for dinner."

Kellen shrugs and selects a sugar and cinnamon twist. "Not much else to eat that doesn't need prep work."

Tobias's dark gaze shifts to me expectantly.

I shake my head. "I already made dinner twice this week."

"The first time doesn't count. It was a race." Tobias's thick eyebrows lift. "You lost."

"Shall we consult the schedule?" I set my doughnut on a napkin, then turn to the fridge, where I duct taped a monthly chore chart. A little lightning bolt marks today's date under the section for meals. "Kellen's turn, so doughnuts it is!"

"I don't like these charts that keep appearing in our house," Tobias growls.

"I applaud the attempt at organization." Emil strolls into the kitchen wearing white, fleece pajama bottoms and a t-shirt that hugs his muscles. His frosty eyes settle on me. "Though the presentation lacks finesse."

The comment slips over my head, my attention fully fixed on the way his pajama bottoms sway and bounce. He didn't put on underwear, and it makes my mouth water.

My ice demon has withheld himself, choosing instead to teach me the fun of *foreplay*, which apparently involves *not* giving me his cock. It's been enjoyable, sure, but after the shower upstairs, I vibrate with the need to pounce on him. I want to lick his entire body from head to toe, feel him melt in my mouth like vanilla ice cream, then ride him until his entire body flushes pink.

"You're drooling," Kellen comments as he selects another doughnut.

As I blink back to awareness, the corner of Emil's lip twitches. Is he teasing me on purpose?

I glance down at my very sad doughnut. It will be dry and crumbly when I want something sweet. Bending, I open the cabinet under the counter and pull out a saucepan.

Tobias watches with interest, and even Kellen pauses, his third doughnut halfway to his mouth.

When I walk to the pantry and come back with a bag of sugar, Tobias *tsks*. "Don't you think there are enough sweets?"

"Nope." I dump a cup of white granules into the pan. Rolling up the robe's long sleeves, I turn the burner to medium and grab a wooden spoon. "Mine needs something extra."

"How about mushroom risotto with lemon chicken breast," Tobias suggests.

I snap my teeth at him. "Eat your doughnut."

He glares at the box before he returns to stomping around. "I'd rather starve."

Emil settles onto his stool. "Adie has new magic rocks."

Tobias freezes and spins back on his heel, his lip curled in disgust. "More foolishness?"

I glare at Emil, my desire to ride him turning to a desire to throttle him. "You're such a tattletale."

His white lashes flutter. "If it's nothing to worry about, then there's no reason to hide it."

Tobias stomps back to the counter. "Where do you keep getting these ridiculous trinkets?"

"They're not ridiculous, and they're not trinkets." I stir the sugar faster than necessary, and a couple granules jump out of the pan to land in the fire. The scent of burnt sugar fills the air. "The armband warned me when Domnall and the Hunters were near—"

"Neither of which you avoided, so not really useful," Tobias cuts in.

I raise my voice to talk over the top of him. "*And* the pendants helped me tonight when the Hunters were trying to funnel away my power! If not for them, I would have been drained right away!"

The muscle in Tobias's jaw jumps as he grinds his teeth. He can't find an argument for that one, and it obviously pisses him off.

Kellen extends a hand. "May I see these pendants?"

Reluctant, I dip a hand into the pocket of the robe and bring out one of the clay disks, placing it in Kellen's palm.

He studies it, his fingers smoothing over the rounded edges, the hole in the top, and finally over the swirly sigil I carved into the back. A shiver passes through me, a phantom touch stroking my core. I activated it with my own power in order to form a link with the pendant, and every caress of Kellen's fingers on the pendant finds an echo within me.

"I've seen this before." Kellen flips the pendant over to the blank side. "But it's incomplete."

"It worked well enough tonight." I reach for it, but Tobias snatches it away.

He handles it with less care as he flips it back and forth between his fingers. "What's this one do?"

"It, uh…" I lick my lips, one eye on the saucepan

and one on the catalyst demon. "It gives someplace for my power to go if someone is trying to steal it."

His brow furrows, and he sits on one of the stools. "How?"

I frown down at the melted sugar, checking the color as I try to recall exactly what Xander said when he gave the pendants to me. "Um, my sigil links me to it, and it does something to store my power."

Tobias sets the disk on the counter before wiping his hand on his sleeve. "How do you know the witch you got it from isn't stealing your power for themselves?"

Nervous, I lick my lips again. I trust Tally's men, but how do I convince Tobias and Emil without revealing my source? A quick peek at Kellen gives me nothing. He watches the interaction with his head tilted to the side, a curious light in his eyes as he waits to see what I'll do. It would be easier if he'd just answered my question about whether or not the others know about the small coven he owns.

I glance at Emil, whose impassive expression withholds judgment. He told me to trust, that we must all trust each other. But will my trust in them endanger Xander, Reese, Slater, and Jax? Will it hurt the close friendship Kellen shares with the other two demons?

My heart lurches. I don't want to be responsible for breaking another bond tonight. Losing Philip was more than enough. I will never be able to apologize to Julian enough for what happened tonight.

My wings rustle against my spine as my eyes sting.

Emil's quiet voice breaks through my rising panic. "Adie, the caramel's done."

I stare at the sauce. At some point, I stopped stirring, and it looks darker than I usually make it. With a frown, I lift the pan and sniff it. It smells fine, no hint of burnt sugar. Unsure, I spoon some out, but before I can blow on it, Emil leans across the count, grabs my wrist, and pulls the spoon to his mouth.

His lips close around the molten liquid, and eyes locked on mine, he pulls back. "It tastes fine."

"Hmm." I waggle my spoon at him. "I didn't say I'd share with you."

"You were worried you ruined it." He licks his lips and eyes the pan. "Those are some serious thoughts you were having, to be distracted while making caramel."

I puff my cheeks out for a moment before releasing a sigh. Turning off the burner, I set the sauce on a trivet to cool. "I met some witches at the bakery."

Tobias rolls his hand impatiently. "The fae-touched man. We've met."

I flinch in surprise before remembering the time Torch grew big and escaped his oven. I forgot Reese was there that night. Even in the heat of the moment, I guess his odd eyes stood out. "Right, at the bakery."

"No," Tobias says slowly with infinite patience. "When Kellen started gathering up all the little witches in town and stuffing them into one of his haunted houses."

"Not *all* the witches," Kellen defends. "Only the ones with potential."

"Potential for being desperate enough to sign a demon contract." Emil reaches across the counter and hooks a finger in the rim of the saucepan.

Distracted, I whack his knuckles with the spoon still in my hand. "So, you all know about the witches?"

Emil snatches his hand back and licks a drop of caramel from his fingertip. "Of course. He needed to make us aware of the potential backlash."

"Is that where this came from?" Tobias pokes the pendant in front of him.

Relieved not to have to hide it from them, the tension eases from my shoulders. "Yep! They gave me the armband, too."

Emil and Tobias turn angry stares on Kellen, and Tobias growls, "They're not even properly trained."

Kellen straightens with affront. "Hey, they're doing okay! They've made great strides since you last saw them."

"Have they been tested?" Emil presses. "Have they been recognized by the Council of Merlin?"

The Council of *What*?

Kellen waves away the idea. "Those pompous assholes don't know a good thing when they see it."

Emil glances at Tobias. "That means they *failed*."

Kellen stabs a finger against the counter. "Those old farts are using outdated methods that can't keep up with change."

Tobias stands to plant his hands on the counter and leans forward. "They're proven methods that have worked for centuries."

Kellen turns to me and points at the others. "*This* is why I'm the only one with a TV in the house!"

Confused, my focus shifts between the three

men before I settle on Kellen. "Because they agree with this council group that grades witches?"

"Yes, exactly!" He nods emphatically, then reaches across the counter to snatch the pendant and hold it up. "They'd *never* approve something like this."

Tobias's arms fold over his chest. "That means it's dangerous."

"It's ingenious!" Kellen produces a needle from somewhere, flips the disk over, and scratches his sigil into the blank side.

With a quick prick of his finger, he empowers the rolling storm cloud. An answering tingle rushes through my core, a light shower of static sparks that bring with it a spurt of energy.

Kellen slips it into his pocket and grins at me. "Don't worry, Adie, if something happens to you, I'll keep you anchored."

"Excuse me?" Tobias scowls at Kellen's pocket, then at the demon himself. "What are you talking about?"

"What our fluffy, little succubus is failing to articulate"—Kellen swoops over and loops his arms around me in a tight snuggle—"is that these pendants link her to the wearer. If Philip had something like this, his power would have gone into them instead of being pulled back to the demon plane. We could have popped his head back onto his body, returned the power to his core, and he would be up and running."

Not realizing the enormity of the gift Xander and the others gave me, I stiffen in Kellen's embrace. I need to compensate them in some way. This is too much for a gift.

Kellen coos against my temple. "I'm sorry, that was bad of me to be so cavalier about Philip's passing. But don't worry, he'll be back soon enough."

Emil dips his fingers into the caramel pan, and I stare at the empty trivet. When did he steal that? I glare as he licks the sauce from his fingers.

Ignoring me, he spins on his stool to bring the caramel farther out of reach. "So, if I put my mark on one of these, I'll own a piece of Adie?"

I bristle. "No one owns me."

Kellen talks right over my protest. "Yes, exactly."

Silent, Emil extends his hand, and Kellen produces two more disks. I twitch and shove him off me. When did he pick my pocket?

Unrepentant, he passes one to Emil and shoots

the other across the counter where it comes to a spinning stop in front of Tobias.

Emil produces his own needle and gets to work scratching in his sigil. Where the hell are they stashing those things?

"Now, wait a minute." I lift a hand to stop him. I don't like the idea of being owned. Xander didn't phrase it like that. I should ask him for more information before the others mark their disk. I'm already under contract to these men. This feels more permanent. "Tobias is right, this sounds dangerous."

Tobias's expression turns contemplative, and he lifts the pendant, rolling it between his fingers.

"Tobias, it's not safe, rig—" I cut off with a shiver as a flurry of snow melts in my core.

Emil pokes his bloodied finger into his mouth and holds the needle out to Tobias.

"I suppose it's good to take risks every so often." And with that, he takes the needle and lifts his pendant.

STOLEN

The next few days pass at a tension-riddled snail's pace.

No phone calls from Domnall to apprise me of the situation, and Julian remains frustratingly unavailable. When I call HelloHell Delivery, it goes straight to voicemail, none of the imps stepping in to fill Philip's shoes.

On day four of radio silence, Reese arrives with Tally and takes up his post at the corner table. It makes me nervous, but what can I say? Tally warned her men of the danger Domnall presents. Ultimately, it's their risk to take.

Even so, I keep an eye on him from the kitchen pass-through as I ice my latest creation.

When a customer suggested I sell more baked goods, it presented a perfect opportunity to try out edible garnishes. With summer ending, I want to add fall-themed flavors to the menu, and cookies come to mind. I plan to start out small, as decorations for the cupcakes. If they sell well, or I get enough requests, I'll offer some on their own.

Cookies present a fun alternative to cupcakes. They don't go stale as quickly, so I can make them in advance and stack them easier for storage. And the flat surfaces provide intriguing options.

"Master." A piping bag filled with yellow frosting nudges my arm, jolting me out of my thoughts.

"Thank you, Jesse." I finish the dark-brown outlines on the miniature leaf and place it in front of the small imp. "Just fill in the empty spots like we practiced."

Jesse gives me a pointy-toothed smile before she hunkers over her decorating station. A tray full of practice cookies rests off to the side, while a handful of sellable ones wait to be added to bite-size cupcakes. When I have two dozen, I'll send Perry out with a tray of the samples to pass around to the customers out front and gauge their reactions.

As I pull a card-sized rectangle cookie in front of myself, I blink at how surreal this all is. How can I be here, calmly decorating desserts, while an unknown number of Hunters roam the city set on killing me?

It feels wrong on so many levels. How did I even get on their radar? Is it because of the bakery? Did one of them stumble across me by accident?

My mind flickers back to the alley, to the old woman. For a moment, a shriveled sack of skin overlays her image, turning my memory into a ghoulish mixture of life and death. The rattle of her bone stick drums against my ears, and I shake my head, focusing instead on that moment when the two discussed my feathers.

Succubi and incubi feathers are worth a lot on the black market. I keep all of the ones I shed in a box at Landon's house, in case I ever need fast cash. Even small, they're better than any human-made aphrodisiac.

"She's weak, just like they said." The old Hunter's voice rattles around in my mind.

Julian's words follow. *"Feathers like those go for a pretty penny on the black market."*

At the time, I brushed it aside, but now the comment and response overlap each other in my mind, melting together until the Hunter and Julian speak to each other. Logically, I *know* that's not how the conversation played out. Julian had arrived later. But *why* did Julian arrive so late? What kept him and Domnall away for so long? Who was actually responsible for telling the guys the timetable escalated?

"Feathers like those go for a pretty penny on the black market."

It's not unheard of for demons to hunt their own. Collectors exist among demons, individuals who take pride in acquiring rare and exotic demons, or body parts when the demon itself isn't available. I had thought Tobias such a demon when we first met, but since getting to know him, I no longer worry about that.

Is it possible my cousin is trying to dip his toe into the black market? Is he tired of the stripper business?

My hand clenches around the piping bag, and frosting squirts out in a giant blob. No, I don't want to believe that.

"Master?" A small, nut-brown hand pats my arm, and a moment later, Jesse hops off her footstool and wraps her thin arms around my waist. A gentle purr thrums out of her, like a small version of Tac's rumble.

"I'm okay." Hand trembling, I set the piping bag

aside and pat the top of Jesse's hairnet. "Everything's okay."

A warm body presses against my back, and the purring increases. The tickle of a hairnet-covered beard tells me it's Kelly before he wraps thickly muscled arms around my shoulders with a quiet, "Master."

"Guys, the customers can see us." Despite my protest, I don't fight off their hugs, and soon, Iris abandons the cupcake station to join the huddle.

"Master is worried." Iris wraps her arms around me from the opposite side as Jesse. "Master has taken one of us in memory. We are honored."

A quiet shush comes from Kelly, but I lift my head to stare into Iris's soft eyes. "What do you mean?"

She blinks slowly. "Philip passed, but you respected him and accepted a piece of him as part of yourself. It is a high honor."

Philip was *always* offering me his energy. I'm not sure how what I did in the alley is different, but I don't argue. If the imps think it's a big deal, then to them it is. "Philip was a good imp."

Iris smiles proudly, and images flicker through my mind of rainbow glitter and curtains, of lamps with fringe and throw rugs with long, thick fibers that would bury my toes if I stood on them barefoot. With it comes a sense of possessiveness and the comfort of home.

A contented purr rises from her, and Iris's head drops to my shoulder.

Confused, I blink the images away. What was that just now? The lamp reminded me of the one we bought when I took the imps shopping, but I haven't had a chance to visit the house yet to see how they've settled in. Guilt immediately follows that thought. I need to make more time for them. Do they have food? Do I need to take them shopping again?

I pat Jesse's head again to signal the end of the snuggles. Reluctantly, they move back, and I focus on Iris. "How are the mini cakes?"

"They should be cooled." She hurries to the racks that line one wall.

I turn to Kelly. "Can you bring out a serving tray from the pantry?"

"Yes, Master." His thick-soled boots echo as he hurries down the hall toward the back of the shop. He returns quickly, a rectangle platter balanced between his large hands.

Jesse pulls her plate of acceptable cookies closer and studies them. "There are only twenty, Master."

I peek out of the pass-through, doing a quick headcount. It's crowded for a Thursday night, but not everyone will want a sample. "I think we'll be fine."

Iris delivers the tray of small cakes, and the smell of cinnamon and ginger rise from them. I want a flavor that says fall, but not necessarily pumpkin pie. With that in mind, I add smoked cardamom icing to the top, drizzle it with honey caramel sauce, then top it with one of the small cookie leaves.

Around me, the three imps coo with excitement.

I quickly frost the next nineteen and fill the platter Kelly sets on the counter at my elbow. When I run out of the nice-looking cookies, I frost a few extras and top them with the less pretty cookies, passing one each to Kelly, Jesse, and Iris.

They chitter with excitement and carry them to the island, where they set the cakes down like little pieces of artwork to be admired. I leave the rest on the counter for the others when they come back to the kitchen for a break and lift the tray to take out to the front.

Martha looks up from her place at the espresso machine and hums a welcome that alerts Tally.

The pink-haired demon finishes her transaction

before she glances over her shoulder, and her mahogany eyes light up. "Is that the new flavor?"

"It is. There are samples on the decoration bar if you want one." I peer around the shop. "Where's Perry?"

"He went to sweep the front entry. It's been windy and leaves were coming inside with the customers." Her feathery pink brows sweep together. "He is taking his time, though."

My heart leaps into my throat, and once again, I see Philip's head flying free from his body, only now, Perry's surfer blond hair overlays the memory. No, not one of *my* imps.

I set the platter on the counter as I step around it, gaze fixed on the front door. I can't see Perry through the large front window.

Reese's head lifts in alarm as I hurry toward the front door, and he rises from the booth, leaving his sketchbook open and abandoned on the table. He meets me at the door, and I'm selfishly glad to have him here. I might be powerless against a Hunter, but Reese is filled with human magic. He can take a stand where I can't.

When he meets me at the door, urgency fills his whisper, "What's wrong?"

"Perry hasn't come back." I grab the door, but Reese stops me with a hand on my arm.

The band around my bicep sings at the contact, and he quickly moves his hand to the door. "I'll find him."

"But what if—" I cut the words off before I voice the worst.

Darkness flickers over Reese's left eye, where the splash of brown disrupts his blue iris. "I'll bring him back. Stay here."

Cold wind rushes into the bakery as Reese shoves the door open and steps out. I hover nearby, disliking letting him go out there alone, but mindful of my promise to Kellen this morning when he dropped me off at work. I swore I'd stay inside the bakery until one of them came by to pick me up.

No foolishly making myself an easy target.

After three minutes, Tally calls Iris up to take over the register and joins me by the door. From the stares the customers send our way, we're making them nervous, but I can't bring myself to return to the kitchen or pass out the samples we worked so hard to create.

At the five-minute mark, Tally's phone chirps, and she pulls it from her pocket. She scans the screen, then tucks it away without responding.

She grasps my hand and tugs me toward the back of the shop. "Come on."

I look from her back to the empty front door. "Did Reese find him? Are they coming in through the back?"

We pass the cash register, and Tally pauses to tell Iris, "Pass out the sample cakes along with some coupons, then ask everyone to leave. We are closing early."

"What?" Heart in my throat, I plant my feet and swing back toward the door. "I need to—"

"You need to stay calm." Tally's cool hand grips me tighter, impossibly strong. "Come to the kitchen."

My voice rises. "Where's Perry?"

The air around Tally's shoulders shimmers as her gossamer wings lift through her clothes as if they're a mirage, or her wings are some sort of special optical illusion, my eyes playing tricks on me. They spread wide, a pink cloud of cotton candy sweetness that rolls over me and out toward the tables and booths.

"Tally, what are you doing?" I hiss with a frantic glance back at the humans who fill our shop.

They look disinterested in our struggle though, confused but pleasantly amiable as Iris walks around passing out the sample cakes and coupons, with some quiet excuse on why we have to close early. They drift out of the shop, one-by-one, never once looking back toward the kitchen.

When the last customer leaves and Iris locks the door behind them, I yank my hand from Tally's. "What's going on?"

She turns to face me, her eyes wide with sorrow. "Adie, I am so, so sorry—"

"No! You said the Hunters don't care about imps!" I stumble back a step. "You said they were safe!"

She rushes forward, hands out in supplication. "We will find Perry, I promise."

"How can you promise that?" My wings burst from my back and tangle in my chef coat. "What if they already—"

"Master, calm." Iris's arms wrap around me, and when I struggle, her flesh turns soft and malleable, shifting with my every moment.

Martha joins her, and the two imps manage to stop me from running out to the street.

Slowly, I sink to the floor. No, not Perry. Not one of my imps. Tears stream down my face. "I promised to keep him safe."

"You will keep that promise." Tally crouches in

front of me. "But for now, you need to go to Dreamland. You need to find the Hunters who have him."

"I can't!" I wail. "I'm broken!"

"I will take you." Her wings fold forward, latch onto my core, and wrench me from my corporeal form.

RIDING A NIGHTMARE

I arrive in Dreamland with a scream of agony, my skin ripped from my body, my nerves laid bare.

"Adie, focus!" Tally yells, but her voice sounds garbled and far away. "Take form!"

I struggle to follow direction but can't remember what form is. Terror floods my mind as I feel myself dissipating into the gray mists.

This isn't how it's supposed to be. Existing in Dreamland is my birthright, why is it rejecting me now?

"Tally, what did you do?" another voice joins us, deep and slithery, like the monsters that hide under the bed.

"I don't know what went wrong!" Cotton candy softness surrounds me, soothing some of the pain. "Adie, you need to focus. Form a body. Now!"

"She's still tethered to the human plane. Your witches gave her those stupid magic pendants."

Something tugs in the center of my being, and suddenly, I can think again. Arms and legs form, a body to house my core, and I lie panting on the ground, staring up at the unfamiliar faces above me.

A tiny pink demon with a feathered ruff around her neck and bright, mahogany eyes gazes down at me with concern, her tufted tail wafting back and forth. Gossamer wings unfurl behind her, stained glass come to life.

In stark contrast, the other crouches beside me on all fours, talons digging into the misty ground. Large, floppy ears and an elephant truck sprout from his head, and liquid, black eyes study me. Scales cover most of his body, with a thick swath of gray fur down his spine, which narrows into a tufted tail.

My focus shifts between the two before I settle on the pink demon. "Tally?"

She nods and reaches down to help me stand, careful with her small claws. "Adie, I'm so sorry. I didn't even think about the pendants. Mine stays with my body."

"Because your body is a construct not of the

demon plane," the other demon hisses, and Tally cringes.

On my feet now, the other demon is huge, its shoulders level with my head. One of the biggest baku I've seen in Dreamland. Most are closer to Tally's size, small and easy to catch. Which makes him old, far older than me. Possibly as old as Landon to amass so much power from eating nightmares.

He awkwardly lifts one hand to hold out my pendant. "It should be safe to put this back on now."

"Thank you." I take it and gingerly slip it over my head, half afraid I'll lose form again.

Instead, it settles warm against my breastbone, and for a moment, the human world overlays Dreamland. I see my corporeal form sprawled out in the bakery, my imps protectively surrounding me. Tally's body is there, too, limbs awkwardly splayed like a marionette with its strings cut.

The imps look around, large, fearful eyes searching as if they sense my presence, before one hurries to the phone next to the cash register, lifting the receiver.

The bakery fades from sight as the mists reform, washing the world out to gray once more. We stand in the lobby of an old apartment building, the reception desk crumbling and the doors to the elevator locked open.

While Dreamland resembles much of the human world, it's slower to change. It takes years of dreaming to bring a change to the landscape. Here, the bakery doesn't exist yet.

I turn to Tally, the brightest spot of color in our immediate surroundings. "What have you been eating?"

Her ruff rises defensively in an attempt to make her look larger as the other baku lets out a trumpeting laugh. "My sister has a sweet tooth."

"Ah, so you're Aren?" I turn back to him, my eyes narrowing. "The pervy voyeur."

Now, Tally titters, a higher-pitched giggle than the laugh I'm used to. Reconciling her demon form with the one she wears on the human plane will take some getting used to.

Aren's tail snaps, banishing what remained of a bank of mailboxes for a moment before it reforms. "It is hardly my fault if you undress while I am guarding my baby sister."

Tally's hands move to her hips. "And I've told you I have nothing to fear from Adie. She's not like other succubi."

Other succubi and incubi occasionally hunt

baku for sport, feeding on their energy so the baku can't grow as large as Aren. I never found the appeal, much to my cousins' dismay. It makes me sick to my stomach in the same way feeding on humans does.

Aren's large ears flap in annoyance. "Why did you rip the succubus from her corporeal form, sister?"

Memory swamps me, followed by guilt. "Perry." I turn, stride from the building, and scan the gray city beyond. "We need to find Perry before the Hunters hurt him."

The two baku follow close on my heels.

"Hunting the Hunters sounds interesting." Aren lifts one large paw then the other in a restless prowl as he, too, searches our immediate vicinity. "But how will you find him here? Unless they knocked him out, he is unlikely to be dreaming."

"Adie owns his contract. She should be able to follow that here, where the magic is stronger." Tally turns to me. "You must focus on Perry's energy signature. It will lead us to his location."

Focus on his energy signature? I have no idea what that even means.

I bought his contract from Julian at the same time as the rest of the imps. I wasn't there when he first took form on the human plane, and of all my imps, Perry kept himself the most distant, always in the background while the others clung close.

But Tally stares at me with confidence, as if this is something easily done, something completely normal. Which means it's another basic demon trait I somehow managed to miss out on in my eagerness to escape the demon plane.

The gray mist tickles my ankles, circling my bare calves. I spent so many years here, but it doesn't feel like home. The bakery feels like home; the mini mansions I share with the guys feels like home.

The thought of them makes the energy in my core spark to life. Emil's icy chill, Kellen's crackling static, and Tobias's chaos. In there with them, I find Philip's unique signature, the spark of excitement in the ordinary.

But that's not where my imps will be. I haven't taken their energy. I pull back, searching for that tattered thread I broke long ago in my hurry to take corporeal form.

There I find finer threads tied around mine. Rainbow and glitter for Iris, the scent of espresso and a mother's hug from Martha, Kelly's ruggedness, and Jesse's excited, pointy-toothed smile. Fainter, I pick out Perry's laid-back surfer vibe, a cool swish of ocean and sleepiness, a yearning for something more.

The others' bright tethers almost make his invisible, and I pluck at the narrow thread until it unravels from the rest. Once I free it, it grows stronger, fear, anger, and confusion a gentle thrum that laps against my senses, a wave rolling against a shore before pulling out to sea.

My eyes open, expecting to see the line that connects me to Perry, but only gray mist greets me. My feathers stretch and spread, testing the thickness of the air. Too small to truly fly, still growing into their true form, but prepared to find Perry.

I turn my focus back on Tally. "I feel him, but it's faint. I'm not sure where to go."

She nods as if she expected this. "They've taken him away from the bakery."

"Walk in a circle." Aren paces around us, and the mist parts before him, coiling in on itself to move out of his way. "See if the feeling grows stronger."

Following the suggestion, I pace across the street to the other side, where the rolling gray rises up into a tall building, another old apartment complex the city tore down years ago to make room for trendy boutiques like my own. Here, lights still flicker in the windows, its residents still dreaming of its existence.

The vibration of Perry's thread grows weaker, and I make a large half circle on the way back to where the baku demons wait, pausing halfway when the sensation grows stronger. Just to verify, I back away in the opposite direction, testing the line. When the vibration grows fainter once more, I return to my original position.

I stare down the long, empty street that leads out of the city. "He's this way."

Aren wraps his long trunk around Tally and lifts her onto his back before he lopes to my side. She looks tiny perched atop the hump of fur at the base of his neck, a speck of brightness riding a nightmare. His large paws shake the ground as he moves, the mist parting before him once more to create a clear path. Dreamland seems almost sentient of his presence, something I've never seen before.

One of Aren's large, liquid eyes rolls toward me. "Lead on, Adeline Boo Pond."

"Right." I refocus on Perry's thread, then walk forward, listening to the quiet hum of his emotions.

When the sensation begins to fade, I circle until it grows strong once more and change course.

Aren and Tally stay by my side. Sometimes, Aren even lopes ahead to break through the sides of buildings when the more direct path leads through them.

We pass shadowed living rooms and bedrooms, some with humans in them, oblivious to our presence. When Tally trails her claws through the air above a sleeper, Aren lets out a snort of reprimand.

What does she see that pulls at her attention? Obviously not a nightmare, or she wouldn't look the way she does. What does a baku with a sweet tooth eat? Happy dreams? Dreams of romance? Do the sleepers wake with a sense of loss, unfulfilled and unsure why?

A baku's purpose is to feast on nightmares, to chase away the terrors of human sleep. Over time, like Aren, they take on the form of those nightmares.

Does that make Tally evil? I can't balance that in my mind with the sweet demon I've become friends with.

After what feels like hours of walking, we reach the outer edges of the city, or what I believe to be the outer edges. Shadowy forests flow outward from here, with a wide strip of road flowing down the middle. If we continue onward, we'll eventually reach the city where Landon lives. But our path cuts to the left, following the perimeter.

I frown at that. If it leads to the left now, why didn't we cut through more of the city earlier to follow a direct path?

Then the sensation changes, heading back toward the heart of the city, and I swear. "They're in a car. They're on the move."

"They will have to stop at some point." Tally kicks her heels against her brother's shoulders to push him back into motion.

His large ears flap back to smack her in the sides in response. "I am not a beast of burden, sister."

As the two squabble, Perry's location veers again, and I turn with it to hold his position. Why would the Hunters come all the way out here only to head back into town?

I reach up to grasp the pendant around my neck, focusing on the connection it offers to my corporeal form. For a moment, the mist clears to reveal the human plane. We stand in a warehouse area of some kind, with rows and rows of metal rolling doors. Above the doors, numbers count down the units.

A low growl comes from behind me, and I spin, coming face to snarl with a guard dog. Its lips pull back, baring sharp teeth, its legs braced to leap. Beady, black eyes focus on me, the growl deepening.

Something red marks its short golden fur between its eyes, and I step forward for a better look. A symbol of some kind. My eyes don't want to focus on it, slipping and sliding away, but I force myself to look, to see.

The growl intensifies and the dog crouches, then leaps forward. I release the pendant, feeling the phantom brush of fangs on my skin before Dreamland swamps my vision in gray mist. A flicker of red catches in my peripheral vision, and I flinch back, half expecting the dog to have followed me here, but when I look, all I see is gray.

Shaking it off, I walk forward once more, and Aren and Tally's argument falls silent.

Tally's bright eyes lock on me. "Did they stop moving?"

I focus on Perry. "No, not yet. But they seem to be holding steady now." I point the way.

"Come, we will move faster if I carry you." Aren crouches low to the ground, one arm extended to offer a step up.

I stare at him in surprise. I can hyper-speed faster than he can run, but I'll lose focus on Perry and risk overshooting his location. It's also an unnecessary use of energy if he's offering a ride.

After a moment, I murmur a quiet, "Thank you," and climb up onto his back.

He remains stoically still despite my ungainly scramble, my knees and feet kicking against his slick scales as I pull on his fur. When at last I sit atop him, his broad back makes it difficult to use my legs to hold my position. Not stable at all. If I'm not careful, I'll fall right off.

"I can't wait to tell the other baku a succubus needed my help," Aren snorts out, and Tally bops him between the ears.

I fist my hands in his fur, pulling my wings in tight to my back so I don't fly off once he leaps into motion. "If you help me find Perry, you can tell the others whatever you want."

His trunk lifts with an excited trumpet. "What way should I go?"

"Forward and to the left." He shifts position, and I nudge him with my knee until he faces the right direction. "Straight ahead."

"Hold on tight." He barely waits for me to firm my grip before he leaps forward.

The mist of Dreamland parts. Buildings shift and slide out of the way, taking their human inhabitants with them until a clear tunnel forms before us. The thrum of Perry's string grows stronger, and elation builds.

We're going to find him. We'll make it in time.

A crackle of static sparks against my chest, and I lose focus for a second. Perry's thread begins to slip away, and I grasp it tighter.

We're almost there.

I release an excited breath, and it frosts in front of my face. Another crackle shoots through my body, followed by a lick of lava.

My vision wavers, black dots peppering the landscape.

"How close?" Tally twists to peer over her shoulder, and her lips part. "Oh, no. They're calling you back."

Dazed, I lift a hand to my forehead. "What?"

"Take off the pendant!"

More lava heats my core, followed by a landslide that slams me flush against Aren's back. Soft fur tickles my nose, and I lose my hold on him.

As I begin to slide off Aren's broad back, I frantically reach for the pendant.

The human plane blinks in and out of focus before a black hole opens in my gut, trying to yank me back to my corporeal form.

I'm not going to get the pendant off in time.

Desperate, I search the surroundings for some marker to let me know where we are. Perry's stopped moving, he's close, I can feel it.

A familiar set of glass doors flicker into focus before the misty city rips away, and I slam back into my body in the bakery.

BARRIERS

"No!" I bolt upright.

Emil, Tobias, and Kellen surround me, each clutching the pendants around their necks. They drop them in unison as soon as I regain consciousness. Behind them, my imps huddle together in a clump. Tally's body still lays on the floor, lifeless and abandoned.

Desperation slams through me, and I scramble to my feet.

Static pricks against my arm a moment before Kellen grips it. "Adie, are you all right? When we arrived, you were unresponsive."

I whirl on him. "I was searching for Perry! The Hunters took him!"

His expression softens. "Oh, honey, we'll find him."

"But I know where he is!" Energy sings through my limbs, ready to hyper-speed out of there.

Kellen's hold on me tightens. "Calm down. You can't go running off without backup."

"Fine, but we have to go *now*!" I strain toward the door. "They're after the imps!"

"They won't get them," Emil soothes. "Not while we're here."

"Not *my* imps!" I succeed in freeing myself, but lightning fast, Kellen catches me once more. I struggle against him. "They're at HelloHell Delivery! Julian and Philip aren't there to protect the others!"

Tobias curses under his breath. "They must have forced Perry to reveal the location."

At that moment, the human magic detector on my arm prickles to life, and my talons shoot out, ready for an attack.

On the floor, Tally gasps, then bolts upright, her head whipping around as her eyes refuse to focus. "Adie?"

"I'm fine, but we have to go *now*!" I tug against Kellen, who holds me with unbreakable force.

He looks to the others, and Emil nods. "It could be a trap."

"One of us should stay here, just in case," Tobias agrees.

"I can fly there faster than you can drive." Kellen yanks me closer. "Adie, if I help, can you fly?"

Confused, I stare up at him. "I can hyper-speed faster than you can fly."

He shakes me gently. "You need to conserve your energy to fight if it comes to that."

Yes, I need to be strong. The Hunters have magic I don't know how to counteract. My gaze falls on Tally. "Reese."

"I'm calling him now." She shifts to her knees, then to her feet as she fumbles her cell phone from her pocket.

Kellen frowns. "What about Reese?"

"He was following them, too." I pat his hands to let him know I have my emotions under control. He's right, I need all of my energy to smite these assholes.

His fingers slowly uncurl from my arms as if not quite believing me.

As soon as I'm free, I shrug out of my chef coat, my wings slipping free from their hiding place next to my spine. My feathers spread and rustle, heavier than they were before, but I don't have time to think about it now.

Expression troubled, Tally pulls the phone away from her ear. "He's not answering."

"Keep trying. When you reach him, let him know what's happening. He may be in danger, too." I turn to Kellen. "We should leave out the side door. We'll have to climb to the roof."

"I'll stay behind," Tobias volunteers, stepping to the side.

I turn to him in surprise. Of all my men, he's the one I thought would seek out a fight the most.

His thick eyebrows lift. "If I go, I'm liable to bring down the building if I unleash my power. That place is a deathtrap."

"It's up to code," Kellen protests as he yanks off his shirt.

"Only because you bribe the inspectors." Tobias tosses his car keys to Emil, who catches them with ease.

"I'll meet you both there." Emil strides for the door without waiting for a response, and I tug Kellen toward the kitchen.

"Tally, can you try to reach Julian, too?" Kellen calls over his shoulder.

I freeze, hand on the swinging door. "No, don't."

Kellen's lips part, but I hold up a hand to stop him. "Someone didn't tell you guys about the change in plans when we last faced the Hunters. That could only have been Domnall or Julian. Right now, they're together, and we don't know who we can trust. Our first mission is to protect the imps. We can decide what to do after that."

He gives a tight nod.

Tally's sad gaze meets mine in acknowledgment before she turns to my imps. "Okay, we're all going to go to the pantry. We're on lockdown until Tobias or Adie tell us otherwise, okay?"

They chitter quietly, their attention fixed on me. I want to go to them, to comfort them. One of theirs is missing, someone I promised to keep safe. I'm failing them right now. But I can't stay. If I do, more will die.

I catch Tobias's eye. "Protect them."

His head dips. "I'll destroy the entire city before I let harm come to them."

Tears sting my eyes, and I force myself forward before they fall. There's no time to break down now. Not when so many lives hang in the balance.

Kellen and I push out the side door into the alley. The storm from earlier settled in, and heavy clouds hang over the city. The wind blows hard, leaves scuttling down the narrow walkway.

Kellen looks around. "There's no fire escape."

"We need to climb."

Facing the side of the building, I kick off my clogs, crouch, and leap as high as possible before digging my talons into the brick. Clay and mortar crumble beneath my fingers and toes as I climb quickly.

I reach for the edge of the rooftop, and a heavy mist surges past me. Kellen lands lightly on his feet before he bends and extends a hand to help me the rest of the way up. From his back, thunder clouds spread into wings with sparks of lightning dancing in their depths. A storm god come to Earth.

Up here, the wind blows more fiercely, whipping my hair into my face. I push it back to study the sky. "Are you going to be okay with this storm?"

The last time a heavy storm struck, its siren call almost convinced Kellen to join it in building a hurricane to wipe out part of the city.

Static-filled hands cup my cheeks as he gazes down at me. Lightning flashes across his eyes, and his body vibrates with the rumble of thunder. "The storm in you is more alluring than anything nature can create. Fly by my side, and I'll never be tempted to stray."

My chest tightens, but before I can respond, he pulls me to his side. His legs bend, and my wings snap tight to my body a moment before he launches us directly into the storm.

Since coming to the human plane, I haven't flown, only glided for short distances or used my wings to gain a few extra feet in height when needed. Now, the world spins out at a dizzying distance below us, the gray landscape of concrete and brick a harsh welcome should I fall. But Kellen's hold on me stays firm, his cloud wings not interfering with mine as they spread to help support my weight.

Unerringly, he finds the updrafts in the storm, arrowing us across town to where HelloHell Delivery's office resides. Far below, small, toy cars move through streets on a miniature replica of a city. One of those will be Emil, speeding to meet us.

Do others hold more Hunters? How many do we face? Will we arrive in time?

Mist turns the city hazy, icing my body with tiny drops of water. Off in the distance, thunder sounds, and fear shivers through me as I search for an answering flicker of lightning in the wings that mingle with mine. While I'm glad to have Kellen by my side, I don't want to be in the sky when the true storm strikes.

From this vantage point, all the buildings look the same, so I have no clue we've arrived until Kellen angles us downward.

Parked cars line the street, none distinguishable from the others. I'd really like for something easy to happen in life. Is it too much to ask for the Hunters to paint their evil logo in bright yellow on top of their car? That would make crushing them like a soda can so much easier.

We land on the roof, and my wings snap back to their hiding place along my spine as I head for the access door, I break the lock and rush into the stairwell fire escape, surrounded on all sides by cement walls. While the doors in the stairwell don't have handles on this side, I'm more than willing to smash my way through that obstacle at the moment.

Kellen's heavy footsteps follow close on my heels, and we jog down the two flights of stairs to Julian's office.

When I reach for the door, he stays my hands. "Do you feel any human magic?"

I pause and realize the numbness of my skin from the flight obscured the tingles the arm cuff emits. Now that I pay attention, my bones prickle with all the magic that surrounds the area.

With a tight nod, I take a step back and scan the area around the door, searching for the places my eyes refuse to focus.

"I don't see any spells," I whisper after a moment. "Do you?"

He shakes his head, then presses an ear against the fire safe door. "I hear chittering. They're panicked, but still here."

Far below, a door slams against the wall of the fire escape, and the arm band's vibration increases. "Kellen, Hunters are coming."

"That means they haven't gotten inside yet. I'll hold them off while you get the imps out." He steps to the edge of the platform and grips the metal handrail. Lightning crackles from his hands, and the small hairs on my body lift in response. "Take them to the roof. Emil will handle it from there."

My heart slams with panic. I endangered Kellen by bringing him here, so I should back him up. But that leaves the imps to fend for themselves, and they're so much less capable than my storm god.

I force myself to turn away, trusting him to protect himself.

Energy courses through my arms, and I slam my

palm against the side of the door's hinge. It rips off, bouncing against the wall before it clatters to the cement landing. I take out the remaining two, then rip the door out of its frame, tossing it down the stairs past Kellen for an added barrier between him and the Hunters.

He flashes me an admiring grin. "You're so hot right now."

Blowing him a kiss, I hyper-speed through the doorway and slam up against an invisible wall.

With a hard bounce, I crash through Julian's office door. Frosted glass barely hits the floor before I'm back through the shattered opening, talons out and ready to fight.

Reese's wide, mismatched eyes meet mine from the safety of a large circle. Around him, imps pile one on top of the other in a tangle of limbs, fishnet, and glitter.

"Adie?" Reese questions, as if unsure he trusts what he sees.

A loud bang comes from the office entrance, and the circle chalked onto the carpet glows brighter. The imps bleat with panic, some of them losing their shapes. A headache forms behind my eyes as I force myself not to look away.

I step up to the edge of the invisible wall.

"Reese, I need you to let the imps out on this side. I can take them to safety."

He squints. "How do I know it's really you?"

I pat my chest. "Because you can see me."

He shakes his head, bangs falling over his eyes. "Sometimes what I see isn't real."

"You're going to have to trust yourself this time. I'm going to get these imps to safety. You, too." I hook a thumb toward the fire escape. "Kellen's here as backup. We're going to all get out of this."

"Kellen?" His eyes flicker past me, searching for the other demon.

"He's holding off the Hunters who circled around the back to pin you in." I lift a hand, not quite touching his barrier. "Come on. Let me help. We don't know how many there are."

His focus shifts from me back to the entrance. "If I drop the barrier, they're going to get in."

"How?"

His head swings back to me, and he blinks. "What?"

"How will they get in? Are we talking explosives? Some kind of big magic?"

He frowns. "It's just an office door. They'll kick it in."

"Oh." Well, look at me overcomplicating things.

I follow the curve of his barrier. The cubicles that once created an aisle now lies in shambles, thrown out of the way to make room for the spell. The chalk circle butts right up to the front door, the barrier itself the only thing keeping it from opening.

If it's just a matter of keeping the door closed longer, that's easy enough to accomplish.

Grabbing one of the cubicle walls, I test its weight. It won't do much by itself, but if I angle it right, and give it the proper support, it should do the trick.

Power hums through my limbs, and I quickly make a stack of walls. "When I give the signal, drop the barrier and haul ass up the fire escape. Don't touch the metal railing."

"What are you going to do?"

I roll my neck and bounce on the balls of my feet. "I'm going to hold them off. Just get to the roof."

"I'm not sure—"

"You've been enough of a hero tonight, Reese. Time to let someone else take a turn."

I count the breaths between each bang against the door as the Hunters try to gain access. They're taking turns using brute force. If the offices weren't closed for the night, someone would have already called the cops. As it is, they can make as much noise as they want, short of an explosion, and even that might go unnoticed. Humans are pros at ignoring danger.

Pound, pound, pound. Pause.

Pound, pound, poun—

I slash my hand through the air, and the barrier drops a second after the last blow.

Energy sings along my bones as I move into hyper-speed, slamming a pyramid of cubicle walls through the floor to create a physical barrier to replace the magical one.

When the next pound comes, the walls shake but hold firm, and I turn to rush the stragglers out the back door.

Ozone hangs heavy in the fire escape, and static crackles in my hair. Kellen stands where I left him, a field of lightning filling the stairs below.

"They're out!" I yell. "We're heading to the roof now!"

He lifts a hand in acknowledgment, and thunder crashes, shaking the stairs.

"Don't bring the building down!"

He waves without looking back.

A few of the smaller imps who lost their shape trail at the back of the line, too scared to move quickly. I scoop them up, their soft bodies oozing over my arms. They bleat with panic as I carry them as best I can.

Thunder shakes the stairs again before we make it to the roof. Kellen's expending more power than necessary to hold off the Hunters. He's having too much fun letting loose.

He better remember to get his beautiful ass out of there.

When I step out last, I discover the storm from earlier fully arrived and hail pelts us. Already, white covers the roof, and I search for Emil. Only my ice demon can be responsible for this.

I find him near the edge of the rooftop, his white hair whipping in the wind, and behind him, an ice bridge forms like something from an animated movie, all swooping arches and beautiful filigree. It leads to the next building over, where I assume we'll use the fire escape to reach the ground.

He sweeps an elegant arm toward his creation. "Your chariot awaits."

THEY'RE NOT BABIES

"When I suggested we put them somewhere safe, I didn't mean *here*," Emil growls as the imps shuffle into our living room.

"As long as the Hunters have Perry, they're not safe, even at my other house." I settle the unformed imps near the coffee table, and they slither beneath it to disappear into the shadows. "When Kellen returns, we can see if he has another house we can settle everyone into."

Once Kellen knew everyone was safe, he flew back to the bakery to inform the others while we hijacked the HelloHell Delivery van from the parking lot and stuffed all the imps inside. I drove with Emil behind me in Tobias's fancy, useless sports car, ensuring no one followed us.

"Where will they sleep tonight?" Emil folds his arms over his chest. "I'm not sharing my room."

"The basement?" I say hopefully. "I'm sure there's enough furniture down there for everyone to find something to sleep on."

His lips purse. "I was planning to reuse that furniture."

"No, you weren't." I flutter the pages of a new catalog filled with dog-eared pages. "You're planning to buy new stuff as soon as you convince the others it's necessary."

His disparaging gaze lands on my floral sofa wedged in front of the fireplace and completely out of place among the leather and dark wood motif of the rest of the room. "Our living arrangement has changed. I feel we can be better organized."

"Which doesn't involve excavating anything that's in the basement." I go to stand in front of him and walk my fingers up his cool chest. "You were so amazing tonight. You're a real artist, you know?"

Snow flits across his pupils. "I'm not weak to flattery."

"It's not flattery when it's the truth. I'm not trying to butter you up." I pinch his chin. "They're staying the night, end of story."

His eyes narrow. "If anything goes missing, you'll be held responsible."

I try not to cringe. I just brought a dozen mischief imps into a house filled with shiny treasures. It's impossible for nothing to go missing.

"Adie, do you need help setting things up?" Reese asks, his gaze not quite fixed on me. Instead, he focuses on the kitchen archway, his eyes tracking something that only he can see.

I refuse to ask. If we have ghosts, I don't want to know.

"That would be great, Reese. Tally will be here soon with everyone else. If we can get something ready, we can figure out food, then plan our next move against the Hunters." I look to Emil. "Will you wait up here until they arrive?"

"I am not a babysitter."

"And they're not babies." Jaw set, I rise onto my tiptoes. "They're scared and out of their comfort zone. So, pull up your big girl panties and deal."

His nostrils flare, but he remains silent, which I take as agreement. I understand my stuffy ice demon doesn't like sudden change, but I need him to take one for the team right now. If I could, I'd ask him for help in the basement, but he'd create more work, wanting everything in its place. Quick and dirty is what I need right now.

I clasp Reese on the shoulder to pull his attention back to the real world. "Come on. Let's get to work."

When we enter the kitchen, Tac lifts his head from his place under the kitchen table, his toy knight flopped over one arm where he was napping on it. He blinks saucer-sized, green eyes at us in greeting.

Reese misses a step and catches himself against the island. "Do you see the demon cat?"

"Yeah, that's Tac." I make kissy noises at the beast. "Hey, you big, beautiful monster, can you help Emil watch the imps in the living room?"

His tufted ears swivel for a moment before he crawls out and lumbers to his feet. Reese takes a step back, his eyes wide with fear, but Tac ignores him as he prowls forward to shove his giant, wedge-shaped head against my chest.

I rub between his ears with both palms before shoving him toward the archway.

One fury wing nips me in the shoulder as he leaves, long tail swishing behind.

Concerned, I call after him, "They're not toys. Be nice to them!"

With a quiet chuff, he vanishes from view, and a moment later, nervous chitters float from the front room.

Reese stares after him. "Will they be okay?"

"They'll be fine. Imps are pretty resilient as long as they're not mortally wounded." I stride to the basement door and pull it open, then flick on the lights. "Use the handrail. The steps aren't evenly spaced."

The bare, overhead bulb no longer flickers like it did when I first moved in, but the long, narrow staircase is still creepy as shit, the steps uneven and rough, with empty backs that someone could reach through to grab your ankles.

He peers over my shoulder. "This reminds me of a horror movie."

"I thought so, too, the first time I came down here." I grab the handrail and start my descent. "I've gotten used to it, though. I have to do laundry down here every week, so I've had time to explore. There's a ton of furniture. Enough to fill multiple houses."

As the walls of the ground floor disappear to reveal the sheet-shrouded jungle below, Reese gives a low whistle. "It's like a treasure trove."

"That's Emil. Dragon hoarder of furniture."

Since I moved in, I've cleared a path from the

base of the stairs to the washer and dryer at the back, ancient machines that never saw use until I arrived. The guys waste money sending all their stuff to the cleaners. Which isn't to say they never come down here.

Kellen once replaced everything I own with pink tracksuits. Lesson learned. I no longer leave my laundry unsupervised.

With a couple hours to waste guarding my wash, I've spent some time peeking under all the shrouds and have a fairly good idea of what we can grab to use for tonight.

Unfortunately for the imps, Emil didn't hang onto a dozen beds, but there are couches and recliners down here, too. With a little creativity and sharing, everyone will be able to sleep somewhere moderately comfortable, which is probably better than the sleeping bags on the floor they're used to at HelloHell Delivery. Those cubicles served as both office and living space.

I still need to have a word with Julian about how he treats his employees.

The reminder of my cousin brings a sinking sensation to my stomach. Do I really believe he tried to set me up?

A week ago, I would have said no way in Hell.

But a week ago, I didn't know he used to hang out with Domnall. It was a slap in the face, the reminder I've only known Julian for the last few decades, while he has centuries of shadowed history that informs his actions. I'm not really anyone to him in the broader scheme of things, only a drop in the sea of his life. The realization hurts. Immortality can be so cruel.

"Adie?" Reese's quiet voice breaks me from my thoughts. He stands with his hands at his sides, staring at the piles of furniture, unsure where to start.

"Sorry, I was just…" I rub a hand over my eyes. "It's been a shitty week, you know?"

"Yes, but it will get better." He speaks with the certainty of experience. "Hunters have lots of tricks, but their magic takes time to set up. It relies on ritual and preparation. Perry's still alive. If they plan to harvest him for body parts, they can't do that until the full moon."

"What?" I straighten in surprise. "How do you know that?"

"We have one of their books." His lip curls as if the idea disgusts him. "To harvest demon parts, they need a full moon."

"I didn't realize that." Some of the tension eases.

We have time. "That's helpful that they can't do anything until a full moon."

"Oh, they *could*." He blinks at me slowly, as if this should be obvious. "They just don't *think* they can, and so they can't."

"Huh?"

"Sixty percent of human magic relies on belief. If they believe they need a full moon, then they do. And the book they use, that they teach new members with, is very specific about needing a full moon. They also need a goat, which is just stupid."

"A goat?" I shake my head. "Never mind, I don't want to know."

"It's for the best." He shrugs. "It doesn't end well for the goat."

I cover my ears. "I don't want to know!"

He grins and mouths something.

I drop my hands back to my sides. "What?"

"We have three days to figure out where they're holed up. They'll have set warning spells to detect if demons near them, though."

Three days to track them down and save Perry. Not a lot of time.

It's a good thing I know where to start.

By the time Kellen and Tobias arrive with my imps and Tally, we have enough soft surfaces for Julian's displaced imps to sleep. I expended more energy than I like hefting around the heavy, solid wood pieces and curse Emil's expensive taste in quality furniture. But we managed to find four beds, two couches, and a recliner. They'll have to cuddle up together, but at least it's something.

When we head back upstairs, boxes of cakes fill the kitchen table. Tally clearly emptied out the bakery cases before she left, and the imps all crowd around, chirping at each other as they stuff their faces. Guess that takes care of dinner for them. Blue and pink frosting cover a few lips, and the kitchen smells like an odd combination of coconut oil and sugar.

It sets my mind to thoughts of summer, of beach-themed cakes and margaritas, when fall hasn't even set in yet. Who knew imps could be so inspiring? I bet Kellen would love a pina-colada cake. Would I do a pineapple cake with coconut-rum icing? Or would that be too heavy? Maybe coconut cake with rum frosting and candied-pineapple shavings.

My fingers itch to start experimenting. I need a notebook to write these down.

Fingers snap in front of my face, and I jerk back with a hiss.

Tally lifts her hands, palms out. "Sorry, I didn't mean to startle you, but you weren't responding."

I brush at the dust on my clothes. "Sorry, what was the question?"

Her pink brows pinch together. "I don't see Perry. Was he not at HelloHell Delivery?"

"He had to have been. He's what led us there." Guilt rushes through me. How can I be thinking of cake recipes when one of my imps is missing? "But by the time we circled back to street level, the Hunters were gone, Perry with them."

"I'm so sorry." She enfolds me in her arms, the scent of clay that clings to her blocking out the sense of summer. "We'll find him. It can't be too late. We can go back to Dreamland, try again—"

"No." I push her back, not wanting comfort right now. "I think I know where their base is. But it's guarded."

Reese steps up to Tally's side. "We can help with that. If Xander and I can go in first, we can take down their alarms without them knowing."

My pulse trips with excitement. We discussed the storage place I saw in Dreamland while moving furniture around and what I recalled of the marking on the guard dog. Reese is pretty sure it matches the ones in the Hunter book they own, which means they're following their standard training.

Knowing their methods in advance gives us the upper hand.

Tally turns to him, one hand on his chest as her head lifts toward his. "You will be safe?"

He cups her cheek with a tenderness that makes my heart ache. "We've faced Hunters before. We know how to deal with these bastards."

I turn away from them to go find my imps among the strippers. They're easy to spot, standing out from the others by their differences.

They abandon their cakes to circle around me with gentle coos of, "Master."

"I'm okay." I pat whichever body parts I can reach. "We're going to have a slumber party tonight, okay? You guys are going to sleep in my room upstairs."

"Master is kind," Iris sighs.

"Generous," Kelly agrees.

"The best Master," Martha adds.

"Shiny," Jesse chirps.

A chitter rises from the group, and they agree in unison, "The shiniest."

"Come on, I'll show you the way. And if you're

very good, and all my stuff is still in its rightful place in the morning, I'll take you back to the mall, okay?"

"Kellen will come, too?" Iris asks, her eyes bright with interest.

I frown at her. "Kellen is mine."

She gives me a beautiful smile. "Kellen pleases Master."

"Well, yes, I suppose. We can ask if he wants to come." I herd them ahead of me, then glance back. "Tally, Reese, can you get everyone else settled in the basement?"

"Of course." With a clap of her hands, Tally turns to the table and the demolished cakes. "Time for bed, everyone."

Grumbles rise, but I trust the baku demon can handle them.

I pass Emil, Tobias, and Kellen in the living room, where they hid away from the imps. "I'll be right back down."

"I'm going to make tea." Tobias strides for the kitchen. "Anyone else thirsty?"

"Hot chocolate sounds good," Emil murmurs. "I'll help."

Kellen flops down in his chair. "Whiskey for me. Just bring the bottle."

Tobias lets out a low growl but doesn't object to the command. Instead, his dark gaze shifts to me in question.

"Coffee sounds good. Some for Reese and Tally, too?"

Emil pauses next to the archway to the kitchen. "They're staying?"

"For a little bit. I'll explain in a minute."

I usher the imps upstairs, pointing to the bathroom on the first landing and cautioning them away from Emil's door. It's closed now, and since I didn't see Tac downstairs, I can only assume he hid in Emil's room.

When we reach the turret, I worry if they'll all fit on my bed, but once I move my nest to the floor, they all clump together just fine, Kelly and Iris spooned together, with Martha on the opposite end and Jesse curled protectively in the middle.

The Hunter book on my nightstand catches my eye as I turn off the lamp, and I grab it on my way out. While I haven't been able to decipher anything except the pictures, Reese might recognize the markings in the margin.

I trot back downstairs, flipping through the pages to see if the symbol on the guard dog is there.

The demon writing squiggles and crawls like

usual, and I glare at it for being so illegible. If it would just *stay still* maybe I'd have a chance to educate myself before going into battle.

On the brittle pages, the writing halts, then slowly flows backward, forming a picture.

FIE-FI-FO-FUM

Shocked, I stare at the book as the picture becomes clearer.

The scent of blood wafts up from the pages, screams echoing in my ears. Then the scene begins to play out like a freaking movie, and my heel misses the next step.

I trip, the book flying from my hands as I flail and stumble down the last few steps before landing heavily on one knee. Pain shoots through my body, but it barely registers as I scramble after the book.

"Adie, honey, you okay?" Kellen demands as he comes to my assistance.

"I saw something!" I crawl to where the book lies. "Kellen, I *saw* something!"

"Okay?" Confusion colors his voice as he places a hand on my elbow and helps me stand. "What did you see?"

"I don't—ow!" Pain spikes through my leg when I take a step forward. "Ow, ow, ow."

"You fell pretty hard. You might need to expend some energy on that one." He helps me over to the couch, propping my legs up. "Hey, Emil, come be helpful!"

The ice demon appears at the end of the couch, pinching the handle of a steaming cup between two fingers. A pink, bendy straw pokes out of the top. "What happened?"

"Adie fell and hurt her knee. Put your hand on it until she heals."

His eyes narrow into frosty slits. "I am *not* an ice pack."

My eyes widen, lip jutting out as I stare up at him. "It hurts."

"Then don't fall." But he sets his mug on the coffee table before he settles on the couch next to me, drawing my legs onto his lap.

His palms cover my knees, frost nipping at my skin through my slacks. Crystals crawl down my calves and up my thighs like lace stockings, and my bare feet turn blue. It burns against my flesh before sinking in to crawl along my bones toward my core, replenishing some of the energy I burn to heal my stupid knee.

As soon as it fades, new ice forms, and the process repeats. My entire lower body goes numb after only a moment, but I'll happily pay that price as the pain fades.

With his hands occupied, Emil eyes the mug on the coffee table with longing, and I lean to the side to grab it for him. Already, the cocoa has cooled even though he was careful to touch the handle as little as possible.

Wishing I had the power to reheat it for him, I adjust the bendy straw and hold it to his lips. He drinks quickly, frost creeping down the straw and the mug turning cold before he slurps up the last bit.

A chocolatey drop clings to his lips, frozen in place, and I swipe it free, pressing it into his mouth where it belongs. His cold tongue rolls around my fingertip, teeth closing gently to hold me in place a moment longer as he licks away every trace of sweetness.

My pulse jumps, imagining all the things that tongue could do to my body. His pale-blue eyes meet mine, shimmering with an icy promise. The ice on my thighs flows higher, toward the juncture of my legs, and my knees tremble with the desire to part.

A scuff from the kitchen pulls my attention to

the archway where Tobias strides into the living room carrying a tray of mugs and a green bottle of whiskey. It breaks the fragile moment with Emil, and I set his mug aside with regret. Someday soon, my ice demon and I will finish this teasing dance he's embarked on.

Kellen hurries over to Tobias and snags the bottle of whiskey, then joins me and Emil on the couch for a change, edging in at my back. Static crackles down my spine, little lightning bolts that burrow under my skin and into my core. He's charged from the storm, the energy he expelled at the office barely denting his reserves.

He wiggles until he shoves one leg between me and the couch, then shifts me to recline against his chest. His hands slip under my shirt, fingers spread wide over my stomach for maximum contact.

Between the two demons, I feel a bit like crackling ice. Not unpleasant, but not comfortable, either. I don't usually skim from more than one of them at a time. Their conflicting powers war within my body before settling in my core. But I need the energy, and Kellen needs to offload some of his before the storm outside convinces him to join it.

No matter how sweet his words earlier, I don't trust the siren call of the storm not to lure him back to the sky. Especially after he already felt its sweet caress. I might even sleep in his room tonight. Or try to. Kellen's not the best bed partner once he passes out.

Tobias sets the tray on the coffee table and eyes our cozy setup on the couch as if trying to figure out how to wedge himself in, too. But there really isn't enough room, so he hands me a mug already topped off with cream and sugar before sitting in his usual chair.

I frown at the distance between us, not liking the space but unable to resolve it. Maybe I should take a look at Emil's furniture magazines and dog-ear a couple pages of my own. I'd be willing to move my floral couch back up to my room if it meant getting a large sectional we can all cuddle up on.

After a few minutes, Tally and Reese return from the basement and join us in the living room, taking seats on my sofa.

Reminded of my original purpose, I disentangle myself from Kellen and Emil to grab the book I brought down. "Reese, do the symbols in this mean anything to you?"

He catches the book I toss him, frowning at the symbol partially obscured on the dirt crusted cover. "This is the mark of the Hunter."

"Yeah, it's a demon book about them."

"A demon book?" Interest fills his eyes, and he flips it open, his eyes instantly sliding to the side. "What the…"

"You can't read it." Tally pats his arm in sympathy. "Human minds, no matter how clever, just aren't designed to take it in."

Well, that's good to know. I struggle to focus on human magic symbols. Knowing humans struggle with our language makes me feel a little better.

Reese covers the writing with his palm to focus on the symbols in the margin. After a moment, he nods. "Yes, these are some of the symbols for entrapment. They're incomplete, though." He flips a few pages and pauses again. "And these are for protection. But, again, they're incomplete."

If the person who made the notes was a demon, that makes sense. They wouldn't have been able to focus enough to fully replicate the magic. But even just a little is enough to alert a demon to a spell's purpose.

"I can show you the book we have, if that will help." Reese lifts his palm to uncover the demon text once more and shudders before closing the book. "I'm not sure you'll gain anything from it, though."

"Can you help take down the Hunters'

protection spells when we find them?" Tobias cuts in.

Reese nods. "Yes, and any trap spells they have in place, too. If we take that away from them, then they should be easy enough to deal with. Without preparation, Hunters are at an extreme disadvantage."

Something that was bothering me rises back to the surface. "But they couldn't have had any preparation when they went after Julian's imps today."

"No, they wouldn't need it." He casts us an apologetic smile. "Imps aren't powerful. They can be taken down with a taser."

For now, I'm going to ignore how he knows that and ask a more important question.

"Why would they go after them to begin with?" I hug my elbows close, and Kellen rubs a soothing hand over my back. "They don't have much in the way of magic for someone to steal."

"Hunters can't abide *any* demon to exist on the human plane. Tonight would have been about simple extermination."

My stomach rolls. "Then why keep Perry alive?"

"For information." Sympathy fills his eyes.

"What I said earlier still applies. They'll keep him alive for now."

"But why?" I shake my head, not understanding.

"Because it's a trap, honey." Kellen grips my shoulder. "They know you'll come for him."

"I don't know why, though." Tobias leans forward, elbows on his knees. "No other demon would risk their life for an imp. How can they know Adie will?"

How indeed? The unease in my stomach grows. Only people who know me personally would know I'm soft for my imps.

As if called by the thought, the front door bangs open, a smoky voice drifting into the room. "Fee-fi-fo-fum, I smell the blood of a witch inside."

THE OBVIOUS CULPRIT

"*Fee-fi-fo-fum, I smell the blood of a witch inside.*"

Before the last sibilant whisper enters the room, I have Reese up the stairs, shoving him into my bedroom before I hyper-speed back downstairs.

I crash onto the couch, my head slamming onto Emil's lap as my feet shove into Kellen's face. Emil lets out a pained grunt, and Kellen stares cross-eyed at my toes under his nose.

Tobias stands, hands loose at his sides and ready for combat, as Domnall rounds the entryway wall, an evil grin on his face as he searches the room.

His dark eyes sweep over the five of us before they settle on Tally, and his lip curls. "Oh, the baku is here. You stink, little demon. Don't you think it's time for you to run back home?"

I bristle at his tone, but Tally simply relaxes, her arms spread over the back of the couch like a queen. "Domnall. How unpleasant to see you again."

I stare at her in shocked surprise. How does Tally know Domnall?

"The feeling is mutual." He stops next to the coffee table, ignoring Tobias's formidable form. "Don't you think you've played on this plane long enough?"

"I don't think you want me back in Dreamland right now." Tally's fingers flex, the shadow of claws kneading against my floral couch. "I might have a change of taste in dreams. And even you need sleep."

A low growl of warning escapes Domnall, and the smell of burning forests fills the air. On reflex, I drag Emil's arm over my chest to breathe in his frosty, clean scent.

Baku and Devourer stare at each other in steely silence, neither willing to bend.

Julian skips in from the entry. He zeroes in on where I sit with Emil and Kellen, darting forward with arms thrown wide. "Cousin!"

In his enthusiasm to embrace me, he manages to wiggle his way onto Kellen's lap, which I suspect was his goal in the first place.

He hugs my legs to his chest. "I heard you rescued my imps. Thank you so much." He squeezes harder, on the verge of pain. "You should have called."

With a glare, I pull myself free to sit up. "Why? You never answer your phone, anyway."

He pouts but doesn't protest. His call log is stuffed with all the messages he declined to answer. Instead, he twists to bat his lashes at Kellen from only inches away. "You were there, too, right? Let me *thank you* properly."

Kellen stands, Julian rolling off his lap to bounce against my side. "I was there for Adie. Your thanks aren't needed."

Julian throws an arm over my shoulders. "Oh, *my* thanks aren't needed, just sweet little Adie's, right?"

"Stop it," I hiss.

Julian's always been upfront with his desire to feed off my demons, but propositioning Kellen right in front of me goes too far.

Domnall's attention finally shifts away from Tally to land on my cousin. "Shouldn't you save those lips for me, pet?"

"But you're hoarding all that delicious energy."

Julian's head drops to my shoulder. "What's a hungry incubus to do?"

Domnall's head tilts to one side, his eyes narrowed. "Are you really that hungry, pet?"

Tension fills the arm across my shoulders, but Julian's voice remains playful and pouty. "You know I am. I've been by your side since you called me. There's been no downtime to go hunting in Dreamland."

In answer, Domnall crooks a finger.

Julian lets out a tense laugh. "Right now?"

Domnall's brows lift in question. "You said you're hungry, right?"

"That I did."

As Julian slides off the couch, I resist the urge to yank him back. I've been on the receiving end of Domnall's power dump; I don't want to watch my cousin go through that. But I resist the impulse. Julian asked for this. He's aware of what he's getting into.

Julian circles around the coffee table, stops in front of Domnall, and winds his arms around the demon's neck, offering up his mouth. "Give me all you got, darling."

Domnall isn't gentle or sweet as he enfolds Julian

in his embrace. This is not two lovers coming together. No, despite Julian's open offer, Domnall fists a hand in the incubi's white curls, tight enough to pull tears from the corners of his eyes, and grips his chin with the other, forcing open an already willing mouth.

My stomach rolls, nausea twisting in my gut and acid burning in my throat. I huddle closer to Emil, unable to watch as Domnall's mouth covers Julian's. But I sense it as the power in the room shifts, the burning forest pulling back on itself, the breath-stealing weightlessness of a backdraft before it strikes. I remember the overwhelming suffocation, the thick coat of ash in my throat and lungs, the crackle of my bones as I burned from the inside out.

An unwilling whimper escapes, and Emil's cold arms slide around me. He pulls me into his lap, tucking my face to his neck where frost kisses my lips and steals into my mouth. It melts on my tongue with a purity that leaves no room for fire, and I gasp it in deeper, wanting it all the way to my core.

Julian's thready chuckle brings my attention back to the present, and I lift my head as he pulls away from Domnall, his palms lingering on the other demon's chest. "Delightfully forceful as always, darling." He licks his lips. "Thank you for the meal."

Domnall pats him on the head, ruffling his curls. "I'll give you even more once we locate the witches who escaped."

"I look forward to it." Julian turns to where I sit. "But first, I'd like to check on my imps. They're here, right? There's no way to miss the smell of coconut body oil."

I give a jerky nod. "Yeah, I'll take you to them."

Reluctant, I climb off Emil's lap and edge past his knees, keeping my distance from Domnall. Empty of power or not, I want nothing to do with him.

Kellen meets me on the other side of the couch. "I'll join you, too. I want to make sure they know not to touch anything."

Julian joins us and grips Kellen's arm. "Going to put the fear of electrocution into my imps?"

Kellen grins and doesn't push him away. "Something like that."

I frown at the contact but stay silent. Julian's knuckles are white with how hard he grips Kellen's arm, but the two men play it off as casual bromance.

When we walk through the kitchen, out of sight of the living room, Kellen casually grabs the large stock pot from the counter. I pulled it out to make stew for tomorrow's dinner before everything slid sideways. Why does he want to take it with us to the basement?

I walk ahead of them to open the basement door, glad to find lights still on below. When searching earlier, I found a few more glass table lamps. I set them up for the imps to use, not wanting to force them up and down the uneven stairs in the dark.

The door swings shut behind us, and Kellen whispers, "Just hold it in a little longer."

Julian grunts in response, and I hurry down the stairs to be out of their way.

They barely make it to the bottom before Julian crashes to his knees, then drops forward onto his hands. Kellen thrusts the stockpot under Julian's mouth, and he clutches it tightly as he vomits.

Thick sludge hits the bottom of the pot with a wet splat, bringing back the memories of wet ash from when I did the same.

The heaving continues for long enough that the imps still awake trickle over to see what's happening. When they discover their owner being violently ill, a chitter of alarm goes up, and the rest swarm over.

They huddle around Julian, and a steady hum thrums through the air to comfort him.

At last, Julian sits back on his heels, his face

ashen with sweat glistening on his brow. Eyes closed, he pants, the sound more a wheeze than actual breathing. Black dots of ash cling to his lips, and after a moment, they lengthen into worms that try to crawl back inside him.

My gut heaves. Is that what happened when I expelled Domnall's energy, too? Is that why I sometimes sense his darkness lurking in my core? I push through the imps to reach Julian's side, wiping the disgusting stuff away with the hem of my shirt.

Julian's lashes flutter open, and he gives me a weak smile. "Thank you, dear. I forgot how horrible this can be."

I blot his brow with a clean edge of my shirt. "Why did you ask for it, then?"

"Who else would you have take it?" He catches my wrist and pulls my hand away from his face. "This is penance."

My brow furrows. "Penance for what?"

"For being a coward once already, when I left his side the first time." He cradles my hand in his lap, unable to meet my eyes. "I knew he would just find others of our kind to dump his power into, but I didn't care. I just couldn't take it anymore."

Kellen's hand lands on his shoulder. "You shouldn't have had to take it at all."

"It wasn't always like this." Julian shudders and clutches my hand tighter. "In the beginning, it was fun to hunt the evil witches, and taking the power didn't hurt. But Domnall changed. He wanted more. He stopped caring about good and bad. Any witch became fair game. Instead of simply draining their power, he started consuming everything." Julian curls forward, his forehead to my hand as if in supplication. "I couldn't stay, and because of that, he attacked you."

"That's *not* your fault." Yanking my hand free, I push on Julian's shoulders until he straightens. "You were every bit the victim in this, too. The higher-ups gave him this power; they're aware he's abusing it." When my eyes briefly meet Kellen's, he gives a grim nod. "This is on him and on them for not correcting the issue."

One corner of Julian's mouth kicks up as he cups my cheek. "You're too good to be a demon."

"Or maybe demons need to hold themselves to a higher standard." I wipe his mouth again. "Have you really not fed since Domnall came to town?"

"There hasn't been time." He side-eyes the imps. "But I can always—"

Spindling out energy from my core, I press my lips to his and feed it into his surprised mouth.

"Well, this is interesting," Kellen murmurs, but I ignore him, all of my focus on my cousin.

When Julian's hands find my waist, ready to push me away, I press closer. He's weak at the moment, malleable with hunger, and I take full advantage as I wrap my arms around him.

Trembling, Julian relents, his hands slipping to my back as his mouth opens wider. He tastes of ash and death, but under that is coconut and determination, smothered but not doused by Domnall's abuse. I feed that part of him, nurturing it until it flares back to vivid life.

I pull back, and Julian gasps for breath, then shivers with delight. "So, that's what you've been feeding on." His eyelids crack open, and he stares at me through his lashes. "No wonder you're so protective of them."

"This was a special service." I flick him on the tip of his nose. "Don't come around expecting me to feed you again."

"How about a threesome?" He flutters his lashes. "I can teach you how to wrap these demons around your little finger."

"She doesn't need help doing that." Kellen lifts me to my feet. "We've been down here too long. We need to go back upstairs before Domnall suspects something's wrong."

"Right." When Julian rises unsteadily to his feet, his imps swarm in.

They coo and pat any body part they can reach, and he tolerates it for half a minute before pushing them away.

"I'm fine, I'm fine. Don't think this gets you off work tomorrow. Who's driving?" A glittery arm shoots into the air, and he nods in satisfaction. "Make sure Adie gives you the van keys. The catering company is scheduled to arrive at ten a.m. for the brunch. You need to be in server's wear and there at nine forty-five to help unload the trucks. Tiffany, you're in charge of the money."

Seeing my cousin shift into business mode jars me. I forget sometimes he can be serious. "Julian, are you sure you shouldn't cancel the job until after the Hunters are taken care of?"

He brushes off my concern. "We need cash now more than ever. Right, everyone?"

The imps nod in unison, their expressions resolute.

"But the Hunters…"

"They won't go after them again when humans are around." He speaks with the knowledge of past experience. "They only went after them tonight because they knew they were unguarded. They'll be safe enough until nightfall, if the Hunters even bother to try again. Hopefully, we'll have dealt with them before then."

I straighten. "Do you know where they're hiding?"

"Yes, and no. We'll discuss it when we get back upstairs." He nudges the pot of sludge on the ground with his foot. "What do we do with this?"

"I'll dispose of it later." Kellen stares around at the imps. "No one touch this or it will be bad for you." His gaze sweeps over them again. "And whoever took the gold cigarette case that used to be on that stack of boxes"—he points to a towering stack next to the stairs—"put it back or Emil will turn you all into ice sculptures."

Bleating in panic, they scurry back to where we set up their sleeping area, pillows and blankets flying in their mad search.

Julian shrugs and bounces up the stairs with far more energy than he displayed on the way down.

As Kellen and I follow behind, he leans down, static nipping at my earlobe. "How much energy did you give him?"

My head turns until I catch tiny lightning bolts

on my lips. "Why? Do you want to top me off tonight?"

He grasps my hips, pulling me against his erection. "That was pretty hot, watching you two together."

I growl and bite his lip. "Don't even think about it."

His hand spreads static kisses over my lower stomach, long fingers inching past the waistband of my slacks. "Then give me something else to think about."

"You'll have to convince me."

"I can do that," he growls.

"Before you two start going at it, we have plans to make," Julian calls from the top of the stairs. "Hurry it up. We're losing time."

Kellen's hand leaves my pants. "Your cousin's a spoilsport."

"Yeah, but I love him anyway."

After what just happened, I can no longer see Julian as the traitor, and that eases my mind. I should never have suspected him in the first place.

Not when Domnall is so obviously the evil culprit.

CHANGE OF PLANS

"How are your pet imps doing?" Domnall sneers when we rejoin the others in the living room.

In our absence, he took over Kellen's chair and purloined one of the cups of coffee and Kellen's whiskey bottle.

Julian flops down on the couch next to Emil and kicks his feet up on the coffee table. "They're being spoiled right now, so they're just fine."

"How nice for them," he says dismissively. "Now, can we get down to business?"

"Yes." I settle next to Tally with Kellen on my other side. "You know where they're holed up?"

Julian tilts his hand back and forth in a so-so gesture. "We have an idea. It was stupid of them to take one of your imps. It will lead us straight to them, assuming they haven't disposed of him already."

I stiffen at the idea but push it aside to focus on the facts. "I already tried to track Perry through our contract link."

Julian glances over at me in surprise. "You went to Dreamland? Good for you!" Then he frowns, his focus going distant. "How'd you do that?"

"It doesn't matter." No way am I discussing that with Domnall in the room. "What *does* matter is that he was alive a few hours ago. It's how we knew the Hunters were attacking your office."

"That's good. Hopefully, that means they're keeping him alive for their harvest ceremony. They can't perform that until—"

"The full moon. Yes." I make a motion for him to hurry along.

His eyes narrow with suspicion. "Yes, the full moon. That takes time to set up, so they'll keep him wherever they've holed up to make it easier when the time comes."

I nod eagerly. "I think it's a storage complex on the outskirts of town. I saw it while I was tracking him in Dreamland."

His mouth opens and closes for a moment. "You *saw* the human plane from *Dreamland*?"

Impatient, I nod again.

"We need to have a sit down when this is over," he grumbles before turning to Emil. "Might I borrow your tablet for a moment?"

Emil's white eyebrows lift. "Why?"

"All of my imps have a tracker installed. I can log into the app, and we can pinpoint exactly where Perry is."

"Say what now?" I lean forward. "You didn't say anything about a tracker when I bought their contracts."

"It's in the fine print, dear." Julian plucks the tablet from Emil and types something onto the screen. After a moment, he releases an *ah* of satisfaction. "They're at Sure-Lock Self Storage."

"Excellent." Domnall claps his hands together. "We'll strike tomorrow at sunset."

"Why not now?" I demand. "We know where they are. Why wait?"

"This is the *nest*, where they'll be at their most powerful," Domnall explains slowly, as if to a child. "Before we attack, we map out a plan, make sure we memorize the layout of the complex and where exactly they are. Tomorrow night, we strike when they least expect it."

It makes sense, but I hate the added time. What

if they hurt Perry before then? "Why sunset? Won't that be when they're out hunting demons?"

Domnall shakes his head. "Ambushing you at the bakery already failed, so they'll most likely try to lure you out to a location of their choice tomorrow, using your imp as bait. They'll want somewhere secluded where they've already set up their spells. They'll want to meet between three and four in the morning when they're the strongest, which means they'll be sleeping during the day in preparation. When you receive the message, contact us. We'll ambush them when they're feeling safest at the storage facility."

Julian taps the tablet again, lays it on the coffee table, then waits until we all gather around. "This is the top view of Sure-Lock Self Storage. They only have one entrance into the place, with a simple coded gate for security. But there are fifteen rows of outside storage units that can be rigged with spells. The tracker says Perry is around this area." He circles a row at the back. "We won't know the exact location until we get there."

I stare down at the map. "Is there a way to see the numbers on them? When I was in Dreamland, I saw two-fifteen and two-seventeen. There was a guard dog, too."

Domnall swears under his breath. "If they have a familiar, that makes things more complicated."

"How so?" I ask as Julian opens a new window and looks up the storage facility's website.

"Familiars heighten their magic and are more difficult to neutralize." He glances at Julian. "Still have that shotgun, pet?"

I cringe at the idea of killing an animal, even an evil witch's familiar. "If the dog isn't supposed to be there, then let's just call animal control and report a stray dog on the premises."

Domnall blinks slowly. "Huh."

Kellen grins. "We can have it picked up while they're sleeping. Humans won't set it off like one of us would."

"Sounds like a plan." Julian locates the numbered map of the storage facility. "Looks like that's the place, Adie. That gets us closer than the tracker does."

Tobias points to a shadowed area behind the complex. "Someone will need to guard back here, in case they have an escape route into the forest."

"I can do that," Tally volunteers.

"What can a baku do against Hunters?" Domnall sneers.

Tally's cold, mahogany eyes meet his. "Their

magic will not affect me, and I am strong in this form. If they seek refuge in the woods, I will stop them."

"Adie and I can fly in from above while Emil covers the east side of the unit and Tobias covers the west side." Kellen points to the places on the map.

It seems like a solid plan except for one small thing. "How will we get past their spells, though? They'll be set to ensnare demons and alert the Hunters."

We all sit back, stumped on how to deal with this part. Kellen, Tally, and I share a guarded look. Reese's offer fills the air between us. But with Domnall here now, there's no way we can ask Reese or the others to risk exposing themselves, especially not after Julian's revelation that Domnall destroys *any* witch he comes across.

"How are the spells triggered, exactly?" Tobias asks at last.

Domnall rubs his chin. "Most of the time, they sense a demon nearby and activate."

Kellen straightens. "What do they use to apply the spells?"

"They used spray paint at the bakery," I offer.

Domnall shakes his head. "They won't have done that at the storage facility. They'll have used something more temporary that they reapply daily to prevent the humans from noticing. The only permanent spells will be at the actual storage unit."

Lightning sparks in Kellen's pupils. "Are these temporary spells something that might be disrupted by heavy rain?"

A slow grin spreads across Domnall's lips. "Yes, something exactly like that."

Kellen rubs his palms together, sending up a shower of sparks. "Then, it looks like we'll be bringing a storm with us tomorrow night."

∼

After another thirty minutes of working out the details, Julian and Domnall take their leave.

Tally waits until the door closes before rushing up the stairs to where I stashed Reese. She leads him cautiously back down to the living room, as if wary Domnall will burst back in and attack him.

Reese, on the other hand, doesn't seem concerned, his focus on the ancient book in his hands. His lips move as he reads, and it takes me a moment to realize it's the book about the Hunters that the Librarian gave me. Reese's brow furrows as he struggles to decipher something.

Curious, I join them. "What are you looking at?"

"Hm?" Reese's eyes lift, and he blinks a couple times before he focuses on me. "Oh. There's an interesting spell here in the margin, but I'm not quite sure what it does. It might have something to do with what's on the page that I can't read."

"Let me see." I tip the book and see a picture of a demon with giant bat wings and cloven hooves clasping a screaming human close, mouth open to display pointed fangs. He Who Devours. "Oh, this is about Domnall."

His fingers brush over the woodcut image. "Is that who this picture is supposed to be?"

I nod. "Yeah, it doesn't really look like him, though."

"That's because we're no longer allowed to take forms like that on the human plane," Tally explains. "He used to put on quite the show."

My head jerks up. "Wait, that's what he *actually* looked like? I thought the artist was just taking liberties with the whole demon thing."

"The books in the Library record what is. They are not of our making. Though, as you can see, some choose to embellish on them." Tally traces the human magic symbols in the margin. "It was a darker time, and some demons felt these vestiges would terrify humans into leaving us alone."

Emil joins us and stares down at the picture. "Some of us never felt the need. It was a ridiculous idea that only endangered us all."

"That makes sense, then, for what this spell here was trying to accomplish. But like the others, it's incomplete." He pulls out his cell phone, then pauses and glances back up. "Is it okay if I take a picture? I want to consult with Xander on this. He understands these things on a different level than I do."

I shrug. "I don't see why not."

"Our language doesn't photograph, so there's no harm." Emil's hand touches my back. "Are you well, Adie? You feel less than you were when we got home."

"You should have seen her." Kellen joins us as Reese snaps his pictures. "Julian was pretty hard up after he expelled all that nasty shit Domnall dumped into him, and our little succubus here decided to share her energy. I'm going to be dreaming of that scene for the next decade."

I bristle, not liking the idea of Kellen dreaming of my cousin. "Well, I hope you and your hand have fun with that."

"Mmm, jealousy." Kellen reaches for me. "That will add spice to the bedroom tonight."

Emil deftly swings me out of reach. "You need to remain connected to the storm if you're going to use it tomorrow. You can't let it leave the city."

"But…" Kellen makes grabby hands at me. "We were going to go at it like bunnies."

"You can keep it in your pants for another night." Tobias slides up on my other side, hot for Emil's cold. "With your room full of imps, I'm happy to share mine with you tonight."

Emil's arm tightens around me. "No."

Tobias stares at him over the top of my head. "I didn't ask you, though I don't mind if you join."

A low growl rumbles from Emil. "*I* mind."

"Yet you're so easy to convince."

I wiggle out from between them before I turn into a slightly chard ice sculpture. "I promised the imps a slumber party, so I'm sleeping in my own room tonight."

"Adie, what does this section say?" Reese thrusts the book in my face.

My eyes cross as I focus. The scent of death and burning fills my nose, my skin tight and throat parched, while someone screams in the distance. "He Who Devours holds no demonic power of his own, and so he cannot be drained as other demons can. If his corporeal body is destroyed, he will return in form made new to hunt again."

Shocked at myself, my mouth drops open. I read the demon text. I *read* the demon *text*. That means I can read *demon* text. I am going to read so many books once we deal with the Hunters.

Introduction to Sex Demons here I come!

"That's what I thought it might mean." Thoughtful, Reese flips through a couple more pages. "I need to talk to Xander. It would be easier to just borrow the book, but that's probably a no?"

"No," I say numbly, still floored by my new skill, then shake myself. "I mean, yes, you can borrow the book for tonight."

"Excellent." He snaps it closed and tucks it under his arm. "We should head out before the others come looking for us."

"Yes." Tally comes forward to wrap me in her arms, whispering, "Congratulations on learning to read. We will celebrate when this is over."

I squeeze her tightly in return. "Thank you."

She steps back. "I'll see you at the bakery tomorrow?"

"Yes," I say at the same time Tobias says, "No."

Frowning, I turn to him. "You heard Domnall.

The Hunters won't attack me there again, and I need to keep up appearances. We already closed early today."

He scowls back at me, his jaw set in a stubborn line. "It's not safe."

"Then you can be there to protect me." I pat his chest. "You can sit in the front window and look handsome for my customers."

His narrow gaze shifts to Emil, who shrugs. "We don't have any meetings tomorrow that require your presence."

"Fine," he bites out.

"I'll come, too." Reese catches my eye. "I'm sorry we can't assist in the actual battle, but there might be something we can send along to help out."

"I'm sure there is, my tricky witch." Kellen throws an arm over his shoulders. "See, this is why I'm training you. You think on your feet."

"You threw books at us and told us to self-study," Reese protests as Kellen leads him toward the door with Tally trailing after. "I'd hardly call that training."

"Do you have any idea how hard it was to get some of those books?" Kellen ruffles Reese's hair. "The Council of Merlin would slaughter me if they knew."

The front door opens, and their voices fade, followed by the slam of two car doors.

A moment later, Kellen comes back alone and walks toward the kitchen. "I'll deal with the nasty stuff in the basement."

"I don't want that stock pot back," I call after him. Stretching, an ache pulls at my shoulders, making me long for a hot shower and a warm place to sleep. "I'm going to head up."

"I'll meet you in the morning." Tobias heads for the stairs to the right of the large fireplace. "Don't leave without me."

"I wouldn't dream of it." I blow him a kiss. "You're going to pull in a lot of customers tomorrow."

NOT SLEEPING

When I come out of the bathroom twenty minutes later, silence lays over the house. For some reason, I expected some noise with so many inhabitants stuffed under the same roof, but the quiet creaks and groans remain the same, the weight to the air still light with a subtle draft. Not even a hint of baby powder from all the imps.

If I didn't know better, I'd think the last few hours never happened.

I tug the fluffy, pink collar of Emil's bathrobe closer at my neck. He never asked for it back, and I refuse to offer. This kind of luxury isn't something I'd buy for myself, but now that it's mine, I'm reluctant to let it go.

The hem *shushes* along the hardwood floor as I

head for the stairs, but a light farther down the hall catches my eye.

It looks like Tac opened Emil's door, the silly beast. I should tell him not to wake me in the morning. His methods usually involve stomping all over the bottom two-thirds of my bed. I don't want him crushing Martha and Jesse in his enthusiasm.

Walking closer, I touch the edge of Emil's door, making sure I keep my toes on this side of the threshold. "Tac, buddy, you awake?"

The door swings inward, revealing a sea of plush white in the dim light. The low dance of flames from the fireplace casts a warm, orange glow over Emil's numerous, soft comforters. Cords from the electric blankets poke out the back, trailing across the floor a short distance to the nearby power strip. The light on it glows to indicate it's on, heating the bed to toasty warmth, but Emil is nowhere in sight. The furred, beanbag Tac usually lounges on lays empty, too.

Are they downstairs, enjoying the quiet now that everyone settled for the night?

The flicker of firelight pulls my focus back to the bed, and my bare toes curl against the cold hardwood. Those soft blankets look so much more welcoming than the nest I built on my floor. They're warm and heavy, with enough layers to block out the light. With a couple strategically placed pillows, it's almost as good as my pillow cave.

But I promised the imps a sleepover. If they wake without me there in the morning, who knows what mischief they'll get up to?

Shoulders drooping, I turn back toward the stairs only to come to a stop.

Emil leans against the wall, his arms folded over his chest as he watches me through frosted lashes. "If you want to go in, you can go in."

My chest tightens at the invitation, and I shuffle closer. "No, I was just looking for Tac."

"He and his knight are guarding the basement door." When Emil straightens, his body fills most of the hall. "Should I be sad you weren't looking for me?"

My tilt my head to the side. "Do you want me to look for you?"

Slowly, he reaches out, fingertips painting snowflakes along my jaw. "Come to my bed."

Reluctant, I shake my head. "I promised the imps a slumber party. I have to sleep in my room tonight."

He brushes the corner of my lips. "I'm not asking you to sleep."

My pulse picks up speed, but, again, I shake my head. "I can't handle more teasing tonight."

"No teasing." His touch falls away as he walks toward his open door and the inviting warmth beyond.

Unable to resist, I trail after him. "No teasing?"

Turning to face me, he unbuttons his shirt, revealing frosty white skin one inch at a time. "No teasing."

My toes inch across the threshold. "And no sleeping?"

He shrugs out of the shirt and sets it neatly off to one side. "No sleeping."

I inch farther into the room. "This feels like teasing."

"It's called foreplay." With painstaking slowness, he frees his belt. "Close the door, Adie."

With a start, I find myself halfway to his bed, lured by the vanilla ice cream promise of the body he reveals.

Do I want to stay? To finally know what it feels like to hold Emil inside my body? To fully feed on him for the first time? Hell, yes.

Do I deserve it, though, with Perry missing and my other imps scared and alone? I'm not so sure. It doesn't seem right to allow myself pleasure when others of mine suffer.

A sigh of regret escapes, and I turn toward the door to leave. Once this is all settled, I can come back here and take Emil up on his offer, if it's still on the table. My ice demon may change his mind by then.

"I'm sorry, Emil, I don't think this is the right time." I reach for the doorknob. "With everything going on, it just doesn't seem right."

"I understand." The slow slide of a zipper sounds, and I freeze, imagination going rampant. "A lot is happening right now that makes you uneasy."

"Right." I nod, hand tightening on the doorknob as I resist the urge to turn around. "It wouldn't be right to have fun while Perry is missing."

"Hmm." The rustle of comforters shifting pricks my ears. "But is it really fair to Perry to go into a fight at your current energy level?"

Automatically, my focus shifts inward, prodding at the ball of energy at my core. When we rescued the other imps at HelloHell Delivery, the power I used to increase my strength and hyper-speed only brushed the surface of what I currently hold. But what I gave to Julian left an empty space that instinct urges me to fill.

I push the desire aside. "I still have enough."

"You depleted your reserves three times today." His voice comes out lower, with the added sound of skin slipping over skin, and I twitch, head half turning before I abort the motion.

Pulse spiking, I lick my lips. "I skimmed from you while I healed."

"So, you have enough power to go into battle? That's good." A breathy sigh follows, one I've felt against the back of my neck on more than one occasion while his fingers delved between my thighs.

My stomach muscles tighten in response. "Emil, what are you doing?"

"It excited me to see you hovering outside my door." A groan underlays his words. "But I understand your feelings. I'll see you in the morning."

I will my feet to move, to walk out the door, but remain frozen on the spot. My lashes drop, masking out the cold, empty hallway.

With my vision gone, my other senses come to life. The hard, smooth surface of the doorknob. The clean scent of winter and fire. The quiet rustle of a body on soft blankets and the slip of skin against skin.

"Unless you'd like to watch?" The offer nips at the parts of my body not hidden by his oversized bathrobe. "There's no harm in watching, right?"

The air catches in my throat at the visual painted across the backs of my eyelids. Emil's muscular, pale body surrounded by the soft fullness of down comforters. Melting frost glistening on his skin in the firelight. The blush of desire on his face.

"Adie, open your eyes."

The soft command brings my lashes up, and I find myself facing the bed once more. I don't know when I turned or how long I stood frozen, but the sight of Emil sprawled out on his bed steals my breath all over again.

He reclines at the edge of the mattress while facing the door, his strong, muscular thighs spread wide to provide a perfect view of the hard cock he fists. Like the rest of him, he's pale as frost there as well, with a hint of pink at his swollen head where a drop of cum glistens.

My mouth waters at the sight, my fingers curling against my empty palms with the need to touch, to take control.

As if he senses my desire, he gives himself a languid stroke, rolling his hand over the top.

I follow the motion, licking my lips as the drop

of cum disappears. I want to taste that, to discover what his cum tastes like, to feel it roll down my throat. Will it melt part way or land in my stomach still cold? I desperately want to know the answer to that question.

As his hand moves again, his lips part on a shaky sigh. He looks so powerful, so controlled as he strokes himself, his hair still immaculate, his blankets folded just so to perfectly frame his luscious form. It makes me want to bury my fingers in his hair, to push him back and make a mess of his blankets.

My shins butt up against his bed, and his knees slowly close, trapping me in place. We've been in this position before, in another room in a different house. At that time, I desired and resented him. Now I simply want him, all of him, from his sharp personality to his numbing comfort, to his icy dignity. All mine.

Slowly, he reaches up to tug the tie on the robe loose. It gapes open, a heady mixture of warm and cool air slipping inside to curl around my bare body.

My pulse races, my thighs pressing together to ease the ache of emptiness. My eyes skate across his hard planes before dipping once more to his lap. The pink robe puddles across his thighs, accentuating the milky paleness of his skin. "I was going to leave."

"No, you weren't." He cups the backs of my thigh, and I shiver as frost forms, liquid lace that creeps toward the curve of my ass.

"My imps need me," I insist even as I allow him to draw one leg onto the bed.

His fingers slip up my inner thigh but fall away before they reach my core. "You treat them well. They know you care."

My breath hitches. "I don't want to fail."

"You won't." He pulls my other leg onto the bed until I straddle his thighs. Ice nips at my skin, burrowing in to find the core of energy at my center. "You're going to be so strong for them."

My eyes zero in on his lips. "The strongest."

He leans back, inviting, and I follow him down, chasing after his mouth with mine until I lay over him, my nipples hard against his cold chest, my stomach flush to his. Our bodies trap the hard length of his cock, and he grabs my ass to shift me higher until I reach his waiting lips.

The taste of ozone and winter melts on my tongue and a hungry whimper escapes. I didn't know how much I needed this until the first tendril of power slips from him to slide past my lips and down my throat. It burns like ice cream swallowed too quickly and melts before it hits my core. I delve deeper in search of the glaciers that live inside him, hunting for the tipping point of the avalanche and prodding until it crashes into me.

My fingers find his hair, burrowing in to mess up the careful waves. When Emil shifts beneath me, I fist the silky strands to keep him in place. No backing out for my ice demon now. I'll melt him into a puddle and drink it all down.

Large hands cup my ribs, then slide down my waist to mold me to his shape, stealing my warmth and leaving me frost burned. Shivering, I shrug out of the robe, not liking its weight on my back, the way it blocks his chill from my skin.

Ice pools in my core, but instead of lulling me toward sleep, it fills me with energy, like iced tea on a hot day or the first breath of a spring morning before the sun takes hold. I tug on Emil's hair, fretful and in need of more than he gives. Ice ages reside inside him, hidden from my searching grasp. They creak and groan in the hard planes of his body, in the icicles of his fingers as he squeezes my ass.

He urges me higher as one hand finds the crease of my ass cheek, then slips inward until his fingertips brush the heated juncture of my thighs.

His groan creates snowflakes in my mouth that melt against my tongue, and I swallow them down before spreading my legs wider in offering.

Tracing my outer folds, one finger dips deeper to test my readiness, and he groans again to find me slick. It shouldn't surprise him, the silly demon. I'm a succubus. I'm *always* ready. There's no part of my body he could probe and not find it willing to take him.

I roll my hips, my clit grinding against his hard cock before I push back, taking his fingers deeper inside. The shallow penetration acts more like a tease, and I growl with frustration. He promised no teasing tonight.

Reaching back, I grasp his wrist and pull it forward, pressing it to the bed by his head, then do the same with the other. Lips still locked on his, my eyes open to find him staring back, his irises the liquid blue only found in frozen lakes high in the mountains.

My fingers thread through his, pinning them to the fluffy comforters as my body lifts. I shift higher until the head of his cock bumps against the apex of my sex, then follows my slit to my aching center. I pause there, poised over him, and we both hold our breath, savoring the moment.

Slowly, I sink down onto him, my muscles clenching around his cold cock, squeezing every ridge, memorizing every vein. He sighs into my mouth, his eyes fluttering shut with pleasure. When my ass hits his thighs, I spread my legs wider, pressing down hard to take in every last bit of him. Holding him tight within my body, my muscles ripple around his hard length, luxuriating in the sense of fullness.

He squeezes my hands, body flexing under me, and I pin him down harder, expending some of the energy he gave me to keep the dominant position.

Too many nights I've let him toy with me. Tonight, it's my turn.

I pull my mouth from his, using our joined hands to support my weight. My ice demon desires warmth, possibly more than he desires me, and that needs to change. I took enough of his power to allow a flush of pink to spread to his chest, to make it safe to take him into my body, but those hidden caverns of ice remain untouched.

If I fuck him hard enough, long enough, they'll break, become mine for the taking, leaving him warm and cozy until they form again. And I want to give him that, to let him be warm in his own bed without the need for heated blankets.

But not yet.

Eyes locked with his, I delve inside myself and shut off that part of me that feeds on energy.

My bones ring, like a switch being flipped, and his lips part in surprise. "Adie, what are you doing?"

I grin down at him. "Foreplay."

"This isn't how foreplay wor—"

His words cut off as my hips undulate, clit rubbing against him while I keep him buried deep inside, pleasuring myself while giving him minimal friction. He taught me I can come like this, by only stimulating the aching nub at the height of my sex, and I grind against him, my breath coming faster, the blood rushing in my veins as I indulge in pleasure simply for the sake of self-satisfaction.

It feels exquisite, the warmth of my skin and the coolness of his pressed together. Sweat trickles between my breasts and and drops onto his hard abdomen, turning to crystals that roll down his abdomen, then melt where our bodies meet, providing added slickness. His bed is going to get so messy, and I shiver with pleasure at that knowledge.

Pressure builds, my muscles tensing as my orgasm crests, and I rein in the instincts that want to fling wide, to pull in all the energy in the room. Not yet, not until—

With a growl, Emil's patience breaks, his hands twisting out of my grasp. I lose my support, and he catches me before I fall, one hand tangling in my hair while the other grabs my ass. He half sits up, pulling my head toward his, mouth open and seeking. At the same time his tongue thrusts past my lips, his knees bend and his hips pull back before he surges up into my body.

I come in an instant, muscles milking around his hard length, but he doesn't pause to give me time to enjoy it. His cock pistons in and out of my body at an even, steady pace designed to bring me back to the edge of release.

My fingers rake down his chest as I resist the push of power he tries to feed me. He's not formed of storms, and I can deny his energy when I want to. It presses at my tongue, slips against the back of my throat, but I refuse it entry into my body even as I accept the rest of him.

With a growl, he rips his mouth from mine. "Why are you doing this? Don't you want to be strong?"

I gasp and move to meet his thrusts, new pleasure already spiraling up my spine. "I want to be the strongest."

His hand grips my ass hard enough to leave

bruises. Bruises I'll wear with pride. "Then, take my power."

My nails dig into his chest. "Then, give me *more*."

His mouth crashes back over mine, his power an avalanche that pushes to be inside me. So much weight, so much temptation, but he still holds back, and that just won't do.

With one hand, I scrape my nails down his chest, over his hard nipples, then down to his abdomen before I slip my fingers into my folds, finding my clit. I circle the hard nub, building my pleasure faster, and another orgasm crashes over me. I gasp and groan, my inner muscles clutching at him, warmth flooding my womb.

"Adie, please," he groans, and the last of his restraint breaks.

Ice fills the air, the flames in the fireplace banking in an instant. The entire house groans, the supports shifting with the sudden flux of cold. Desperate, Emil grips my hips, his thrusts no longer controlled, but a frantic drive to find his own pleasure.

My back arches, head falling back, as I sense his release near. He bows forward, forehead to my breast, as he gasps out quiet entreaties, his hands frantic on my hips before he suddenly presses down hard. The ice in the air snaps, sharp crystals raining down as he comes.

I release the reins on my instincts, my senses thrown wide, and power crashes into me, swamping my senses as it floods me with the weight of ice ages. My bones crackle and freeze, my body shuddering as I take in all that delicious power, funneling it into my core.

Another orgasm rolls through me, shaking the ice from my bones as my body floods with heat. My wings burst from my back, feathers spread wide as I hold onto Emil, my safe point in the blizzard.

After a few moments, my breathing steadies, and I slump against him, my muscles turning to liquid. "I don't think I can move."

With a quiet laugh, he falls onto his back, taking me with him. "Just for the record, that wasn't foreplay."

"Maybe not for you." I tuck my head into his shoulder, his skin warm beneath my cheek for the first time since we met. "But it was great foreplay for me."

MAGIC CONFETTI

At the bakery the next day, Tobias definitely draws in the soccer moms, something that both pleases and pisses me off. Good thing I had the forethought to take away the extra chair at the two-person table I stuck him at before we officially opened for the day. More than one person has cast him an appreciative glance, but none have been brave enough to drag a seat over to join him.

It helps that he emits a *Do-Not-Approach* aura as he sips his cappuccino and focuses on the laptop he brought along.

Tally arrives to work on time, sans witches, with a promise that Reese and Xander will follow in a couple hours.

As Domnall predicted, the Hunters contact me soon after we open shop. I don't know what exactly

I expected, but it certainly wasn't a phone call on the bakery's landline.

When the phone next to the cash register rings, I lift it with my usual greeting, "Boo's Boutique Bakery, Adie speaking, how can I make your day sweeter?"

"Listen, demon," a muffled male voice comes from the other side. "We have your *friend*. Meet us at three a.m. at West Glover High School, or you'll never see him again. Come alone."

The line goes dead, and I gently set it back in the cradle before smiling at the customer who steps up to the counter. "How can I make your day sweeter?"

∽

At five, Reese and Xander arrive. Unlike the others, they have no qualms about dragging chairs up to Tobias's table and sitting down. Reese settles a long box next to Tobias's laptop, and the three men hunker over it in deep conversation.

I peek over at Tally who runs the espresso machine while Martha takes a break with the others in the kitchen. "What's in the box?"

"I do not know." She sets the current order on the bar and calls out the customer's name before joining me to stare at the demon and witches. "The four of them were up all night in the kitchen. I could not get near it, and they were all asleep when I left this morning."

I rise onto my tiptoes to try to see into the box. "No idea what they were working on?"

"They said something about giving you more time." She shrugs. "They are amazing men who I often do not understand."

I touch her arm. "Are you sure you want to come with us tonight? It's going to be dangerous."

"You are my friend. Perry is my friend." She wraps an arm around my waist, turning my light touch into a hug. "If I stand to the side when I can help, I do not deserve that friendship."

My eyes sting at the sentiment. I don't know how I got lucky enough to earn Tally's friendship, but I won't betray it. Martha comes back out of the kitchen, and I give Tally a squeeze before I leave the register to join the guys at the table.

I stop next to Tobias's chair, and without thought, I run a hand over the back of his neck, ruffling the fine hairs there as I study the long box.

Inside, it holds a bunch of innocent-looking cardboard tubes a little over a foot long. I extend a hand over them, and the warning band on my bicep kicks up from a gentle vibration to a full-on shudder that travels through my entire body. The warning screams *Big Magic*.

I snatch my hand away without touching them. "What do these do?"

Reese hooks a finger on the lip of the box and drags it closer. "We're calling them Kickbacks."

"No, we're not. They're Reflection Wands." Xander slaps his brother's hand away before lifting out one of the tubes. It looks a lot like the leftovers from a roll of wrapping paper and just as threatening. "Do you know the Rule of Three?"

My brow furrows. "The karma thing? Like, whatever I put out into the world comes back threefold?"

"Yes, exactly. There's a spell that helps enforce that rule when the universe isn't working fast enough." He taps the side of the tube. "In here are a hundred of those. If you find yourself caught in a binding, you just aim the top end at the spell, twist the bottom, and it blasts out the spells inside. It will reflect the magic back on itself threefold and give you time to get out. But it only has a ten-foot radius, so you have to be pretty close and know where you're aiming."

"You made us confetti cannons," Tobias says drily.

Reese wiggles his fingers in the air. "Magical confetti cannons."

I twitch at the word *magic* and glance around the shop, but no one pays our table any attention. And even if they did, they'd just think we're New Age Pagans. Sometimes, it's nice to live in a more open-minded time where witchcraft is becoming a recognized religion instead of a burn-them-at-the-stake offense.

Steeling my nerves, I reach into the box and lift out one of the magical confetti cannons. It vibrates in my hand, and I turn it around until I find a little arrow Sharpied onto the side that says *This End Out*. The arrow points to the end facing my stomach, and I hastily flip it around. "Will this work in the rain?"

Xander nods tiredly, rubbing the large bags under his eyes. "Yeah, it's a strong blast, but you'll still need to move fast."

"I can move fast." Returning the tube to the box, I spot the top of a can of spray paint. "What's this for?"

"If you can see the markings, you can disrupt them, but you have to be careful." Worry fills Xander's expression. "A change in lines can shift a spell from holding to killing. I don't recommend it, but it's another alternative if you're truly trapped."

"Sounds dangerous." Tobias cups my hip, thumb stroking the top of my ass. "We don't want to go from bad to worse."

"I thought of that." Reese pulls a sketchpad out of the satchel at his hip and flips it open to a fresh page. He folds the bottom third up to create a square, then fishes out a Sharpie. Popping the cap off, he begins to draw. "This is the most commonly taught glyph for entrapment. There have to be three of them positioned around you in a triangle to work, so if you disrupt one, the spell fails."

The more he draws, the more my eyes hurt to watch until they eventually slide to the side.

"You aware we can't see that, right?" Tobias growls in frustration.

"One more second." The permanent marker squeaks over the paper some more before Reese caps it and stuffs it behind his ear. Setting the sketchpad on the table, he presses his fingers to the edges of the bottom half of the paper and slowly shifts it down. "Tell me when you can focus."

After a couple seconds, the paper comes back into focus, a solid inch of ink-free paper bisecting the symbol he drew. "I can see it."

Tobias grunts in agreement.

"Huh, that's farther apart than I thought it would be." Reese creases the bottom of the paper to keep it in place.

An odd assortment of circles, triangles, and jagged hatch marks make up the symbol. I have no idea what it all means, but I can *see* it. I grab his shoulder to give him a light shake. "That's clever!"

"Well, I was pretty sure it would work." Reese retrieves his pen. "I mean, it's nowhere near as complicated as your language. It doesn't physically move away from untrained eyes."

"Yeah, it's a pain in the ass," I mutter under my breath.

Tobias pinches my ass. "It's simple if you know what you're doing."

When I glare down at him, he stares back, unrepentant. *Someone* isn't getting snuggles anytime soon.

As if he reads the thought, he pinches my ass again. Harder.

"As you can see, aside from the locking ring, this symbol is all straight lines." Reese interrupts as he points at the various parts. "So, the easiest way to disrupt it is with an *S* shape."

Using the pen, he demonstrates by drawing a backward *S* over the symbol.

I study the way the curved lines disrupt all the straight angles. "Does it need to be backward?"

"Hm?" Reese blinks down at the sketch pad before his focus shifts to his brother. "Did I do it backward?"

Xander lifts a tired hand. "Which hand am I holding up?"

Uncertainty fills Reese's voice. "Left?"

Tobias and I exchange a glance. Xander's clearly holding up his right hand.

But Xander doesn't look surprised as he fishes a couple bills out of his pocket and passes them to Reese. "Go buy yourself some sugar and caffeine. You're going back to bed when we get home."

Swearing under his breath, Reese stands and walks over to join the line at the counter.

I watch him go, concerned. "Is he okay?"

"He just hit his wall." Xander rubs his eyes. "When he starts seeing things backward, he's too overloaded and needs to shut down. He'll be fine."

"Is that because of his…" I wave my hand in front of my face.

"I don't know." Xander grabs the sketch pad and

flips to a new page. "We used to think he hallucinated, so he was on all these medications to stop that. Then, we figured out he was actually seeing real things no one else could. It got better without the meds, but sometimes he really does see things that aren't there."

Dismayed, I lean against Tobias as my focus returns to the counter. "How do you tell the difference?"

"I can't. I don't see what Reese does. Tally helps, but she's not always with him." Xander focuses on the paper as he draws. "The backward thing is pretty easy to identify, though, once I'm aware it's happening."

After a few more minutes, Xander lays the sketchpad flat on the table once more. "This is the symbol for energy drain. You'll note how it's all curved lines."

Tobias and I bend over the drawing. Indeed, there's not a single straight line in it. The more I stare, the more it reminds me of a spindle, similar to how I store energy in my core. Almost like a vortex, all leading to the center, which Xander left oddly blank.

I point to that part of the drawing. "Why does it seem like something should be here?"

He hums with appreciation. "Because there

should be. This is where the practitioner puts their mark to identify who the energy funnels into. I left it blank because, even with the gap to keep it inactive, it's not a safe spell to be tracing, especially for me."

Tobias leans back. "Why especially for you?"

"Reese and the others have to put conscious thought into imbuing the spells with magic." He touches the bottom half of the circle, and it briefly flares to life before it hits that gap of blank paper and dies. "When I draw the symbols, the magic just happens."

"That's because you're naturally gifted." Reese places a plate with three cupcakes onto the table, sets a cup of black coffee beside it, and settles back in his abandoned seat. His odd, mismatched eyes focus on me and Tobias. "That's why I usually map out the complicated spells, or Slater and Jax do it. Big magic is made up of smaller magic. Like this one." He points to a smaller circle that touches the edge of the larger circle. "This is a spell for finding."

I frown. "Then why can we see it? Shouldn't it push our eyes away?"

He points to the larger circle that surrounds everything. "This is the locking ring. It works to contain the magic within it. If it were removed, each of these smaller spells would act independently." He points to a couple symbols not contained within their own circles. "And these would be meaningless. They're the conditioner symbols. It's like a complex math equation. Each piece offers unique information, which, when combined, result in a specific answer. Because the smaller spells all link in some way to the locking ring, they're inactive unless the locking ring is complete. Does that make sense?"

I shake my head. "Not really."

"It doesn't matter, so long as you understand the basic design." Xander lifts the Sharpie and holds it poised over the page. "Since this one is all curved lines, the safest way to disrupt it is with straight lines."

He draws a "Z" over the symbol, then pushes the bottom of the page up until the two halves connect once more. The drawing stays as just a drawing, easy to focus on.

Only one problem with this whole thing. "If we can't see the spells when they're active, how will we know whether to draw an *S* or a *Z* over it?"

"That's the kicker." Xander flips the sketch pad shut. "You won't be able to tell until it's activated. And the Hunters will most likely use these two spells in conjunction with each other. You'll be going in blind, which is why the spray paint should be a last resort."

Reese sips his coffee. "You can make an educated guess, though. Most likely the entrapment spells will be on walls, while the draining spell will be on the ground."

"Why?" I want as much information about the situation we're going into as possible. "Does that make them more powerful?"

Xander shakes his head. "Not at all."

Tobias's hand tightens on my hip. "Then how do you know that's how they'll place them?"

Reese peels the wrapper off his first cupcake. "Because that's how they're taught to place them, and if nothing else, Hunters are very firm in following their dogma."

I nod slowly. "The belief behind the spell."

He smiles up at me. "Exactly so."

"What does that mean?" Tobias asks.

I pat his shoulder. "I'll tell you about it later."

"Speaking of belief." Reese fishes around in his satchel and pulls out the demon book on Hunters. "Thank you. This was enlightening."

I accept the book and tuck it into the large pocket on my chef coat. "I'm glad it helped."

"It more than helped." Xander reaches into his

pocket, then sets a small, gray ball on the table. "It inspired this, which you might find handy."

When I pick it up, my bones vibrate with the amount of magic the marble-sized piece of clay holds. "What does this do?"

"Usually, Hunters stop siphoning your energy right at the point where you're almost out of power, but before your corporeal form is destroyed. That way, they can harvest your body parts with some power intact." Xander shudders, his gaze briefly flicking over to the counter where Tally assists customers. "It's a delicate balance, and sometimes they don't always stop the spell before the demon is drained. When that happens, you don't return to the demon plane. Your body is destroyed, and all of your power goes to the person who set up the spell. They then portion it out to re-empower their existing tools."

I shiver with apprehension. Energy is what makes a demon, not the actual body. What he describes is a living hell, a demon's consciousness chopped into pieces, each one aware, but lacking the ability to reconnect with the whole.

"If you're trapped and almost out of power, and it looks like they won't stop the spell before you're destroyed, break it between your teeth to activate the spell." He reaches across the table to grab my hand, his gaze serious. "But *only* use it as a last resort. It will lock the remaining power within your body, stopping your corporeal form from being destroyed, but if you're mortally wounded before the spell wears off, you die. No returning to the demon plane, no forming a new body. You're just gone."

Terrified of its potential, my fingers convulse around the small orb. If something like this got out, humans could destroy demons permanently.

A low rumble emits from Tobias, the beginnings of an earthquake awakening. His thoughts must run parallel to mine.

Xander releases me and holds up both hands. "I didn't entirely make this spell on my own. The beginnings of it are already in your demon book. But I can assure you that I did *not* write it down. No record of how to complete it exists outside my mind. Not even Reese assisted me with this one. It's too dangerous if it gets into the wrong hands."

Tobias tenses, muscles coiling tight, and I grip his shoulder in warning, afraid he'll wipe Xander out right now to prevent the spell from ever being leaked.

Xander slowly leans back in his chair. "I also

took the liberty of adding other incomplete symbols to the book, to mask the true intention of that specific spell. It won't be recreated. The one in Adie's hand is the only one that will ever exist."

"I trust you, Xander." I dig my fingers into Tobias's rock-hard shoulder. "Thank you for this gift."

He glances back to the counter. "Tally values your friendship. She would be sad if you ceased to be. If we could do more to ensure you come out of this intact, we would."

My gut tightens. I'm worried about tonight, too, about everything that could go wrong and the possibility that one of us, or more, might not come back.

MAGIC IN MY BAG

At dusk, we leave Reese and Xander at the bakery to keep the store open and protect the remaining imps while Tobias, Tally, and I walk down the few blocks to meet up with the others at Fulcrum.

As we near the club, loud music pulses from the open doors, and a line forms around the block. For some reason, I expected the place to be dark, but Kellen also needs to keep up appearances if we have any chance of catching the Hunters unaware.

High on the building, the neon sign with the word Fulcrum on it slants upward with a line underneath, like a teeter-totter, while below, the windows flash bright then dark as the strobe lights follow the pulse of music.

We walk straight to the front of the line, and the bouncer sweeps us through without a second glance.

No boob flashing necessary for me today. He must recognize Tobias, though I can't imagine he comes here often.

Inside the club, people loiter in the hall, making it difficult to pass until Tobias takes the lead. Then the masses part with ease, a high heel breaking here, two drunks bumping against each other there. Little accidents that move the humans closer to the walls for one reason or another. My eyes widen in awe. I've never seen his catalyst power so active, or so precise.

I hug the satchel with our secret weapons protectively against my chest and stick close to Tobias's back, Tally just as close behind me.

Perfume and the musky sweat of too many bodies packed together hangs heavy in the air, with a roil of emotions intermixed. Lust, anger, greed, all a heady bouquet that would tempt me if not for the promise of blizzards that currently lives in my stomach. I let the feelings roll along my skin like the touch of a friend's hand that taps me in passing without time for a visit.

The hall opens into a large room packed with dancers. A bar selling drinks takes up one side, while directly across from us, a tower rises above the crowd, the DJ inside swathed in bright blue and red strobes. On a platform below him, six of Julian's stripper imps dance in full body, white pleather that appears painted on and turns them into gyrating glow sticks under the black lights. I have to give Julian props. They certainly do draw a crowd. A small mosh-pit convulses at their feet, arms lifted in the hope of catching the attention of one of them.

When I angle toward the employees-only hall, Tobias touches my arm and gestures to the cordoned-off VIP area instead. I frown at that, not liking how public it is. It's one thing to talk witchcraft in public. Quite another to discuss breaking and entering and likely murder.

But in this noise, no one will hear our conversation.

Tobias catches my hand to keep me close as he ignores the obvious path around the dance floor in favor of striding directly through it. A few dancers overcome the effect of his power to push forward, arms flapping as they mime dancing, but he ignores them, eyes fixed ahead.

Behind me, a scuffle breaks out, and I peer over my shoulder to find Tally farther behind, fending off the unwanted attentions of a man who wears nothing but fishnets and a thong. Tall and skinny, he towers over the small demon, using his long arms to bar her way.

Before I can leap to her rescue, the tiny woman solves the problem herself by simply picking him up and tossing him back into the crowd. The move brings a smile to my face.

I have the coolest friends.

At the VIP section, the crowd grows thicker, and not even Tobias's weird mojo can conveniently tip people out of our way. Some trip, but their neighbors stand so close that they easily stay in place.

With no other choice, Tobias uses brute force to shove his way through. At first, angry voices rise around him, but as soon as the humans get an eyeful of his hotness, their tone switches to something far more grating on the nerves. Desire.

I grip the back of his belt to keep from being separated from him as we move forward. A cool hand touches my shoulder, and I know without looking that Tally had the same idea. Most of the humans who surround us are women, dressed in skimpy outfits designed to catch the attention of potential sugar daddies. They won't appreciate added competition. I catch more than one spiteful gaze cast in my direction.

On any other night, I'd answer those challenges and prove how very much Tobias belongs to me. But there's no time for pettiness now. Not when we need to save Perry.

At last, we break through, and the security guy next to the cordoned-off area unclips the red, velvet rope to let us through. Set behind the enormous speakers, much of the VIP section remains out of sight of the onlookers, providing a semblance of privacy only slightly quieter than the dance floor. Kellen, Emil, Julian, and Domnall sit on the edges of the plush, black leather couches, their focus on a poster-sized piece of paper laid out in the center of the large, rectangular coffee table.

As we near, Domnall's head jerks up, eyes greedy as his nostrils flare. Then his attention shifts to Tally, and his lip curls in a sneer. Did he smell the added witch magic in my bag? I'm suddenly grateful for Tally, whose presence masks our new tools. Somehow, I don't think Domnall will be open to using human magic to fight the Hunters.

His dark eyes shift to Tobias. "You're late."

"It's dusk. We're here." Tobias strides to the couch where Emil perches.

I move to wedge myself between Kellen and Julian, who sits entirely too close to my storm demon. Static crackles down my side, and when I meet Kellen's eyes, lightning skitters across his pupils.

I frown with concern. "Are you doing okay?"

He pats my knee in reassurance and sparks zap through my slacks and skate along my bones. "She's a mild storm, as far as storms go."

I grab his hand, ignoring the *snap, crackle, pop* where our skin touches. "You're not encouraging her to grow, are you?"

His gaze moves to the ceiling. "That would be irresponsible."

I grip his hand harder. "I'll ground you if I have to."

His attention diverts back to me, and the rumble of thunder shakes the couch. "I could build the storm inside you, make it great enough to swamp the city."

I toss his hand back into his lap and shift closer to my cousin. I want to be powerful, but not like that.

Kellen doesn't seem to notice my rejection, his eyes distant as he hums quietly to a tune only he hears.

"He's not going to be much use if the storm distracts him this much," Julian murmurs, quiet enough that the others won't hear but loud enough to travel over the music.

"He only needs to keep the storm over the city. We can take care of everything else."

"If you're done whispering over there?" Domnall snips from the opposite side of the table. "Based on the attack at HelloHell Delivery, we know there are at least five Hunters to contend with, but there could be up to eight. They travel in groups of three to increase their magic."

I search my memory of the attack. There were at least two at the front door to Julian's business, taking turns trying to break in, and I recall at least two sets of feet in the fire escape. If one stayed in the car with Perry, that's five. We took down four when they attacked me at the bakery. Would another three have stayed behind during the attempt to exterminate the imps? That doesn't seem likely. Not if they're fanatical about wiping out demons.

Domnall points to the printout, which turns out to be a blown-up layout of the storage facility. He taps the two entry points on the row of units where we identified the Hunters rented space. "Two will be awake on lookout while the others sleep. Here and here. We need to take them out fast."

"That means direct kills, darling," Julian points out. "No leeway for you to play."

Domnall grins. "There will be enough left over for me to have fun. And I can always drain the bodies afterward."

I shudder, recalling the mummified husks left when Domnall drains the witches after death. If I never watch that happen again, I'll be a happy demon.

"The baku will be positioned behind the unit." Disgust fills his voice. "There's a chance they have an escape route out the back. They'll blow through the wall if they need to, which should give plenty of noise as a warning."

Tally gives a confident nod. "They will not get past me."

Domnall ignores her. "The most likely places for traps are at the entrance to the storage facility." He points to a rectangle next to the gate closest to the main road. "If we trigger their early warning system, we lose the element of surprise."

Kellen shifts restlessly. "The storm's been raining directly over the storage facility since early this morning. It should have disrupted, if not destroyed, any temporary spells they set up, and they won't have been able to reapply them with the constant downpour."

Domnall nods. "I'll be able to sense if they're still active and give warning."

I was worried we'd miss an active spell in the storm, unable to notice when our eyes naturally skipped over the markings. But if Domnall can actually sense the magic, that makes everything so much easier. Providing he decides to tell us.

"That leaves the lookouts. Which is where Adie and Kellen come into play." Domnall rubs his hands together in glee as he stares at us. "You'll fly in from above and take them out before they even know you're there."

My stomach is rolling with an unease I try to ignore. The Hunters are evil. They need to be destroyed before they hurt my people. They're not innocent humans being preyed on. They're full participants in the paranormal world, accepting the risks they take in their quest for more power.

Julian touches my knee. "Will you be able to do this?"

I nod stiffly. I *have* to do this if I want the people I love to be safe.

"Are you sure?" he presses. "I can take your place and fly in with Kellen."

My head turns toward him, and I force steel into my voice. "They kidnapped one of mine. I *will* protect him by any means possible."

As we pull up to Sure-Lock Self Storage, the storm rages, rain pelting against the windshield. Stuffed into the tiny back seat of Tobias's sports car with Kellen, my skin vibrates with the low-level electricity he emits, and every hair on my body stands on end. It's an active struggle not to absorb all the excess energy, but I don't want to skim even a drop if it will damage Kellen's link to the storm.

Emil parks next to a sleek, red muscle car and turns off the ignition.

The others arrived ahead of us as we dropped Tally off at the back before driving around to the front.

Through the heavy rain, the sign for the storage facility casts a white pool of light over the minimal parking area, but the office at the gate lays dark, already closed for the night. The post in front of the gate holds a password protected lock to provide after-hours access to renters. A security camera mounted on the side of the office hints at security that doesn't exist. According to Julian, the owner stopped paying the security company, and the cameras are all for show. I don't know how he discovered this, but it makes our lives easier. We won't need to worry about our secrets being exposed to the public.

Perhaps that's why the Hunters chose this location over the nicer places located farther into town. It makes it easy to set up shop in a place where no one checks to see what's going on in the storage units after dark.

When we climb out of our car, the rain instantly plasters my clothes to my body. I eye Julian, who fares better in his ridiculous black duster.

Domnall slicks back his wet hair. "How about we shut off the waterworks? If the spells aren't eradicated by now, more rain won't make a difference."

"One does not simply shut off a storm," Kellen growls through clenched teeth as he strips out of his sodden dress shirt. "I released her an hour ago, but she's decided to stay."

"She's wooing you, mate." Domnall claps him on the shoulder with a wide grin. "After this is over, you can have a spot of fun."

"No fun." I strip off my hoodie. The low-cut

tank top I wear beneath offers plenty of room for my wings to slip free from their hiding place. "We get this done, then head home."

"You're a real sour puss for a succubus." Domnall grabs Julian by the back of the neck and gives him a hard shake. "What are they teaching the young ones these days?"

"You'd have to ask her mentor." Julian shrugs out of his grip on the pretext of checking the knives strapped on either side of his body, under his arms. The hilt of a sword peeks out at his hip, and I wonder if it's the Hunter's blade he took from me at the bakery. "I had no say in raising her."

I brush the comments off. What Domnall thinks of me means nothing. I reach into the car and pull out the satchel full of party supplies. Glad Reese chose something weatherproofed, I sling the strap over my shoulder. I was hesitant to take it from him, but now, I'm glad I did. I don't know how well the cardboard tubes will hold up once they're exposed to the elements.

Domnall frowns at the bag but says nothing as he strides toward the gate, a simple chain link on wheels with an electric lock.

He stops in front of it, searching the area beyond

for a full minute before he lifts a hand to beckon us forward. "Looks like the rain did the trick."

When we join him, he turns to me and Kellen. "You two are up now. Let us know once you've eliminated the lookouts."

I check my pocket to make sure my cell phone is secure. As Kellen does the same, I catch Domnall's eye. "Make sure you answer. We don't want another mixup in our plans."

His thick brows sweep together. "What are you going on about, now?"

"The disaster that happened last time," Tobias growls. "When Adie was caught because you changed the plans."

Domnall turns to face him fully. "Don't blame me because you were too slow to arrive."

Ice crystals bead on Emil's face. "We would have arrived sooner if we'd actually been informed."

Domnall's focus shifts to Julian. "Pet, weren't you in charge of that?"

Julian's lips part, but I raise my arm to cut him off. "Now isn't the time to play the blame game. We have a mission. Let's get to it."

"At least one of you is thinking straight." Domnall circles a hand toward the sky. "Up you go."

Kellen pulls me against his chest, strong arms banding around my waist. "Ready?"

No, I'll never be ready for something like this. My heart races, while a storm of terror rolls my stomach. Tonight, I go into battle with the intent to kill, and every part of my being rebels against that.

Kellen's head drops next to my ear. "You don't have to do this. You can wait in the car."

"No." I wrap my arms around his waist to hug him tight. "I'm ready."

Because no matter how scared I am to fight the Hunters, I'd never be able to live with myself if something happened to the people I love while I stood on the sidelines.

Kellen's muscles ripple, and he launches us into the storm.

SOMETHING SWEET

Flying just below the clouds, Kellen and I circle the storage facility, eyes open for any sign of the Hunter lookouts. The storm masks any light we might have gained from the moon, and the wet ground turns everything reflective, making it difficult to pick out details from above.

The rain hinders my ability to glide, too, and I keep a hand connected with Kellen for added support. Occasionally, lightning flickers through the storm clouds that sprout from his back and zap me with more force than I'm comfortable with. It's a different type of energy than what I drain from him, elemental and raw.

Untameable.

Kellen points downward. When I follow the line of his arm, I spot a Hunter huddled under the eaves of a building two away from the one at the far back where they rented a space. I nod to let him know I see them, and we circle back to the other side.

Motion near the rear fence line catches my eye, and I point. This one seems focused on the forest, and I worry they spotted Tally in the woods. Her pink hair doesn't exactly blend in with nature. Neither do my white wings, for that matter. If the Hunters look up, they'll spot us easily. Good thing humans rarely look for danger from above. Not even when they should know better.

We make a couple more loops in case Domnall was wrong and the Hunters placed more than two members on lookout duty, but the rest of the complex remains empty. No one wants to be out in this storm if they don't have to be.

Kellen motions from himself to the Hunter at the fence, and I nod, searching the ground one last time for my target. Now that I know where to look, I find the person with ease. My heart pounds, blood rushing through my ears loud enough to drown out the distant roll of thunder. My talons lengthen, and I release my hold on Kellen, focus intent on the Hunter.

Without his support, I fall fast, my wings not strong enough to sustain me in the air. I spiral down, using my wings to direct my descent, and crash down in front of the Hunter.

My legs ache with the impact, and I rise to my feet, wings spread wide to block off escape.

The Hunter's soft blue eyes widen in shock. "An angel?"

"No." I slam his head against the wall, and his eyes roll back in their sockets before he slumps to the hard cement.

I stare down at his still body, my gorge rising. He's just a kid, his cheeks still rounded with the remnants of baby fat, his limbs gangly on a body not yet finished growing. So young. Not old enough to be truly evil, right? Retracting my wings, I crouch at his side to flip the wet hair away from his forehead. I don't know the ways of Hunters, but this child can't have killed already. Surely he hasn't participated in the atrocities against my kind.

Gently, I press my fingers to the side of his neck, relieved to find a pulse that still beats strong. Blood seeps from the back of his head, and I inspect the wound. I didn't use super strength when I knocked him out, and his skull feels solid under the gash. I can't leave him here, though. If he wakes, he'll act against us, and if Domnall finds him, his magic and life will fuel the demon.

Rummaging through the kid's clothes, I find a wand similar to the one the old Hunter used against me at the bakery. The bones rattle against the handle, making my skin crawl and anger burn in my blood. These are the bones of my people. But age turned them yellow, too old to be a tool of this Hunter's making. I find a notebook, too, and stuff it in my satchel to pass along to Tally's witches.

I unclip the walkie-talkie from his waistband, then drag him to the nearest storage unit, spindling power into my limbs to break the lock and open the door. I stuff him inside, out of sight and safe from the elements. As a last thought, I pull out one of the confetti cannons, point it at him, and twist the bottom. Silver pieces of paper fly out, fluttering and landing in a circle around his still body. It won't stop him from leaving, but if he tries any spells, they'll bounce back on him, in theory.

The cell phone in my back pocket buzzes, and I dig it out to find Kellen's number on the screen. Swiftly, I step back into the storm, slide the storage unit door shut, and twist the broken lock into place. Being locked inside won't hurt the kid, and I'll make an anonymous call to the manager in the morning to let him out. Hopefully, tonight will scare him away from the allure of demon hunting, because it's unlikely he'll face someone with my soft spot in the future.

My phone buzzes again, and I lift it to my ear and press answer as I duck under an overhang. "Mine is taken care of."

"Are you all right?" Kellen demands. "What took you so long?"

I peer through the darkness toward the front gate. "I stashed the body in case someone comes before we finish."

"Good thinking." He grunts, and the sound of something being dragged comes through the speaker. "Are you *okay*?"

My chest tightens at his concern. "I'm fine." A beat of silence fills the line. "Really."

Kellen's voice returns, quieter now. "I thought it would be harder for you to take a life."

A hard ball forms in my throat. "I've taken a life before, Kellen. I knew what I was signing up for."

The man's gentle, hazel eyes still haunt my dreams. It was the last time I allowed myself to truly feed on humans, and the reason I starved myself to the point of needing to order one of Julian's imps as a meal. A choice that led me to Tobias and the others.

"Okay, stay where you're at," Kellen instructs.

"I'll be there soon. I'm going to call the others to let them know the lookouts are taken care of."

"Okay, I'll be waiting." Shivering, I tuck the phone back in my pocket and move away from the storage unit, back to where the Hunter laid in wait.

The rain already washed away the blood, like the attack never even happened. No one who passes by will know a life was almost taken here.

While I wait, I study the nearby buildings for any places where my eyes refuse to focus, but find none. Either the Hunters are overconfident in their ability to hide from us, or we'll find the main traps closer to their hiding place.

Through the rain, I make out the dark forms of the others as they stride toward me, and I pull my shoulders back, trying to exude confidence I don't feel. I already failed my first mission. Will my hesitation cost us in the battle to come? At the beginning of this, Emil, Tobias, and Kellen offered to take care of this entire issue for me. But the Librarian said I would be needed, so I insisted, and when they took Perry, it became personal.

In my heart, I believe I'll be able to kill if it means protecting someone I love, but a cold assassination without provocation is another issue altogether.

Domnall reaches me first, his hungry eyes sweeping the empty space around me. "Where's the Hunter?"

"Stashed him. You can drain him later. We should keep moving before anyone notices they've lost communication with him."

Annoyance clear on his face, Domnall's attention shifts past me. "I suppose you stashed yours, too?"

A moment later, Kellen's static-filled hand touches my back. "Seemed the safest option."

Julian comes up along Domnall's left. "Don't pout. You know you like to see them all stacked up at the end."

Domnall rubs his chin. "I do like a good pile of bodies."

Emil and Tobias stride past them to stop in front of me. Tobias's eyes search my face, and his tense expression eases at whatever he finds before he glances back to Domnall. "Do you sense any magic ahead?"

"Hard to say with all the magic right in front of me." His dark gaze fixes on me. "Neat trick using the baku to hide behind. I think it's time you tell us what's in that bag of yours."

I shift the satchel so the bag hides behind me. "Just some backup in case something goes wrong."

"*I'm* the backup." Domnall thumps a fist against his chest. "Demons shouldn't mess with dirty human magic. It will twist you."

Domnall's a prime example of how power twists, but I don't think it had anything to do with the humans who practiced it. "If it's all the same to you, I'd like a secondary backup in case you're busy."

"She's young, darling," Julian pats his arm soothingly. "Allow the trinkets."

"For now," he concedes.

Emil strokes my arm. "Are you okay to continue?"

"I'm fine." I catch his hand and bring it to my lips. "I'm strong."

His thumb skims across my bottom lip. "So you are."

"Touching as this all is, we have witches to exterminate." Domnall stomps past us, Julian close on his heels.

At the second to last bay, Tobias and Kellen separate to cover the north exit while the rest of us keep to the south. Emil and I fall back, putting distance between us and Julian and Domnall. If someone triggers a trap, we won't all be caught, leaving two of us on the outside and still active.

However, we make it to units two-fifteen and

two-seventeen without incident. Tobias and Kellen meet us from the opposite direction, and we all stare at the closed metal doors with suspicion. This feels too easy, even to the inexperienced. For a Hunter's base, their security is underwhelming.

Domnall finally lifts a hand to point at the door to two-seventeen. "That one."

Emil, Tobias, and Kellen all step forward as one, power flaring between them.

I frown, searching the surroundings for any sign of spells the storm broke. There should be sensors here, traps in case demons get this close.

I turn to Julian. "Is Perry's tracker still here?"

He pulls out his phone, and we huddle together to block the rain as he opens the tracking app. The little dot for Perry blinks right in front of us, confirming we're in the right place, but the entire setup feels off.

Delving inside, I search for the thread that connects me to Perry through our contract. It's more difficult to find on the human plane, the thread fainter, the emotions duller, but I catch nervousness, apprehension, and guilt.

And the thread leads behind us, to the south.

My eyes snap open in time to watch Emil reach

for the lock on unit two-seventeen, and I lunge forward. "Wait!"

The explosion blooms in slow motion, a spark of light that sprouts fingers made of flame that swat the three men aside. Pressure comes next, a wall of air that shoves outward. Julian reaches for me, arms spread wide and eyes filled with horror, but not even hyper-speed can save us as the blast tosses us into the air.

An instant later, I crash back to the ground, and searing pain shoots through me as the back of my skull slams into the cement ground. Dots of gray fill my vision, and my head rolls to the side. Domnall lays on the ground beside me, eyes closed and blood running from his ears.

Feet appear between us, and I follow the legs attached to them until I meet a pair of heavy-lidded eyes filled with regret. Rain plasters his blond hair to his head like a surfer just come in from the waves.

His name forms on my lips. "Perry?"

He looks away as another person appears beside him, an older man who sports a necklace made of bones. He nods in satisfaction and pats Perry on the shoulder. "Your plan worked. Bring the girl and this one." He nudges Domnall with his shoe. "I'll take great satisfaction in destroying him for the good of our people."

Perry nods. "What of the others?"

The older man looks toward the burned out shell of the storage unit. "Their forms are too damaged. They won't survive on this plane long enough for the ritual."

"No," I whimper and force my body to sit up.

Perry kneels by my side. "I'm sorry, Adie. For what it's worth, you were a good master."

He pulls out a brown bottle and pours liquid onto a cloth. I struggle to crawl away, to escape to where Emil, Tobias, and Kellen lie, their bodies still on fire from the blast.

Perry catches me with ease, the cloth covering my mouth and nose. Something sweet and slightly chemical fills my senses, and weakness washes through me a moment before gray floods my vision.

PROMISES

"*Wake-up, Boo. This isn't the time for napping.*"

Around me, Landon's living room comes into focus, but it's not the space where I last saw him. The couch is floral and well-padded, with blankets and pillows taking up the spaces we don't occupy. The pizza boxes stacked on the coffee table come from a restaurant that closed years ago.

Blinking, I stare at the old tube TV with the VCR below it and a stack of animation VHS tapes waiting to be marathoned. My arms tighten around the purple, sequined pillow in my lap, the tiny plastic disks pricking my bare arms.

We had spent many nights on this couch, the TV a constant drone in the background, until I finally fell asleep and Landon carried me to my room.

Being back here now brings a sense of comfort,

of safety, and I snuggle into my corner. "What movie are we watching?"

In the opposite corner, Landon stretches out, feet up on the coffee table and one arm along the back of the couch. A lazy hand scratches his taut stomach. "The Lion King."

I pull my knees up, squishing the pillow against my stomach. "Can we fast-forward past the beginning?"

"No can do." As he shakes his head, his long, white hair sways, the monarch yellow tips curling around his shoulders. "You can't skip the origin story."

"It's depressing." I frown at the blank television screen. "I like the part where they fall in love."

His head turns, yellow eyes bright in the shadows of the room. "You can't ignore the bad and only focus on the good. It's a package deal."

"Yes, I can." I lean to the side and grab the remote control from his lap. "That's why we have fast-forward."

"Always in a hurry." He releases a heavy sigh. "You're going to miss out on a lot if you don't pay attention."

Pain spasms up my arm, and the remote falls from my hand. My fingers curl into my empty palm, talons sprouting to knife through my flesh and hit bone.

Landon studies the blood dripping onto the cushions, and *tsks* quietly. "We have to burn those pillows, now."

The acrid scent of charred polyester fills the air, making my eyes sting, and when I glance back down, only a liquid pile of goo remains of the cushion. The more I stare, the more they resemble twisted bodies, limbs thrown wide and motionless. Ash flutters like snowflakes in the air, and I choke on a sob.

"Oh, here comes the canyon scene." Landon nods to the blank TV. "Make sure to pay attention. This is a defining moment. The great betrayal and loss."

"Boo, you can't linger here. Wake-up."

I flinch, head whipping toward the brightly lit kitchen where only Landon's butterflies flit about. Twisting, I peer behind the couch, but Landon and I are alone.

Landon's feet drop to the floor, and he leans forward, eyes intent on the blank screen. "Look at the little cub run. Too weak to face his enemies alone."

My gut clenches, bile burning in my throat.

Fog curls along the floor, washing out the color in the room and blurring the lines of the entertainment center.

A blue butterfly floats past my face, drawn to Landon like a moth to the flame. He catches it with ease, popping the little jewel into his mouth with a crunch. A red one follows. He nabs it by the wing and offers it to me.

It struggles in his hold, delicate wings flapping, and I shake my head.

"You're weakening, Boo. Take the energy."

The voice tickles my ears, and I lift a hand to swat it away.

Landon glances back to the TV and sighs. "Such iffy guardians, don't you think?" His focus shifts back to me. "Maybe I was wrong to ask them to look out for you. You're safer here where I can protect you."

My lips part in shock. "What?"

"Ah, here we go." Leaning forward, he shoves the butterfly past my lips.

It tastes like pennies and snaps against my tongue like pop rocks. Landon's face blurs and thins, hollows forming in his cheeks and his hair shortening. The floral couch flickers, then fades away, gray fog taking its place.

I stare at him in confusion. "Landon, what's going on?"

Worry creases his brows. "You're not in a good place, Boo. You need to wake-up before the Hunters steal all your energy."

"Steal my…" My heart slams hard in panic. "Landon, I messed up. Tobias, Emil, Kellen, they're—" I can't bring myself to finish the sentence.

He grips my arms and shakes me. "Take care of yourself for now. Worry about them later."

"But it's my fault. Perry. The Hunters—"

"Stop." The command holds power, and my lips clamp shut. "You can't focus on that. You need to *wake-up*. Help is coming, but you need to do your part, too, or more people will be hurt."

Tears flood down my cheeks. "I don't know what to do."

"Oh, Boo." His arms fold around me. "I'm too far away to save you this time. You need to be your own hero. The power's inside you. All you need to do is take it." With a gentle kiss to my temple, he pushes me to arm's length. "Now, *wake-up*."

Pain explodes across my face, and my eyes snap open, a growl already on my lips.

Domnall stares down at me, hand raised, ready for another slap.

I glare up at him. "Do that again, and I'll rip your balls off."

"About time you woke up." He paces away from me as I slowly sit up.

Cold cement floor, metal walls, and the bright halogen bulbs overhead indicate we're in another storage unit, though probably not Sure-Lock Self Storage. Based on the way my eyes slip and slide around the room, spells surround us. My hand drops to my hip, then pats around.

"If you're looking for your bag of tricks, don't bother," Domnall sneers. "Your precious imp made sure to take it before he tossed us in here."

My hand shifts to my arm, oddly bare after wearing the metal cuff for so long. I should have noticed right away that my bones didn't vibrate with all the magic around us. Muscles protesting, I climb to my feet. "How do you know Perry's the one who put us in here?"

He scoffs. "How many imps could possibly be working for the Hunters?"

"You were conscious, and you just let him manhandle you in here?"

Domnall pulls his jacket open to reveal a scorched hole in his shirt the size of a basketball, the skin beneath still red. "I was a little busy recovering from the *hole* in my gut."

"What about Julian?" I spin, searching the small room for my cousin. "Where is he?"

Domnall shakes his head. "I didn't see what happened to him after the blast."

I stride for the door, only to come up short at an invisible barrier. "So he could still be out there, wounded?"

"If he was wounded, he'd either be in here, or he was destroyed."

At Domnall's dismissive tone, I turn on him in anger. "Don't you care, even a little?"

Nonplussed, Domnall blinks at me. "I can find another of your kind easily enough." Then, he grins. "In fact, you'll do just fine once we get out of here, and I consume these Hunters. That is, if you survive that long."

Red edges my vision as my blood boils with rage. How dare he have so little regard for Julian? How dare he assume I'll step in to take his place?

My fingernails lengthen into talons, and I clench my fists to fight back the urge to rend and maim.

Not yet. I might need Domnall to escape.

He smirks as if reading my thoughts before he walks to the door. "Hello? Anyone out there? We're awake now if you want to come taunt the evil demons!"

I hold my breath, ears open for any sign someone waits outside, but I hear nothing.

The adrenaline from earlier drains away, leaving fatigue in its wake, and I sway on my feet.

Domnall glances back over his shoulder, and one thick eyebrow lifts. "How low are you?"

I lift a hand to my forehead. "What?"

"Low, pet," he says slowly, as if to a child. "How much energy do you have left?"

I delve inside, focusing on my core, and dismay rolls through me. Kellen's lightning and Tobias's chaos are already gone, and only a few ice crystals remain from the vibrant ball of energy I took from Emil. Once those go, the drain will latch onto the part of me that creates my corporeal form.

My hand lifts to my neck to find it bare.

"If you're looking for that ugly necklace, your imp took that, too." Domnall's lip curls with disgust.

"I told you it was stupid to play with human magic. The only good thing a witch can offer is their life."

It wouldn't matter anyway. Not with Emil, Tobias, and Kellen gone. The pendants that anchored me to them would have been destroyed in the blast, the link broken when they were killed. I only hope they were cast back to the demon plane where they can gather themselves and heal. My mind shies away from any other possibility, unwilling to believe the Hunters strong enough to catch their energy and bind them in death.

Staring at the floor, I admit, "I'm low. At the rate they're draining me, I won't last much longer. What about you?"

"Nothing to drain." His shoes scuff against the cement. "Julian took all the power I held, so aside from this magnificent body, I have nothing for them to steal."

My head jerks up. "What are you talking about? I've felt your power before."

He leans down, face close to mine. "And do you feel it now?"

Unwilling, I let my senses drift out and find only blankness where he stands. Not even the gentle brush of life that humans let off. Just nothingness. "How is that possible?"

"I wouldn't be a very good boogeyman if the Hunters could just drain me and cut me up for parts, now would I? I take their power and use it against them. All they can do is destroy this body." He rubs a hand over the hole in his shirt. "I'll just pop back into the demon plane, then come right back to kill more of them. That's why they threw me in here with you. As long as I'm trapped, I can't grab the silly buggers. Which is why it's good you're almost drained dry."

I rear back. "Why?"

"They want you weak, pet, not dead. They'll be by soon to carve up your pretty ass."

Ice slides down my spine. "It's not the full moon yet. We have another day."

He casts me a derisive look. "Sorry to burst your bubble, pet, but you took a nice long nap. I thought they'd start carving you up before you regained consciousness."

"That's not possible," I whisper through numb lips. If that much time had passed, someone would have come for us.

Tally was nowhere near the blast, surely she could have located us through Dreamland. Or her brother Aren. I whip around, searching the corners for shadows, but find none. The only shadows in the room are the ones cast by me and Domnall. How big does a shadow need to be for a baku to use? How long does it need to stay in one place? I don't know enough about the dream eaters. When we get out of this, I'm going to have a nice, long talk with Tally.

My mind whispers *if* we get out, but I push the thought away.

Instead, I focus on the room around us. Or, rather, the parts of the room my eyes *refuse* to focus on. Six points on the walls, two on the left and right near the floor, and one on the back wall and the door near the ceiling, triangles building triangles to cage us in.

I search the floor for the draining spell. When I have no issue focusing, I switch to the ceiling. The halogen lights make it hard to focus regardless, but the gap of ceiling between the center bulb and the far left one seems especially difficult to stare at.

Pressure builds in my temples, and I look away before I add another ache to my already pain riddled body.

If rescue hasn't come for us after a day, then we'll just have to free ourselves. Which means I can't let them take any more of my power. Even as the thought crosses my mind, another ice crystal bleeds away from my core.

Kneeling, I pull up my pant leg, then sag with relief when I see they didn't get my last line of defense. I dig the clay marble out of my sock. If I do this and die, that's it for me. But if I get any weaker, I won't be able to fight them off, and that will be a much more painful end.

Domnall wanders over. "What do you have there? More human magic?"

I roll the warm ball between my fingers. "It will hold me in my body so I'm not cast back to Dreamland."

He crouches to study it, and his nostrils flare. "Smells powerful."

My fingers tremble. "It is."

"Good. I need power." He plucks the marble from my fingers, tossing it into his mouth.

I lunge at him. "What are you doing?"

He leaps out of immediate reach. "Not like I can rely on your sorry ass to get me out of this." The crunch of clay sounds loud in the small space, and a shudder rolls through him. "Oh, that's the good stuff."

The smell of burning leaves fills the room, and he rolls his head, neck cracking.

"You asshole! You just said they can't actually harm you!" I grab the lapels of his jacket. "That was my only chance!"

He brushes me off with ease. "You never had a chance, even at your fullest power. Maybe after a few centuries, but we'll never know. You're just too weak."

My eyes burn, but I refuse to let the tears fall. I can't believe my last moments will be spent with this sadistic asshole.

A clank sounds at the door, and we turn to face it.

The door rattles open to reveal Perry on the other side, my missing satchel slung over his shoulder. His blond hair rustles in the night wind, the moon full to his left.

Sadness makes my eyes prickle once more. "Perry."

"Adie." Regret flickers across his expression.

I shove my hands into my pockets to hide their trembling. "Can you at least tell me why?"

Domnall throws his head back with a groan. "Oh, my god. Not the bad guy monolog."

"Perry's not a bad guy," I hiss at him.

"He's about to deliver you to the butchers, pet. He's bad."

"He might be misguided." I turn back to Perry. "It's not too late."

"Oh, Adie." He sighs with regret. "It was too late the minute you bought me. I'm so *sick* of being owned, of being powerless. Do you have any idea of the hell imps go through just to gain citizenship? I'm sorry you have to die, but it's a price I'm willing to pay to be free."

My chest fills with a heavy weight. "So, you're canceling our contract?"

"Seems so." He motions to Domnall. "Back of the room with you."

I swallow past the tight knot in my throat. My hands tremble, and I press them over the aching emptiness that forms in my chest. "I promised to take care of you, Perry. I can't break that promise."

His gaze shifts back to me. "Don't worry, Adie, death will solve that."

"Yes, it will." I find his thread with ease this time, grasping on to the crash of waves against a distant shore and spiraling out the last of my power.

Our contract exists on a different level from human magic, somewhere in the space between the human and demon plane, and the magic that keeps my corporeal body locked here does nothing to stop the hooks I cast out and latch into Perry.

His eyes widen in shock, and he stumbles where he stands. "Adie, what are you doing? You promised to take care of me."

I step closer to the invisible barrier that separates us. "Yes, for better or worse. You're my responsibility."

My heart stutters, but I refuse to look away as I tear Perry's power core from his body. Empty now, he crumples to the ground with a sickening thud as energy floods down the line, following the only path left open. It crashes into me, an ocean wave that tastes of salt and sunshine, of dreams and determination.

I take everything that created him. No returning to the demon plane. No second life. No second chance.

Shuddering at the sudden influx, my wings burst from my back.

"Well, that was unexpected," Domnall murmurs. "Look at you, growing up."

My feathers rustle, their weight heavy on my spine. Glancing to the side, I find them larger now, with hints of snowflakes and storms riding the edges of my feathers. A shadow of darkness mixes in with hints of sunshine and ocean foam. This should be a time for celebration, but it brings me no joy, not at the cost of one of my imps.

As fast as they appeared, I pull them back into hiding along my spine. "It doesn't matter. We're still trapped."

"Well, I think I can help with that," a cheerful voice calls, and Julian steps over Perry's body. He scoops up my satchel, digging out a confetti cannon. "How exactly do these work, now?"

PULSE

I shift back and forth on my toes, overwhelmed with happiness to see my cousin still standing. "You point the open end at the spell, then twist the bottom."

Julian twirls the cardboard tube. "Seems a bit anticlimactic, but okay." He eyes the invisible barrier. "Where's the spell."

I point to the bottom right corner. "There's one there."

"Point and shoot. Got it." Julian walks to the corner, aims the tube, and twists the base. Silver confetti bursts out, and he lifts his eyebrows. "Well, that was pretty. Is that it?"

When I extend a hand, my knuckles knock against the barrier. Pushing along it, I find the weakened point near the floor. Teeth gritted, I try to shove my arm through, and pain rolls up my arm, slivers of glass that cut without leaving a mark.

I pull back with a shake of my head. "It's not enough."

Domnall snorts. "I told you not to rely on human magic."

"No, it's working, it just needs more help." I eye the wall, marking where my eyes begin to resist seeing. "Julian, there should be a can of spray paint in the bag, too."

He pulls the satchel forward and digs around inside. "Found it."

"Okay, this is an entrapment spell, so you need to paint an *S* over it."

"Easy enough." Julian pops the top off the can of black spray paint. "Only one problem."

I frown. "What's that?"

"I don't know where to paint."

"Right here." As close as I can get to the spell, I draw a circle around it to indicate the size. Based on the experiment with Reese's notebook, I'm within an inch of the spell's edges. "And make sure it's an *S*. No straight lines."

Julian pauses, can lifted and nozzle pointed. "What happens if I use straight lines?"

"Changes the spell."

Julian rolls his eyes. "To what?"

"I don't know, possibly something deadly, so make sure you draw it super curvy."

Julian swears and makes a couple practice S shapes before he takes a deep breath and presses the nozzle. The black paint mists in the air, slowing as it hits the barrier, but penetrating nonetheless. By the time Julian reaches the downward swoop of the S, the paint moves at a normal rate, and the original symbol comes into focus, exactly as Reese drew it at the cafe.

He completes the bottom curve just to be safe, and I test the barrier once more. The entire section on this side feels softer now, like taffy, malleable but still not allowing us to pass. It must be because they used a double barrier. Removing one piece still leaves five other parts to complete the triangle.

I jump and run to the opposite corner, waving my arms in a circle to indicate the next spell. "Do this one, too."

Julian repeats the process with a new confetti cannon, followed by the spray paint.

When I test the barrier again, it feels crackly. Still there, but damaged enough that when I shove hard, my hand makes it through. Knives of pain bite through my flesh, but I keep going. With one part of my body free, the rest of me yearns for escape, no matter how much it hurts.

I fall out the other side, crashing to my knees with a wheeze of victory.

Domnall shoves his way through the barrier with a grunt, managing to stay on his feet. He claps Julian on the shoulder. "Good to see you alive, pet."

Julian still wears his witch hunting outfit, though it's charred in places. A long tear bisects his duster on the right side. His hair is shorter, too, the pink tips burnt away, and ash smudges his cheeks.

Lurching to my feet, I rush to his side, shoving Domnall out of the way. He doesn't deserve to touch my cousin. My arms wind around Julian's neck in a tight hug. "I thought you were gone, too."

His cheek rubs against mine. "It takes more than a small explosion to take me out."

I peer over his shoulder, surprised the storage place looks almost exactly like the one we attacked the night before, only here the doors are painted blue instead of orange, and everything is in slightly better condition. "Where are we?"

"Opposite side of town." Julian's hold on me tightens. "Do you know that there are actually eight storage facilities in town?"

Nose against his neck, I drag in the precious smell of coconut body oil. "How did you find us?"

Reluctant, he gently pushes me back. "Tally and Landon. They teamed up to locate you through Dreamland. She's with him now."

Relief rushes through me that she's safe, followed by a swamp of sadness for those who aren't. I want to ask about Emil, Tobias, and Kellen, to demand if they've returned to the human plane yet, but I bite back the desire. There's time enough to make preparations for their return.

First, we need to take care of ourselves.

Pain cuts through me as I glance down at Perry, and Julian eyes drop to the body as well. "Your imp."

My hand spreads over my stomach, where his energy crashes inside me. "Apparently not as loyal to me as I was to him."

"I'm sorry, love." Julian leans over to press a kiss to my cheek. "You can't save them all."

"No." But maybe if Perry's life had been better, he wouldn't have come to this crossroads.

Or maybe greed would have driven him here regardless.

Domnall's head lifts as he sniffs the air. "Witches."

I tense, and Julian reaches into his coat, pulling out two knives. We move to stand back to back, searching our surroundings.

A few doors down from where we were held, shimmers in the air push my eyes to the side. I pretend not to notice as I reach into the satchel at Julian's side and pull out a confetti cannon. Energy unfurls inside me, not much, but enough to lend me speed as I point the tube at the shimmer and twist the base.

Tiny, silver pieces of paper shoot out, taking the shape of a person before whatever spell masked him falls. My pulse spikes at the unexpectedness of his appearance, and I hesitate.

My cousin does not.

His warmth at my back vanishes, and he appears in front of the witch in the next heartbeat, his blade swinging through the air. Blood splatters the side of the building, followed by the wet thunk of the Hunter's head and body landing in two separate pieces.

Julian twists, the bottom part of his face painted red, and his eyes widen. "Behind you!"

I spin, arm swinging, and throw the cardboard tube still in my hand at the approaching Hunter. It bounces off his chest, ineffective, and we both stare at it for a moment in surprise before his gaze lifts back to me.

My stomach tightens as recognition sets in.

The last time I saw the kid, I stuffed him into a storage shed. Looks like his buddies freed him, and by the gun he points at us, he's not the innocent I mistook him for.

Domnall shouts with excitement, springing toward the Hunter.

Maybe he's not scared of a gun, but I am. The energy I stole from Perry curls through my limbs, not enough for hyper-speed, and certainly not enough to outrun a bullet.

Desperate, I dive to the side, hitting the concrete hard as the shot rings through the air. I roll and tumble, then slam up against the storage units on the opposite side from the one that held us.

My head jerks up. Domnall is still a few paces away, and the kid takes new aim, his jaw set with the determination of someone who knows death will strike and decides to take as many with him as possible.

The air in my lungs turns heavy, my chest struggling to rise, and then the ground shakes.

The Hunter stumbles.

The gun flashes as it goes off.

The bullet slams into the metal door two feet from my head, my ears ringing with the blast.

Domnall's hand stretches out for the Hunter, but the ground rolls. The kid falls back, right into Tobias's grasp as the catalyst demon steps around the corner of the building.

Tobias's eyes meet mine, his pupils blown wide until only the void stares back. Rage contorts his face, and he grabs the Hunter's head on either side, twists, and pulls. The ground at his feet opens, and the Hunter's body vanishes. Tobias drops the head in then strides past Domnall, his steps determined.

With one hand braced on the metal door, I force my shaky legs under me and rise to my feet. One wobbly step turns into another, then I'm running, flinging myself at him. He catches me with ease, and I plaster my mouth to his, tasting the copper tang of the Hunter's blood before I push deeper, thirsty for the taste of lava and landslides. My fingers drive through his thick, wavy hair, pulling him closer, never wanting to let go again.

"Before you start humping, we still have more witches to take care of," Domnall interrupts.

I lift my head, eyes searching Tobias's face. "I'm so happy you're back. I wasn't sure how long you'd be held on the demon plane."

His hands tighten on my ass, and he nips my bottom lip, his teeth sharp and demanding. "We never left. It takes more than that to kill a demon of destruction."

Relief leaves me dizzy, and I look around. "Where are Emil and Kellen?"

At that moment, lightning shoots down from the sky, followed by terrified screams.

Julian twists around with a curse. "Well, that's not subtle."

"Better hurry, or we won't get any of the kills!" With an excited smile, Domnall lopes around the building in the direction Tobias came from.

With a last look at me, Julian follows, the ragged ends of his duster flying behind him like wings.

I press another kiss to Tobias's precious lips before I wiggle free of his hold. If Emil and Kellen are still in danger, I need to be there to help. Tobias catches my hand, and for a moment, I think he'll try to stop me, that he'll tell me to stay put.

Instead, he tugs me into motion, and we run toward the fight, our fingers linked together.

More lighting flashes, static heavy in the air as we near. The screams die away before we reach the confrontation, and frozen mist snuffs out the charred remains of the last three Hunters. Smoke carries the scent of burned flesh and ozone to us as we slow to a walk.

Domnall kicks a half-burned head. "We missed all the fun."

"That's what happens when you get yourself caught," Julian says as he ducks into yet another storage unit. His voice floats out. "Hey, there's a goat!"

My eyes sting when I spot Emil's white hair and Kellen's strong back. Without letting Tobias go, I run toward them.

Emil turns, his whited-out eyes clearing to blue as I crash into him. Frost nips at my front as I pull my ice demon closer. Our lips meet, and I welcome the cold of winter that numbs my tongue. Then Kellen joins us, tasting of lightning and the storm of creation.

At last, the tears fall, grateful they made it through this fight safely.

"As touching as this reunion is, did you happen to keep anyone alive?" Domnall grumbles. "I'm a bit peckish."

My three demons exchange guarded looks before Kellen steps back "Sorry, mate, seems we killed them all."

Domnall nudges one of the bodies with his boot. "And ripped off all their heads. A bit overzealous, if you ask me."

"We wanted to make sure they wouldn't get back up," Emil says, his voice cold.

Domnall side-eyes them. "You know I can't drain them like this."

"Our bad," Kellen says without a hint of remorse.

"No matter." Domnall rolls his shoulders. "I'll get enough from the last four."

I break away from the guys, counting the bodies. Including the ones we already took out, we're at eight, the maximum Domnall said we could expect to face. "This is all of them."

"No, my little succubus," Domnall drawls, an evil glint in his eyes. "I'm talking about the ones you got all your toys from."

My throat goes dry. "They're not evil. You have no jurisdiction over them."

"*All* witches are evil, eventually. And they all belong to me." He flexes his fingers. "And with the taste of their magic you gave me, I'll be able to track them with ease."

Panic rings in my ears, blocking out all other sound. *No, not Tally's men. Not my friends.* Red blurs my vision, my body moving before conscious thought forms.

Domnall slams against the side of the storage unit, my hand buried in his gut. Fire fills his body, scorching my flesh as I shove my arm deeper, talons reaching for his heart.

He stares down at me, eyes wide with shock, then laughs. "Stupid girl. You think you can kill me like this?"

"No, she can't," Julian says as he steps up to my side.

Domnall's amused gaze shifts to him. "Ah, pet, tell your little cousin what a big mistake she's made."

"You can't kill him by ripping out his heart, Adie." Domnall's chortle cuts short when Julian reaches into his coat and pulls out the sword I took from the Hunter. "You need a blade made to slay demons."

Domnall's eyes narrow. "Pet, what do you think you're doing?"

Julian hefts the long sword. "Righting a wrong."

"You know I'll just come back," Domnall hisses. "And when I do, you'll be first on my list."

"No, you won't. That spell you stole?" I close my hand around his heart, enjoying the frantic beating.

"It locks you to the human plane. If you die here, you cease to exist everywhere."

His eyes widen. "Wait—"

With a hard tug, I rip Domnall's heart from his chest with a wet pop.

"Goodbye, Domnall." Julian brings the sword down with enough force to separate Domnall's head from his shoulders and bury the blade deep into the wood siding of the building beyond.

His heart continues to beat for a few moments longer, his body not yet registering the death, before it slowly stops.

This was a good revenge, one Julian deserved to share.

My cousin releases the hilt, his body sagging against mine. "I've wanted to do that for *centuries*."

I hold up the heart. "Do you want a souvenir?"

"Oh, yes." Julian takes the offering and drops it into the satchel still on his shoulder. "I'm going to have that bronzed and use it as a paperweight."

"Seems fitting." I grab the sword hilt and yank it from the wall. "I want this."

Julian ruffles my hair with affection. "Maybe in another century." Resigned, I let him take it before

I turn to face my men, and my focus zeros in on

Emil. "I think I need a good cleaning, what do you think?"

"*I* think you are the hottest piece of ass I've ever laid eyes on," Kellen breathes with appreciation. He throws his arms open. "Come on. I have a storm to get out of my system."

Emil cuts coolly in front of him. "I do believe that was an invitation for *me*."

Kellen grabs his shoulder to stop him. "You froze the house the other night."

"And I can freeze it again tonight."

As the two argue, I meet Tobias's eyes, surprised to see pride staring back before he claps his hands loudly to gain everyone's attention. "No one is going anywhere until we deal with all the bodies. We can't just leave them laying around for the authorities to find. And there's the matter of all the blood."

"Spoilsport," Kellen mutters under his breath.

"We can just call in a cleanup crew." Emil pulls his phone from his pocket, putting suggestion into action.

I glance down at Domnall's body, the head that lays a few feet away, and apprehension rolls through me. "Can we bury him in two different places?"

Tobias nods. "Of course."

The ground rumbles and splits open, swallowing the body.

Julian bends to grab the head by the hair. "I think I saw a good spot a couple aisles down."

With one backward glance, Tobias follows after him.

Kellen sidles up to me, one staticky arm curling around my shoulders. "Are you okay?" He touches the clay pendant around his neck. "It terrified me when we couldn't find you."

"Yeah, I'm fine." I lean into his side. "Remind me to search the satchel. I think that's where mine is. If not, I'll ask Xander for a new one."

He holds me tighter. "You did good, protecting my witches. I owe you."

"I didn't do it for you," I say, absolving him of any debt.

"Still, you took a life tonight. I know that doesn't sit easy with you."

More than one. I don't regret killing Domnall. I don't even regret taking Perry's life. Both deaths were just, but they hurt nonetheless. They leave a darkness inside that yearns to be filled.

Turning, I bury my face in his chest and allow myself a moment to let go, tears soaking his shirt.

Silent, Kellen strokes my back, his body

humming with power. After a moment, rain strikes the top of my head, first a couple drops, then a full-on deluge.

Startled, I lift my face, and rain pelts down, washing away the traces of my tears.

Kellen drops a kiss onto my wet lips. "It's not a hot shower, but it's something."

Laughing, I step back, arms open wide to welcome the storm.

(UN)TEMPTED

Restless, I slip from Emil's bed, leaving him asleep. I pull on his pink robe before I pad out of his room and up the stairs to mine.

With the Hunter problem eliminated, my imps returned home to their own house, their eyes large and filled with worry. It took a lot of reassurance to make them go, but I needed my private space to myself once more.

Cleanup at the storage facility went quickly once a van full of wendigo arrived. The corpse-like demon-spirits swarmed the fallen bodies in a ravenous frenzy that left not a drop of blood behind.

Efficient, if disgusting to watch in action.

While they worked, Tobias returned and somehow managed to clean up the storage unit enough to fool the casual eye, promising to return later to wipe it clean of magical paraphernalia.

He *did* lead out the goat they had locked in a cage in there, worried its noise would draw attention. Emil immediately said I couldn't keep it and called someone to pick it up and take it to a local farm.

I stayed outside in the rain, not wanting to see what lay inside, to know what awaited me if Perry and the Hunters had fulfilled their original plan.

Eventually, the question of Perry came up, and the guys took his betrayal with far more stoicism than I expected, as if used to being betrayed by someone they trusted. It made my heart hurt all over again.

Walking to the window, I push open the shutters, drawing in a deep breath of rain-damp air. The storm Kellen called back hovers over our house, determined to lure him to the skies now that it gained his attention twice.

I gaze across the roof that separates our rooms. His window lays open, a perfect frame for his large bed. My storm demon sprawls face down on his mattress, his glorious, golden body bared for any who care to peek in. And peek I do. I'll never get tired of seeing him nude, even if he *is* horrible to sleep next to.

A flicker of red in my periphery draws my attention to the empty backyard, and I search the fog covered grass for movement. After a moment, the yip of a dog sounds from the neighbor's yard, and my eyes return to Kellen's gorgeous ass for a moment longer before I reluctantly close my shutters.

My alarm clock will go off early, life continuing forward regardless of my inner turmoil.

When I walk to my bed, I find the demon book on Hunters laying on my mattress, and I frown, sure I left it in Tobias's car.

I pick it up, and with a flash of light and an all over body buzz, I find myself in the hall of doors at the Library.

Honestly, I'm surprised the Librarian took so long to ring me up. Feet dragging, I head toward the end of the hall. The trek will take as long as the Librarian thinks it should and not a moment less.

I should have just stayed curled up with Emil and his electric blankets.

When I reach the Library, gray fog fills the large room, rolling in small clouds across the ground. Shadowed bookshelves rise in the distance, half-formed and out of reach. Red lights flicker here and there like eyes blinking from the darkness. It resembles Dreamland, but a twisted, nightmarish version that sends a shiver down my spine.

Unlike the rest of the room, the checkout desk remains unchanged, a red scooter blocking one end and an ancient computer at the other. Perched on a stool in front of the computer, the hag clacks away on the keyboard, her long, hooked nose twitching.

I set the book on the countertop. "Thank you for letting me borrow this. It came in useful."

"So it did, so it did." Her head swivels toward me while her body remains stationary, and she regards me from the deep folds of her eyelids. "You did better than I expected."

I grip the edge of the counter. "What do you mean?"

"When I cast the runes, you had a sixty/forty chance of success." A black tongue pokes out of one corner of her mouth before it darts back into hiding. "But you exceeded expectation."

"That would have been nice to know going in," I mutter.

"And set your mind to fail?" She waves the idea away with one clawed hand. "No, that wouldn't do."

"Well, we got rid of the Hunters, so everything turned out okay."

The hag's head spins so she stares at me from a different angle. "Well, of course, Hunters are easy enough to take care of."

I frown. "But you said I had a sixty percent chance."

She snorts, the sound wet and thick. "Not against the *Hunters*." Reaching out, she flips the book open to the picture of He Who Devours. "*This* was the *real* problem, and you nipped it right in the bud, didn't you?" Her hand makes a twisting motion, as if she yanked out Domnall's heart herself. "Delightful and efficient."

My mouth drops open in shock before I snap it closed. "You *wanted* me to kill Domnall? But you said he would *help* me!"

"No, I told you to seek him out." She smacks her lips together. "Not my fault you misunderstood."

The desk creaks with how hard I grip it. "Why didn't you just *tell* me you wanted him dead?"

"And what would you have done with that?" She scratches one sharp claw over the demonic image of Domnall. "You needed to see for yourself the harm such a creature was capable of if left unchecked."

I shake my head in disbelief. "Then why didn't the higher-ups just take care of the problem?"

She leans across the counter, her voice a slithery whisper. "The higher-ups don't make mistakes. To acknowledge his actions was to admit failure."

"That's ridiculous."

"So is the way of those in power. They smear their shit all over town and expect other people to clean it up."

I shake my head again, feeling a bit like a bobblehead doll. "But why me?"

The wrinkles over her eyes lift, creating deeper valleys in her forehead. "Why *not* you?"

"Because I'm weak, and Domnall could have squished me?"

Her hand cups empty air, claws clicking. "And yet you held his heart in your palm and felt its final beat."

"I could have died."

"So is the way of life." She hunkers down to root under the counter, lifting out a slender book. "Your reward."

I eye it with suspicion. "Do I want it?"

She waggles it back and forth. "It's a cookbook. You'll like it."

Curious, I take it from her and flip it open. Sure

enough, recipes fill the right side, while full-color pictures take up the left. "A book on cakes?"

"Very special cakes." She taps one of the titles. "Humans aren't the only ones who can create magic."

I read the title. *Find True Love*. My gaze snaps up. "Are you serious?"

"Well, not every demon can do it, but I think you have talent. Why not give it a go?"

I flip through more pages. *Win the Lottery, Curse Your Enemy, Bring Good Luck*. My heart beats with excitement. I could gain everything I want in life with something like this. I skim one recipe, and the excitement fades. These aren't the usual ingredients, and not all of them can be acquired without causing harm to someone, or something, else.

Slowly, I shut the book and set it back on the counter. "No, but thank you. Killing Domnall was reward enough."

"You sure?" She nudges the cookbook with one claw. "Think of everything you could do."

I tuck my hands behind my back to resist temptation. "I'd rather work for what I gain. Not take shortcuts."

She grunts with satisfaction, and the book

vanishes. "Good girl. Now, go home and get some sleep."

I back away from the counter. "Goodnight, Librarian. A pleasure, as always."

She cackles quietly. "Sleep tight, Adeline Boo Pond. But not too deep. You never know what monsters wait on the edges of dreams."

I freeze in surprise. Yes, I *do* know what monsters lurk at the edge of dreaming. I've seen it, seen its little workers, too, weaving webs of fog to trap the unwary.

My eyes shift to the red lamps, and they blink at me with a hundred eyes.

Turning, I flee back home.

Back to Emil with his electric blankets.

Back to Kellen and his gorgeous ass.

Back to Tobias and his temptations.

Back to my demons of destruction.

Succubus Dreams
The (un)Lucky Succubus Book 5

Adie escaped the Hunters, but not without cost. Nightmares plague her sleep, questioning the choices she made. Or is it something more?

After taking down the Hunters, Adie should be living in bliss. She has everything she wanted, her bakery, friendships, and possibly the love of three powerful demons. But nightmares haunt Adie's sleep, reminding her of the danger her love can bring.

As she withdraws from Emil, Tobias, and Kellen, she leaves herself vulnerable. Something dark stalks her sleep, and it might not be just her own troubled thoughts.

When nightmares come to life, Adie faces a horrible choice, one that could endanger the human world or separate her from the demons of destruction.

ABOUT THE AUTHOR

L.L. Frost lives in the Pacific Northwest and graduated from college with a Bachelor's in English. She is an avid reader of all things paranormal and can frequently be caught curled up in her favorite chair with a nice cup of coffee, a blanket, and her Kindle.

When not reading or writing, she can be found trying to lure the affection of her grumpy cat, who is very good at being just out of reach for snuggle time.

To stay up to date on what L.L. Frost is up to, join her newsletter, visit her website, or follow her on social media!

www.llfrost.com

Printed in Great Britain
by Amazon